LOCAL DEITIES

a novel by

Agnes Bushell

CURBSTONE PRESS

cover design: Richard Mehl

This publication was supported in part by donations,
and by grants from The National Endowment For The
Arts and The Connecticut Commission On The Arts, a
state agency whose funds are recommended by the
Governor and appropriated by the State Legislature.

Nine lines from "Return" and "The Message" by
Carolyn Forché. From the book *The Country Between
Us* by Carolyn Forché. Copyright © 1982 by Carolyn
Forché. Reprinted by permission of Harper and Row.

The Roque Dalton quote is from his poem "Like You"
(*Poems*, translated by Richard Schaaf. Curbstone
Press, 1984).

ISBN: 0-915306-82-4
L.C.: 88-43569

Distributed to the trade by
The Talman Co., 150 Fifth Ave., New York, NY 10011

CURBSTONE PRESS
321 Jackson Street • Willimantic, CT • 06226

For Pat and Ray Levasseur

"The history of the progress of human liberty shows that all concessions yet made have been born out of struggle... Those who profess freedom and yet depreciate agitation are those who want crops without plowing up the ground..."
— Frederick Douglass

The revolutionary is a lost man. He has no interests of his own, no cause of his own, no feelings, no habits, no belongings, not even a name. Everything in him is absorbed by a single, exclusive interest, a single thought, a single passion —the revolution.

—Bakunin and Nechaev

Your letters contain *nothing, but nothing* except for the Workers' Cause. I want you to write to me about your personal life. But not a single word. No, wherever I turn there's only one thing, "The Cause". Even that I wouldn't mind if besides it, despite it, there was a *human being* behind it, a soul, an individual. But for you there's nothing, nothing but "The Cause"....I only need one thing for my inner peace, to see our relationship settled. Our own small apartment, our own nice furniture, our own library, quiet and regular work, walks together, an opera from time to time. And perhaps even a little, a very little baby? Will this never be allowed? Never?

—Rosa Luxemburg to Leo Jogiches

CHAPTER 1

In The Hour
Farthest From God

I

On the afternoon of the day that was so radically to alter her life—and through hers the lives of many others—Annie Pratt, a.k.a. Annie Rousseau, Holly Waterman, Jennifer Maurais, Jennifer Morris, and most lately Bernice Todd, went to a mall twenty-odd miles from her home to shop.

Because she wasn't feeling like herself that afternoon everything seemed uncommonly strange to her, or else uncommonly clear. Shopping malls strike many people as bizarre and unsettling places, even people in the best of mental states, being as they are so redolent of capitalism in this its finest hour. But to Annie on this particular November afternoon the mall was more than merely unsettling. It became her antagonist, a mirror from which each and every one of her fears was reflected back at her. And though earlier at the grocery store she had tried to keep her sunny side up, by the time she arrived at the mall the song that was playing inside her head was no longer one of little Emma's Brownie tunes, but had veered off into something harder and more sinister, not The Sunny Side of the Street, but Strange Fruit.

You would never pick Annie out in a shopping mall crowd. She blends in, she is almost invisible, she has succeeded in becoming invisible: certain things pay off. She never takes it for granted, though. She is always alert for any eccentricity in her dress or her behavior. At the mall there is only one small quirk, one oddity about her. At the grocery store everybody carries one, but here she is the only woman with a list.

She carries it in her right hand, the list of things she has to buy. The list is important, it focuses her. Otherwise she would forget what she was doing, lose her balance here where all the boundaries are blurred and there is no way to mark where one place ends and another begins. She is always afraid she will step outside the line, holding a shirt in her hand she will pass beyond the invisible border between shop and non-shop. Buzzers will sound, plainclothesmen or men dressed in gorilla suits will swoop down from the boughs of the trees—why else have these trees here?—swoop down on her and the shirt ($10.99 on sale, it would be something like that, all the close calls over stupid little things like that), and from trees that aren't even trees at all, but some kind of mutants, trees that can grow indoors, that never feel the real sun or sway in a real breeze.

She stops herself. At the mall she feels she should be cautious even about what she thinks. Anyway she is always cautious.

She grips the list in her hand. Jeans for the boys. Shirts. Socks. Pantyhose for herself. Batteries. Mascara. A birthday present.

She walks into Woolworth's through the invisible barrier, only knowing she has entered the store confines by the smell of popcorn and chocolate candy. The smell is like a curtain she has to push hard against to enter. She notices everything, the dirt on the floor, the lines at the cashiers, the drone of a voice over the loudspeaker. She feels lightheaded. The fluorescent lights.

10

Mascara. A mask. Very important. Tweezers, important too. Batteries. Each item, vital. It is their duty to survive.

Annie stands by the cosmetic rack and tries to concentrate on what she's doing. She finds an eyebrow tweezer and the mascara. While she's there she picks up some lipstick and nail polish. The importance of these things is unquestionable.

Batteries next and pantyhose. Six pairs. Might as well stock up. Then she remembers razors and turns back to cosmetics. They come in a package of twelve. Disposable pink plastic razors. No hairy legs with pantyhose. It was those things, those little things, that bothered her the most.

No, what bothered her was doing the little things by herself. Doing everything by herself. Day after day, week after week, sometimes weeks at a time without even seeing him. Doing everything alone: doctors' appointments, swimming lessons, birthday parties, bedtime stories, buying batteries.

Annie waits at the checkout line with her basket of purchases. She is short but trim. She's in good shape now, not like she used to be. There's a good amount of her, but it's conditioned, toned. She works out, swims, eats well. Her hair is honey blond, short and permed for some wave. Her lipstick is on the red side of pink, her blush is a shade too dark for her complexion. She has china blue eyes under a wide forehead, a heart-shaped face, good teeth.

Today she is wearing the casual uniform of the middle class suburban wife and mother: a mauve Oxford shirt under a pearl grey V-neck sweater, a Calvin Klein jeans skirt, pantyhose, Bass shoes, canvas bag, pearl earrings, wedding band with engagement ring on top. Her nails are manicured and painted pink. Nail polish is also important. God, as Erika always used to say, is in the details.

11

She waits in line and it's all so normal, it's like a dream, the normality of it, and how she fits into it, how she manages to fit in. She is not so lightheaded anymore, but she feels that her face is flushed, that her cheeks are radiating heat. Maybe it's hunger, maybe she just forgot to eat. And thinking this, she tries to remember, turns her face to the candy counter, catches the scent. Not hunger.

In front and behind there are clones of herself. Safety. When a rather unkempt long-haired woman wearing a green army fatigue jacket passes in front of the store, passes in front of Annie's line of vision (a brief passage, she is moving quickly, briskly passing the matrons in her way, even in her movement announcing her difference) the first thing Annie feels, before the wave of envy, is fear.

She goes from store to store now looking for things, winter coats, boys' shirts and jeans. If it's on the list she has to buy it. She goes from one shop to another following the aisles, trying to avoid her own reflection in the mirrors all around her. In one store she buys jeans and shirts. She buys the most expensive since they don't wear out as fast. This much she has learned from having money, first hand experience, not just theory: the rich get better quality than the poor. More quantity, too. When in doubt, buy two. She doesn't even notice what store she's in. She never writes checks. Always pays with cash.

Always cash. Even the van. Cash on the barrelhead. A certain satisfaction in that, to lay the bills on the counter and see their faces. It would have been more satisfying, of course, if she had been dressed like herself. Oh, yes.

She had done that alone, too. Well, why think about it? Why was she thinking about it? It was being at the mall that was doing it to her, making her rave and feel crazy. After all, when was the last time she had dressed like herself? And who cares what she dresses like? Why is she even thinking about these things?

She knows. It is because something is unravelling, something is wrong. Paul talking to her again about surfacing with the kids. The sweep over the summer pushing them farther and farther away from the cities, their own turf, their squads. Isolating them. Going to the post office in the city to pick up the mail and there are the children's faces, her own face, staring down at her from the wall.

She makes her purchases and passes beyond the borderline of the store, stops and sits down on one of the benches under one of the mutant trees. Batteries, mascara, jeans, shirts. Socks. Damn. Forgot the socks. She can't go back. Birthday present for Steve who she still thinks of as Jesse but Steve is a good name too, chosen in honor of Steven Biko and Jess likes it and likes being almost eight, eight today. But she can barely think of him now. It's Mall Panic she's feeling. No air in here. No sky. Outside the store but still inside the store. Trapped in the store, the store all around you, no escape from it, and everything aimed at distracting you, everything geared toward luring you in, seducing you to grab and possess, everything aimed at envy and greed.

Annie needs to see the sky. She needs the sky over her head, lofty, limitless sky, the air around her, wild and untampered with.

She has been told by her own boys that their cousin Steve wants only one thing: anything from the G. I. Joe collection. They lobbied hard. If their cousin could have it, maybe they could too. But it was a lost cause. Her sons could no more have G.I. Joe than little Emma could have a Barbie doll. Second choice was Thriller and Electric Avenue. So it was the record store. And home.

13

A man sits down a little way from her on the bench. He's smoking a cigarette. Sitting on a bench smoking a cigarette. People do sit on benches in the mall and smoke cigarettes.

But it's too intense now, she feels it too strongly. Paul is right, go with your instincts, always go with your instincts.

It was instinct that brought him home last night. Some sixth sense. A warning. He said it was just that Bobby wanted to be home for the party, see his only son turn eight. But Annie knew the party wouldn't have mattered if Paul hadn't decided to change the plans, and he only changed plans when he felt things weren't right. He operated by feel and so far he'd been right.

She's afraid to think about Paul here. She's afraid somebody will read her mind.

And then Annie feels it in her throat, the feeling of being strangled. It's the reason she stopped smoking but the feeling didn't go away. Even now, over a year later, it's there, closing her throat. Maybe nerves. Maybe cancer.

She gets up with her big bag of little boy jeans and little boy shirts and her canvas bag which holds the cosmetics and the pantyhose and the batteries from Woolworth's. She gets up and all around her people are milling about, mothers with babies in strollers, and mothers with toddlers and three and four year olds and the beautiful children are all in the mall eating candy and pizza and picking up the vibes of envy and greed and their mothers are yelling at them or calling to them kindly. Annie tunes in to the voices of mothers, the sounds inside the voices. She hears as a child does what the voices really say. There are a few men around, very few, mostly retirement age. The man on the bench is too young.

Annie stands up and all around her are these strangers. They speak strangely with flattened vowels,

14

dress strangely, think strangely. Oh, what *do* they think? All white, all WASPs, not a single Black face, not a single open face (where is the woman in the army jacket now?), no allies here for her, though her allies wouldn't even recognize her in the uniform of the enemy. And yet, though there was a time all these people would have made her want to scream, all of them looking the same, all of them thinking the same, now they are precious to her. She needs them. They are the sea in which she swims.

Annie has her bags and she is walking away from the bench, away from the tree, away from the man on the bench under the tree. Past the record store and the sound of the Talking Heads, the sounds of Psycho-Killer. But it is as though she has walked through yet another invisible barrier, to something real that she can hear and feel. So she turns back and goes into the record store. Looks first for the exit. Yes, one at the rear that opens onto the parking lot. Now she decides not to buy anything but to weave her way past the record displays (Stop Making Sense wherever she looks, David Byrne in his big suit). She wants Paul, wants to see him and hold him, wants to believe he's all right. (But he's home, she tells herself. Of course he's all right.)

But she stops at the counter anyway. She is being watched. She asks for Thriller on cassette and Electric Avenue. She asks for Girls Just Wanna Have Fun, too, for Emma, who she can see, she can almost see, jumping up and down in delight and clapping her hands and squealing, like a piglet, as Paul once said, our girl squeals like a piglet.

She puts the Woolworth bag on the counter and feels around the canvas bag for her wallet. He's followed her into the store. She can see him in the mirror. There's another one, too, standing in front of David Byrne in his big suit.

15

Now everything is over. Unless she's wrong. Unless this is just another variant of Mall Panic.

Annie hands the cashier two twenties and tells her to keep the change.

She walks with her bags, slowly, almost carelessly, toward the rear door. They don't move. Either store security or there are others waiting outside.

She reaches the door. It is a single glass door. Outside is a cement sidewalk. Beyond the sidewalk, acres of asphalt and automobiles. Beyond the asphalt, a street, a subdivision, maybe somewhere a tree or two. It is late fall. November first. The light outside is very bright.

She sees her blood splattered, beading up in the little holes in the cement.

She holds the bags in her left hand. She turns to the right and pushes against the door with her left shoulder. Over that same shoulder is her canvas bag. In that bag, which hangs under her arm like a shoulder holster, as it was designed to do, her hand is already gripped around the smooth butt of her nine millimeter. She releases the safety with her thumb. It is her duty to survive.

She pushes the door open and steps outside.

November first, the Feast of All Saints.

No one is there.

Annie drove home with great care. She was badly shaken. The flu, or whatever it was she had, was making her rave, her mind was raving. She could slip up now and not even know it. She almost had. What if someone—anyone—in a uniform had been near that door?

She drove home circuitously, according to the rules. Rules had kept them alive for ten years. It was second nature now: double back, circle around, be awake and aware.

Like in LaMaze: awake and aware.

Why had she stopped for groceries first? She had done it backwards. When she got home she would just go to bed. Paul could take the kids to Bobby and Marlene's. He could do that. It would be OK.

Maybe she wasn't sick at all. Maybe she was pregnant.

She had given birth three times, each time in a hospital, each time with Paul beside her, without his bulletproof vest. Each time she had imagined it (she had to): the baby squirming out, the Feds busting in. She doesn't think she can do it again.

Annie knows that when it happens it will happen without warning. Because she knows this, she sees warning everywhere.

She doubles back for the last time, pulls over, waits. Just sky above her, wide and deep. Wide and deep. Words from a song. *The water is wide. I cannot get over.* (It isn't that one, but she starts to sing it anyway.) *And neither have I wings to fly. Give me a boat that can carry two...* And the air is sharp as a tart apple. The trees are bare, most of them, and the last of the wild flowers are drying up in the sun. The sky is above her, the earth under her feet, music in her heart, love. The autumn of the year. It brings her back to herself. She shifts into first and heads for the highway, following the signs west from the suburbs, out toward farm country, flat and open, clean and real.

Paul and the boys were outside behind the farmhouse practicing karate. She could hear their *kiyas* even before she turned off the motor. It was nice not having neighbors for a change. They didn't have to watch themselves here, could yell as loud as they liked, practice all day if they wanted. On the other hand here on the flatlands they were exposed. Nowhere to run, nowhere to hide. No warrens or tenements to disappear into here. Not like five years ago in Philly when safety was being on the fourteenth floor of the fourteenth highrise, block upon block, storey upon storey, people everywhere. Just staying inside, no white face to stir up talk, months of staying inside, pregnant with Emma and George still in diapers...Then they were all converging on the van, the boys making a rush for the parcels, Paul hauling in the bags of food.

"Where's Suzanne?"

"Upstairs. You didn't buy the tanks, Mom!"

"She's sulking."

"Why's that?"

"She has to get her own way all the time."

"No, Tim. She just wants to wear her dress and Papa won't let her. I don't see why, it's just a stupid dress. I think he should let her wear it if she wants to." Brian, the oldest, always trying to negotiate a truce.

"Spare me the details. She's just a little crybaby, that's why." Tim, stuck in the middle. So hard to be the middle child.

"Why don't you shut up, scrub?"

"Brian!"

"OK, that's enough! Enough, understand!" Paul. A whole chorus of male voices. Male egos. She trailed after them up the back steps and into the kitchen. She loved this room, reminded her of a kitchen she'd known as a kid. They'd moved around so much it was hard to remember all the kitchens. But this one was so big and warm, a real room, the heart of the house. Now there was lunch debris on the table and dishes piled up in the sink. She noticed it all without seeing it. Paul was still talking.

"All day long is long enough. Now listen, Brian. Suzanne is wearing pants to this party because it's cold out and because I prefer her to wear pants. I don't know what possessed your Aunt Karen to buy a dress like that for her in the first place and those silly shoes, but I don't like them and I don't want her to wear them. Am I right, Bernice?"

Annie looked up at him from the bag of groceries she was staring into. Mesmerized. Dazed. An arm's length away from everything. Buzzing in her ears.

"Yes, she should dress warmly. It's going to be cold out tonight."

"But, Mom, she just wants to *bring* the dress."

Paul slammed his fist down on the table. "I'd like to *burn* the goddam dress!"

A knot was collecting in her stomach and in her throat. The knot that was in her mind. Why were they fighting like this? Was this the way it always was or was something wrong? What difference did it make what Emma wore, really what difference? And how do you explain to a child that it was all right for Mommy to dress up, but not all right for her? That Mommy dressed up as part of the pretend? Shaved her legs. Wore make-up. Painted her nails. Didn't mean any of it. Hated it.

"How long has she been up there, Hank?"

"Hours. How long have you been gone? What took you so long?"

Maybe he'd been worried about her. Maybe that was why he was being so gruff.

"I bought her a present."

"What did you buy for us?"

"Jeans and shirts."

"That's not presents."

"Don't talk like that to your mother!"

"Go tell Suzanne to come down, Brian."

"She won't."

"Then bring this up to her."

1 9

"Cyndi Lauper? Neat." But behind Tim's back he made a face.

"Neat?" Tim said. "She's disgusting."

"Go on, get out of here, both of you."

She sat down heavily in one of the wooden chairs and watched Paul unpack. She was helpless like this. Every movement was an effort.

" Christ, Bernice, you bought enough cucumbers. What is this?`What are we going to do with all these cucumbers?"

"Are you sure they're not zucchini?"

"No, they're not zucchini! Twelve, thirteen..."

"Good thing we like cucumbers."

"You'll have to make pickles. My mother made wonderful pickles...Where's the rest of the stuff?"

"What stuff?"

"The rice, the bulgar, the beans."

"Oh, sugar, I knew I was forgetting something."

"*Something?* Two dozen cucumbers and you forget the staples? It's a goddam good thing I come home once a week. What do you feed them when I'm gone? Hot dogs and TV dinners?"

"That's not fair. You were eating shit when I met you."

"Yeah. And you were waving a Yippie flag at the Democratic Convention. Great politics. Advanced politics. Organizing women around poetry readings. You thought the People's Republic was sexist because nobody could tie-dye their clothes. And now the great feminist buys her daughter crap punk music and dresses her up like....."

Annie closed her eyes. Closed her eyes, shut her ears. He didn't mean it. He was upset. He didn't mean any of it.

"Next we'll have Barbie dolls all over the house."

"Paul, please stop now."

20

"She's going to start training. I'm going to start her. She's old enough. The boys were five, weren't they?"

"Yes, Brian was. Five. We were in New York then, remember? Paul, I have to go to bed."

"Bed?"

"I'm sick."

"Well, I didn't want to go to this party anyway."

"Come on, sugar. Steve won't have anybody at his party if our kids don't go. And they've been looking forward to it. Take the kids. It'll be fun."

"Fun? Look, I've been alone here with kids all day long and the last thing I want to do is go to a birthday party and have fun."

Annie looked up at him. It was still something of a shock to look at him, her inner picture was so different from what she saw. That was the whole idea, that he didn't look like anybody's picture of him, that he looked entirely different. His hair was trimmed, his thick eyebrows tweezed thin, he wore a goatee and forty extra pounds, flabby pounds: his belly, once rock-hard, was beginning to protrude. There wasn't much he could do about the tattoos on his arms or the scar on his cheek, but he figured by the time it came down to that, he wouldn't wait for them to check out his scars before he let them know who he was. Of course, she didn't look the same, either, didn't look a bit like all those pictures of her that made her look like a dead-ringer for Janis Joplin. But the fundamental, rock-bottom things didn't change. She still couldn't get him to listen to himself and crack a smile. She couldn't get him to laugh. There was too little laughter altogether. And once she had laughed all the time. At that Democratic Convention, for instance, with Brenda and Erika, the three of them, how they had laughed then.

Marlene, Aunt Karen, didn't laugh much either. She cleaned her house and took care of her kids and worried. And when Bobby was gone for days at a time she filled the hours reading Harlequin Romances, hid them all over the house, stashing them like an alcoholic stashes rum. Her secret life, harmless but wrong. But there was no way to show her that. Everything was instinctive with Marlene. Theory didn't mean anything to her. Just the opposite of Paul, though they had some things in common, coming from the same place, growing up in the same barren cold (that was New England to Annie, even in summer, a grim place, humorless, lacking in warmth). They shared a sense of the utter seriousness of life and in both of them there was missing any sense of the middle ground. Neither one of them could imagine it, that in-between place that seemed to Annie to be somewhere broad and open from where you can look out on all the choices, all the different roads, and sit back and imagine taking this one or that, and laugh a little and drink a little wine and admit after awhile that really one isn't that much different from another, all of them leading to the same dead end.

Then Suzanne was in the kitchen skipping-running-hopping to Annie, smiling, Cyndi Lauper under her arm, wearing blue jeans, a t-shirt, sneakers, leaping into Annie's lap, squealing.

"Hey, darlin' puddin', so you've been giving your Papa a hard time today I hear. And you've been just so silly, but he says he wants to start teaching you karate just like your brothers."

"Really, Papa? Just like Brian?"

"Would you like that?"

Then Annie stood up, set Emma down, kissed the top of her head and left them. In the living room Brian and Tim were sitting on the floor wrapping the presents for Steve's birthday. She made her way up the stairs, everything on automatic, everything aching, aimed at one end: bed.

She still had trouble with this set of names. Suzanne, Brian, Tim. Their real names, their secret names, were so much finer: Eli Fidel, Eli after the Black man who had saved Paul's life in Nam; George Raul, for the Soledad Brother, and Fidel's; and little Emma Goldman. The secret names they were never called out loud, though at bedtime she would kiss them goodnight and call them by their true names, the secret names they all had, even Momma and Papa, even Auntie and Uncle and their cousins, all of them having the secret and the pretend, the world divided for them into the secret and the pretend.

She pulled herself up the stairs, undressed as though she were removing weights from her body, and crawled into bed.

Paul woke her once before he left.

"I won't call in tonight. Just sleep."

"No, call."

"Sure?"

"Yes. I want to know that everything's O.K. Did you call there?"

"Yeah. O.K."

He glanced at the clock and then at his watch.

"Talk to you at ten then, unless we're back before."

Annie closes her eyes and listens to the pounding of her head, the puckering of her skin, a hollowish sound inside her ears, the swishing and heaving of her stomach. Later as she hears the van start up she wishes he had remembered to kiss her goodbye.

Later still she wakes up and sees that it's almost ten, the numbers glowing at her, red in the dark. She doesn't need the clock, her body tells her when it's ten, when it's six, when the phone is supposed to ring. Rules are rules. The times the phone didn't ring—everything they could pack up in half an hour, the children wrapped up and carried into the van, some things left behind that were better brought, in New Hampshire, Eli's dog, a mistake anyway, to have him in the first place.

She stretches out her senses, listening for a car on the road, watching for lights. She had been dreaming, now can't remember the dream. She wants to go back to sleep, back to find it. Something was about to happen there, something she had been waiting for, something she didn't want to miss.

Now every corner of the room is stuffed up with darkness. The dark seems to spill in through the slits in the blinds, leak in from the closets, cover up the numbers on the clock. At a distance something is buzzing. Eli's fish tank. They left the fish once. Eli wondered who was feeding his fish, always wondering who was feeding his fish. So sweet, his secret name, Eli Fidel. George Raul. Secrets all through the house, in boxes, in drawers, file cabinets of secrets.

Now she is waiting for the phone. Any minute now and she can close her eyes again, the thickness will lighten, there will be a space within that will open to her and she will see something there, revealed.

She opens her eyes and stares at the numbers glowing in the dark. She sits up and tries to wake herself, but she knows she is still asleep and still dreaming because the clock says 2:48 and that is a mistake, that cannot be right, that is part of her dream that she must wake herself from because the phone must be ringing and she can't reach it, she can't wake herself up to answer the phone.

She grabs the clock in both hands and squeezes it.

2:48. It's no mistake. 2:48. It's no mistake.

No mistake. 2:48.

No mistake.

2:48. 2:49.

II

Just as Annie was sitting up in her bed, scared, feverish, alone, gripping a digital clock in her hands, gripping the clock with fingers that now look unfamiliar to her—the wedding band, the diamond ring, nails painted Moulin Rouge pink—and standing in the room more unfamiliar things, shadowy, the big color TV and VCR, the stereo system, tape player, Bearcat scanner, and through the open door, in Paul's office, other shapes, word processor and printer, xerox machine, cartons and boxes, papers, communiques, their history, preserved, everything saved, and all the other things, so many things, already ghosts (what will she do with Eli's fish?), at the same time Erika was hunched over the wheel of her car, peering through the fog, driving herself home. It is the same hour of the night, a thousand miles to the east.

(She grips the clock. Her first thought: the children. Then quickly: No. It's not Guatemala. It's not El Salvador. This is America. They can't hurt the children here. Nobody will hurt my children. She squeezes the clock so her hands won't reach for the phone. She wants to call the other house, make sure it's not true, that they just crashed out, too much beer, wine, they fell asleep and forgot to call, that's all it is. But she is frozen, she can't lift the phone. Rules are rules. She knows what she must do now. There has never been a mistake yet, every other time the danger was real. But they were always together, no overnights for the kids, no visiting friends, school all day was bad enough, enough of a risk. And always essential things stashed in the van, ready to go at a moment's notice. And still she thinks, she repeats the words: The children are safe. This isn't El Salvador. This is the United States. They don't storm houses with children

25

inside. They don't kill children. They wouldn't do it. They wouldn't dare.)

Yes, just as Annie was half-awake and struggling with paradox under percale sheets, Erika was coming home.

The first thing she notices before she even pulls the car into the driveway is that the bedroom light is out. That's good. Simon's gone to bed. If he's gone to bed, he's gone to sleep. If he's asleep he won't notice what time it is, two-thirty, two-forty-five, two-something, too late. Each time it's later. Each time it's harder to leave. Harder to go and then harder to leave. Going from one world to another, one person to another, going from being one person to being another—too hard. People don't do it much and that's why. Or they do it, but not for long. Or they do it, maybe, without giving a shit.

Erika sits in the car and wonders who she is. At that moment, between worlds, wanting both of them or neither, not wanting to face Simon, but not wanting to turn the car around and go back up the hill she had just come down, she sits still and wonders what she is.

She is tired.

She gets out of the car and steps into the denseness of the air, into its rough, sweet scent, crabmeat sweet, sea mist sweet, a sweetness she knows comes from death. Everything is thick, dense, the leaves thick on the ground, the stillness thick in the air, the trunk of the tree thick, her clothes thick, the light from the living room windows—he left them on for her and the one in the hall. He left the door unlocked too. But the air is so thick she has to push her way through it and the scent of it, the odor, so sweet, all the air around her smelling (or is it only herself?) of sex.

She goes up the front steps. The door handle is smooth and cold. The hinges squeak. Open. Close.

The house greets her. It is warm.

There are three empty beer cans on the table in the living room. One glass. A full ashtray. Shoes and socks and Noah's toys strewn all over the rug—guns and swords and armor. Becky's music on the piano, her geography book open on the couch. The room is cluttered with things, the dining room table covered with newspapers, some new watercolors of Noah's laid out on the kitchen counters to dry. She checks the kids. Asleep, a guard cat or two curled up on each bed.

She undresses in the bathroom, studies herself in the glass. The dark smudges under her eyes look darker, her face looks bruised. But there are no marks this time. The marks are all inside. She retraces her steps, turning off the lights. Slips into bed, into sleep.

"What time did you get home last night?"

"Around one."

"I waited up for you until around one."

"It must have been later then. I had to drive Brenda home."

"How is she?"

"Wonderful. She's really involved in this..."

"Christ! Tell me in the car. I have to be in the office at 8:30 and Noah isn't even dressed yet."

But in the car Simon had other things to talk about. He was out of clean shirts. Could she bring a batch to the cleaners and pick up his suit. She would have to stop at the bank and take out twenty dollars, ten for his suit, ten for gas. He had to work late. He would call around eight and let her know when she should pick him up.

"Becky's concert is tonight."

"What time?"

"Seven."

"Well, pick me up after."

27

"I thought you were coming."

"I can't. I have to work."

"You worked late last night."

"Erika, look. I don't exactly love putting in twelve hour days."

"Why do you do it then? I mean, if you don't like what you're doing."

"Let's not start now. It's fine for you. You don't have to pay the bills."

"No, I don't do anything."

"You don't do anything you don't want to do. You never have. You play every day. You go out with your friends at night."

"You could do that, too."

"Sure I could."

"You could, Simon."

"Get off it, Erika. I don't want to hear your philosophy of life right now, O.K? Enjoy, play, it's all wonderful, do what you want, don't worry, be happy—the song of the grasshopper."

"I'd rather freeze with the grasshoppers than live with the ants. And so would you."

"Well, I'll tell you what. Why don't I stop working for awhile and we'll see how long you like it. Winter's coming. Let's see how you like living in a cold house with no food and no beer and no cigarettes and no warm clothes and no electricity and no gas, eating brown rice. Just like the old days, huh? Maybe we could get food stamps."

"Simon..."

"No, don't 'Simon' me. You keep harping on this—You're never home, Simon. You're always working, Simon—Why do you think I do it? Because I love it? No. It's so you can have the luxury of hanging out with your friends all day and doing whatever it is you do."

"I appreciate it, Simon."

28

"Damn you."

"What did you say that for?"

"Goddam sarcasm."

"I wasn't being sarcastic. I wasn't."

"You don't even know how you sound."

"I just wish you liked being a lawyer."

"I do like being a lawyer. I just don't like being a lawyer seventy-two fucking hours a week."

"So cut down."

"I can't cut down. I have a hundred active cases. How can I cut down? It would be a hell of a lot different if you were making some money."

"I am making some money."

"Some real money."

"It is real money. What do you want me to do, get a job in some goddam insurance company? That bullshit wasn't part of the deal."

"Oh. The deal was I should make the money and then listen to you bitch about it."

"It's only because you're so unhappy."

"Happiness was never one of my priorities."

"Well it's one of mine."

"Fine. So go ahead. Be happy. Be my guest."

They pulled up in front of Simon's office, an old lean brick building recently restored, like most of the old buildings in the waterfront area, and like the others, divided laterally, three-quarters lawyers' offices, one-quarter antique store.

"Come to Becky's concert tonight. She'll be disappointed."

"You'll be there."

"Yes, but she has two parents, though you'd never know it."

Simon got out of the car and stood by the door. It pleased Erika that at least he didn't look like a lawyer, was far too shaggy-haired and unkempt with a suit coat

29

about as old as their marriage and a shirt that was frayed at the wrists.

"If I get a lot done this afternoon, I'll call you."

"Right," she said, knowing very well that he wouldn't. When you're trying to hold the world up with one hand, you don't have much time for piano recitals.

Erika headed the car back across the peninsula, a hilly knee of land upon which the city was built. Everything seemed dimensionless this morning, everything was dank. Wisps of grey sea mist hung suspended like deformed angels over the city. In the east a thick fogbank had moved in, hiding an entire neighborhood, covering it like a shroud. At regular intervals the foghorns lowed.

These conversations with Simon were so predictable, almost pre-recorded. Just punch Start and it runs through the player until it stops. She could change the tape, of course. One sentence. Just one sentence and the tape would change. But she couldn't do it. She couldn't bring the two worlds together, matter and anti-matter. They were totally separate, always and forever separate, except for the place where they met in her, where they touched each other inside her, like the very spot within the fogbank where the ocean met the air. But she didn't know, she couldn't tell, whether this was right or wrong, whether it was better to lie or tell the truth, whether she was protecting him or harming him more. She didn't know or, if she did, she didn't trust what she knew. No amount of thinking helped. She had to do everything by feel.

At this particular set of lights, this particular spot, she can see Marc's building. She can see his bedroom window on the fifth floor. If she closes her eyes she can see into his room. She can see his bed. She can see him in the bed, curled up under a thin green blanket like a child. If she tries very hard, she can see into his dream.

There are nights when, after picking Simon up at eight or nine o'clock, she gets stopped at these lights. Maybe he is silent or asking about the kids or the car, maybe he is looking away at the street or the sky. But she glances up, always glances up, across parking lots and low brick buildings, across streets and the tops of trees, and she sees the light shining from that window like a beacon, like a beacon light far up on a rocky cliff, and she is there, drowning far below it, seeing it and yet being pulled away, pulled out to sea by the sheer force of the tide.

Even now in daytime the blank-faced window tugs at her. It's all that exists on this corner, a quarter mile away as the crow flies, now topped with a ring of mist, but it might as well be trimmed with flashing neon lights the way it draws her, the way it tugs.

She can't resist the tug.

Erika drove to Marc's building. She parked and let herself in with her key. Took the elevator up, opened another door.

He was still in bed, asleep.

She put water on for coffee and went into the bedroom. From the window she looked down at the fog-choked harbor and the narrow cobblestone streets of the old district. She saw Simon's office and the intersection where she had caught the light. She saw the very route she had travelled to get from one place to another, where she had been, how she had come to be where she was. Just a single turn, a single choice. She sat down on the bed and felt as though she had just put time into reverse. Now she should return everything to its proper order, take off her clothes and get into bed, wake herself up and study the light and the smell, get up and get dressed, make coffee again, bring it in to him, say, Good morning.

Erika sits on the bed on the green blanket in the nearly empty room whose bare windows are opened up to dimensionless space. In one corner there is a tall, spindly, dust-covered palm-like plant, across from it a bookcase with an odd selection of titles, his favorite book, *Candide*, in full view in its leather binding. (How many arguments they had had about *Candide*, how often they had exploded at each other over Voltaire!) Open shelves where he keeps his clothes, neat, well-ordered. His closet, where he keeps his shotgun and his shirts. On the floor beside the bed is a saucer with a candle stuck on it, burnt almost all the way down. An ashtray filled with Camel butts. A book, one of hers. He lies curled up in a ball, face buried in a pillow, blanket pulled up to his neck. All she can see of him is his profile and his hair, the great mass of it, dark and curly and long. She sits quietly and studies him with the absorbed attention of an astronomer tracking the path of Halley's Comet: yes, it is here now, but, even as real as it is, in this lifetime anyway, it will never come again.

This is the essence of how she feels about Marc: that he is passing through her life like a comet, that once he leaves, he will never come again. That he is singular and precious and en route to another galaxy. That he is the last man she will ever love.

She sits and looks down at him. She wonders why he has taken this form, why she has chosen him, or he her. She doesn't understand anything anymore. She is so lost she is paralyzed. It has lasted too long but nothing has been resolved. Just sex. I thought that's what you wanted, he had said to her. I thought that would be enough.

Never enough. Never enough. Never enough.

He slept curled up in a ball like a child.

"Come in the morning. I'll go to sleep now and when I wake up, you'll be here."

But he hadn't said that. Go home to your husband. That's what he had said.

She walked through the open rooms, so stark compared to her own, hers and Simon's and Becky's and Noah's, open, bright, empty rooms. Neat. Ordered. Clean. Barren. How you are reflected in your space. And here everything excessive, everything decorative, everything beautiful had been given to him by a woman.

"I like you a lot," he had said to her once.

He wasn't the sort of man to tell a lie.

All you can do, Annie had said to her the last time something like this had happened—fifteen years ago, could it have been that long?—all you can do, sugar pie, is laugh. Just laugh until you cry.

Oh, she was losing it all right, losing control of it, losing sight of everything. She could almost hear Annie's voice, the timbre of it, over the span of a decade and a half. What do you want, darlin'? You got to be clear about that one thing—what exactly do you want?

And she, Erika, answers: I want, I want, I want. Horrible, horrible to want. No point wanting what you can't have, says Marc. Then you're stuck with wanting. Better to want what you have... But if everything you have is dying... You can save it, Erika, he'd say, if only you gave it as much attention as you give me.

She picks up a cigarette and returns to the bedroom. She looks at him as he sleeps. The body of a satyr and the face of a Botticelli angel. Incongruous, like what she wants. She wants to fuse two opposites. She wants to break the barriers down. She wants everything: she refuses to choose.

Not to decide is to decide.

Camus. A poster that once hung in her kitchen. Long ago, when Annie lived there too. When Annie lived with them and they were happy. Before Annie made her choice.

Not to decide is to decide.

The choices that come back to haunt you. The choices that you didn't make. Especially those. Not to decide....

She glances down at last night's paper lying open on the floor. Automatically she begins to read.

EXECUTION REQUIRES SECOND JOLT

The state's first try at executing Alpha Otis Stevens in the electric chair failed today and he struggled to breathe for eight minutes before a second jolt...Stevens, 39, was still alive more than six minutes after the two minute 2,080 volt charge was administered at 12:18 A.M....struggled to breathe during the six minutes in which the body was allowed to cool...At 12:26 two doctors...was alive...The second jolt...

The kettle was whistling. Erika dropped the newspaper and went into the kitchen. She made a pot of coffee for him and left it on the stove. She went out without leaving a note.

Simon had awakened that morning in a bad mood and the argument with Erika hadn't improved it any. In fact he had gone to bed in a bad mood. In fact, he had been in a bad mood for days, for weeks. It was a state of being that he wore like a suit and tie. He put it on in the morning, but he couldn't take it off at night. It had merged with his skin, melded with his bones. It was a rage at the world, at the very nature of the world.

Nothing he could do about it. It was a fact. He didn't understand why Erika didn't see it, or why she only made it worse. Why she didn't soothe it a little. How she could blind herself to the truth or pretend it didn't exist.

Two clients were already waiting for him. Either they were early or he was late. Probably he was late. He greeted them and told them he would be with them in a few minutes. Then he poured himself a cup of coffee and went into his office. He sat down at his desk and lit a cigarette and looked at his day.

And there it was in front of him, hour by hour. This day and the next and the next and the next. Appointments, arraignments, hearings, trials: his calendar was an itinerary of misery, broken lives, embittered lives, wounds. As though he could heal them. Get them some money, keep them out of jail. Get them back on welfare, keep the state from taking their kids away or get their kids back from someone else. Pass the kids around, hope for the best. Send them for counseling, arrange this detail or that, argue for them, plead for them—when what was harming them, what was killing them, wasn't this agency or that landlord or their abusive husbands or the banks or the cops. It was bigger, it was the whole works, endemic poverty, hopelessness, a world that mutilated them from the day they were born, made them drunks, child abusers, petty thieves, psychotics, pathetic half-humans who seemed, most of them, to have no soul.

Soul brother. Comrade. He thought of Paul. At least once a week he thought of Paul. "What is a bank robbery compared with the crime of the establishment of a bank?" Brecht said that; Paul lived it. So just tear it all down and start again. And yet it wasn't coming down. Did he think he was Joshua, that if he just made enough noise, set off enough bombs, stole enough money and rattled enough chains he would bring the walls down? Even so, he hadn't been making much noise lately. Nobody had. Everything was quiet. Everything seemed dead. Maybe Paul was dead.

Why did he think that? Why did he keep thinking that?

He stopped thinking it. He put out his cigarette. He had work to get done. More work than he could ever possibly do. Days and weeks and months of work.

The way he wanted it to be.

At 8 P.M. Simon calls home. No answer. Then he remembers the concert. The auditorium filled with parents. The shuffling of bodies and feet. Kids scratching at violins. The chorus singing "Tomorrow" and "Over the Rainbow". The band. Becky playing her flute.

Erika and Noah are there anyway.

He goes through his mail for another hour and calls again. This time Becky answers. Yes, Mom's home. Yes, she'll come and get him. Yes.

(And while she sat with Noah in the auditorium what did she see, what did she think? The other couples, the other children's parents sitting around her, the men with their arms draped over the backs of their wives' chairs, smiling together, talking together. The time when she and Simon did everything together, when they were inseparable, when their lives were completely entwined. They were in love then, she thought, that must have been it. How long ago was that? When did it stop? And once or twice she imagines Marc sitting beside her with his arm draped over the back of the chair, Noah sitting on his lap. But immediately she erases the image. There are certain things she cannot allow herself to think, there is a borderline over which she cannot step.)

Simon knows when she pulls up in front of the building. He knows when she opens the downstairs door. He can almost hear her on the stairs. He wants to get up and meet her at the door. He wants to take her in his arms and tell her how horrible it was, how horrible it always is. And he wants her to tell him she knows, she knows exactly how he feels, exactly what he's trying to do.

He wants her to tell him he can stop now.

She brings the scent of the night in with her.

"Hi," she says. "Ready?"

"Just about. How was the band this year?"

"It wasn't the band. It was Becky's piano recital. Just the piano students."

"Oh, well how was it?"

"All right."

"How was your day?"

"All right. How was yours?"

"Long. I'm tired."

"Have you eaten?"

"No."

"Want to stop somewhere and eat?"

"No. I want to go home."

"Well, the car's outside."

"I'm sorry I was so gruff this morning."

"It's O.K., Simon. You're always gruff in the morning. Gruff in the morning and gruff at night."

"Sounds like I'm gruff all the time."

"You're probably nice to your clients."

"Somebody has to be."

He knows it doesn't matter what they say to each other. He knows the words don't count at all. She didn't sweep into the room, he didn't take her in his arms. She didn't even smile at him. She hardly saw him at all.

He got in the driver's seat and turned on the ignition.

37

"Erika, there's no gas in the car. Didn't I remind you this morning to buy gas? Do I have to do everything myself?"

Simultaneously they thought: This is unbearable. But the tape was playing. They couldn't shut it off.

CHAPTER 2

Spirit Must First of All Fall into Time

The city in which Simon and Erika lived was not a place where anything would ever be expected to begin. Like the idealized urban setting for a child's *I Can Read* book, like a city created expressly for an *I Can Read* book, a city with such a well-scrubbed underbelly it squeaked, a city so prim and neat it had been dubbed by its more cynical inhabitants Cute City, U.S.A., it did not seem to have the natural fertility necessary for any Event to occur in it. (Ah, but perhaps they said the same about Sarajevo once. Fairytale city of the Balkans, Disneyland of the Empire, Belgian waffles on every street corner and polyglot guides in festive native dress!) Imagine then a city of sixty thousand built on a high-spined peninsula that juts into an island-dotted bay. Imagine a city of red brick sidewalks and low red brick buildings, some dating from the eighteenth century, many boasting a plaque or two noting their status as preserved historical houses and architectural landmarks—Colonial, Federal, Greek Revival, Gothic Revival—an entire city, in fact, that doubles as the country's largest open air museum, replete with walking tours on Sunday afternoons. Imagine a city where the chief of police has to call a press conference to remind citizens that, given a sudden rash of daytime burglaries, it would be wise for working people to remember to lock their doors upon leaving home for the day. Imagine in winter (the air fragrant with the smoke from wood stoves) skiing to work, in summer (the air cooled and scented by ocean breezes) strolling along flower-lined sidewalks. Imagine street musicians but no street crime, dogs that curb themselves, the highest ratio of Volvos per capita in the northeast. Imagine the evening paper's banner headline announcing the city's purchase of two spanking new, state of the art, high tech garbage trucks.

The Night Writer, our civic conscience, prints in black paint on the red brick wall: GOVERNMENT HAS TURNED IDIOCY INTO AN ART.

While the city prospered, the countryside languished in neglect.

Our citizens were like colonialists, our state like a member nation of the Third World. The city dwellers came from away; the rural population—the natives—were stuck where they were, in rusty mobile homes or tar paper shacks, in generational poverty, but at least far enough up country that nobody was likely to see them.

ATTENTION YOUNG MEN!
BONZO WANTS YOU!
ARE YOU READY TO DIE?

Yes, preserved under a pristine sky, frozen in time like its architecture, our city was not a place where anything would ever be expected to begin. Resistance least of all. Resistance to what? To freedom? To prosperity ? To peace?

WATCH OUT
BE PREPARED
YOU ARE LIVING IN THE BELLY OF THE BEAST

The Night Writer knows. Some people don't accept the terms. Some send back their ticket. Some send it back quietly, modestly, without postage due. Others....

As Paul Rousseau's own mother once said: "Nobody likes the government, but not everybody goes around blowing things up."

It is from contradiction that rebellion is born. Rebellion and other things. For if some people attempt to resolve contradiction by making war, others try by making up stories.

There are stories people tell themselves so they can remember who they are. Everybody does this. You probably hear the stories all the time and from the most unlikely people: your mechanic who tells you about the years he spent hitching back and forth across Asia; the paint salesman who mentions in passing the intensity of light in Taos; the gasman who reads your meter and the Japanese characters on your t-shirt because he spent ten years in a Zen monastery in Kyoto. The stories are so real that the day seems to fade back, the stories move in closer, as though they had more strength, as though real life was lived inside the stories, as though the present were merely a long daydream, like treading water, treading time. The stories are precious; like Navajo chants, they help to heal the contradiction that lives in the heart of the world.

Simon Donnis had stopped telling stories. By 1984 only people who knew him well or had long memories could recall that twenty years before he had been one of the student leaders of the Free Speech Movement at Berkeley. If he were forced to refer to that period of his life, he would do so with deep cynicism or, worse, with ridicule, irony, self-deprecation. It was a source of great embarrassment to him that something so obviously hallucinatory as the Revolution could have been taken so seriously, as seriously as in another age men took the idea of the withering away of the state, the dictatorship of the proletariat, the brotherhood of man, the City of God. He still smoked dope and listened to rock music, he still read the Guardian and The Progressive and hated landlords and Republicans and wore his hair long, but the pictures of Ho and Che over his desk had been replaced by a single sentence from, of all things, the Declaration of Independence:

> *Prudence indeed will dictate that Governments long established should not be changed for light and transient causes; and accordingly all experience hath shown that mankind are more disposed to suffer while evils are sufferable than to right themselves by abolishing the forms to which they are accustomed.*

While evils are sufferable. All experience shows. Mankind are disposed to suffer.

Simon was disposed to suffer. People who knew him even superficially—and most people of his acquaintance knew him this way—could say two things about him: he had once been a radical and now he worked hard inside the very system he had once tried to destroy. And it didn't make him very happy. Or at least, it didn't appear to.

The fact was nobody saw him much at all, except maybe on the street in a trenchcoat carrying a briefcase, hurrying to court or back to his office. Always hurrying. People who knew him before understood. Most of them had also made compromises along the way. Only a handful still worked in alternative organizations. Two or three were still trying to organize the poor. Two or three were still involved in food co-ops and free schools, still talked about third party candidates and guaranteed annual incomes. But the underground newspaper had long since folded and the co-operative daycare center had gone non-co-op and the community building was rented out to girl scout troops and capitalistic enterprises and a community theatre group that only occasionally performed the work of Brecht or

42

Clifford Odets. None of these men could scratch a living out of any of it. And they all had kids and it was only so long that they could keep telling themselves that it didn't matter that their children wore only second hand clothes, couldn't have new tricycles or piano lessons, were growing up in slums (though in our city they were referred to as low-income neighborhoods) on streets littered with trash, in buildings filled with roaches and the sounds of domestic violence, in rooms covered with peeling lead-base paint, buying food with food stamps, driving around in uninspected cars, hearing their parents fight about money, fight constantly about money, nickle and diming each other to death, the bills stacked on the kitchen table, the oil tank low, the car battery dead, no milk in the house. When you live like the poor you become like the poor. One day you wake up and you are poor and the glory of voluntary poverty becomes the spectre of real poverty and you think, how are you going to explain to your kids, how are you going to tell them, that with graduate degrees stuffed in a drawer you made them grow up like this because you believed you were making the Revolution.

Yes, people who knew Simon before understood. They couldn't condemn him for cashing in his chips. Anyway they didn't have to. Just looking at him they knew he had paid. Sometimes after talking to him on the street or on the rare occasions when they'd see him in a bar and come over to buy him a beer, sometimes after that they'd go home feeling that they hadn't made such a bad deal after all. Maybe they didn't have many chips left any more, maybe they were bound to lose this hand, but at least they were still playing the game, still at the table, still able to raise hell. So they'd walk home down the side streets of the neighborhood and they'd pass an old building and they'd think about a tenants' union, they'd think about collective ownership, and grant money, they'd envision a playground in the abandoned lot, slides and swings and old people gathered around shaded tables playing checkers, and they'd imagine the block transformed and the people happy and they'd decide to meet with the City Council. Yes, it would start up again, the flow of it like the flow of their blood, the pulse of it. And they'd go home smiling, open a beer, spin it out again for their woman over a joint, go to bed, make love.

If Simon had ever discovered that he had this sort of effect on people it might have been a mini-enlightenment for him. Sometimes the merest glimpse of yourself as others see you has this effect. But although his former comrades had a certain compassion for him, a certain sympathy, let's say, he had only disdain for them. And having disdain for someone, dismissing him as a sap or a fool, even a romantic fool, even an idealistic fool, this dismissal precludes entirely the possibility of seeing anything through his eyes, even the most humble and obvious truth. After all, everyone knows that against humble and obvious truths the best defense is always scorn. So while his former friends left him of an evening to stroll home under the vast sky of possibility, Simon himself would trudge back to his office or, if the hour were late, home to his sleeping children and his indifferent wife. He would roll a joint, too, and open a beer. Then he would sit in front of the TV and watch whatever old movie was on, whatever was on, so he wouldn't have to think or talk, so he wouldn't have to worry about his clients, so he could forget for awhile who he was. And this went on for many years until 1964 was as remote as 1944 or 1924 or 1812 or 1776. Only rarely was he reminded of it, like the night he was in a bar and a kid came up to him and said, "Gee, you must have lived through the sixties, huh? What was it like?"

44

For a second something terrible happened to Simon's face. The kid took a step backward because even he could recognize rage when he saw it, though he was too young to recognize much else. But Simon just rode it, let it rise and fall, let it pass, let it die right there like he had let so many other passions in his life die. All he said was, "You had to be there," and then he emptied his glass and left.

It was in that same bar, maybe it was that same night, that Erika first saw Marc. She was with Simon at the time, one of those rare nights that they went out together and pretended they were still in love. After so many years of marriage these small ruses take on a sweetness, the sweetness of conspirators conning the world. See, they say, we are still together, we persevere, we do not capitulate, we defy the odds. Bittersweet indeed. And so standing together at the bar they saw him. He was wearing a yellow t-shirt with a rainbow embroidered over the pocket on the left hand side, over his heart. The shirt was snug, he was short; he seemed to be all torso and head with that great mass of shaggy hair that curled around his face and down his back. He was busy carrying ice and cartons of beer up from the cellar, but in between trips he would stop and talk to some of the men at the bar. One of these, a big man with a mustache who was very drunk, kept hugging and kissing him and he would smile up at the man and allow himself to be hugged and kissed. Then he would laugh and dart away back to the cellar for more ice. Simon and Erika smiled at one another and watched him. Whatever Simon was thinking he kept to himself, but Erika was magnetized by something in him, his animation, perhaps, or his warmth, which struck her as an angelic presence in the sordidness of the bar. And then as she watched him she sensed something else—an appeal for affection, an appeal for warmth. She stopped herself then because she could

45

not tell, never could tell, whether what she sensed came from outside herself or from within.

What happened after that was really quite remarkable. Erika, who had for years been paying scant attention to her life, distracted as she was by images of global horror—the earth shaking, buildings crumbling, children crying out from beneath the rubble, women falling with dying children in their arms, the earth itself drying up, cracking, men dying of thirst, in prisons being dismembered slowly, armies moving, towns burned, forests leveled, animals erased from the seas and the face of the earth while corporate offices are built on their bones and missiles point upwards to the clouds, giant gun barrels aimed at the sky and the gods of the sky, Jupiter, Jehovah and Zeus, the father gods who betrayed and abandoned us and whom we are now capable of killing once and for all, taking their collected works out along with them—Erika suddenly came to. Miraculously she began to exert her will and her imagination, studying, in respect to him, the myriad implications of a single gesture, a movement as minute as the flutter of an eyelid, a quality as ephemeral as the warmth inside a voice, focusing the intensity of her entire attention on hints and signs, on the one thing that now seemed valuable and important. Ridiculous as it was, Erika, for the second time in her life, had fallen in love at first sight.

Of all writers Erika loved Dostoyevsky best and she would often quote this line of his: In all men, no matter how hardened, there lives a naive and simple hearted child, and it is to that child that we must always speak because it is that child who wants to hear.

It was this naive and simple hearted child that she saw in Marc. Marc the sensualist. Marc the Don Juan. Marc who any hardened woman could peg in a minute, but who Erika, in her absurd nineteenth century naivete, took for an innocent, lonely, lost and unloved.

Erika went back to the bar night after night, to study him, to watch. To him she was invisible, but that was all right. It took her a long time to decide; she waited for a long time.

From all appearances Erika Donnis had everything: an admirable husband; two happy children; a big, old wooden house with its magnificent summer flower garden in back; work that satisfied her, gave people pleasure and did no one any harm (those deft illustrations of obscure wildflowers and commonly sighted birds); and still a measure of wildness, something left in her that had not been domesticated, some spirit that hadn't yet been curbed. She could be seen running down streets with an alpaca poncho flying around her, her hair coming undone from its braid, or riding her bicycle in layers of sweaters and a black beret, everything in her concentrated on speed, or in her rickety jalopy, classical music blasting out of it, sometimes two or more children piled in the back.

Yes, from all appearances Erika had everything.

Ironically, it was just on this matter of appearances that Erika had first entered the political arena of the city. It happened at a community meeting in one of the old Model Cities neighborhood centers, two years into Nixon's first term. She was wearing a blue workshirt, jeans, sandals, sitting with a bunch of freaks, carpenters who had organized themselves into a collective and, rumor had it, joined the IWW (rumor also had it they were communists). The collective was trying to get money from Model Cities to buy and renovate abandoned buildings for poor people to live in. The buildings could be bought for a song, the collective would work for a reasonable wage and take on unemployed neighborhood youth as apprentices. The buildings could be owned cooperatively or sold at low cost, providing home ownership for low income members of the community. (Excellent though the idea was, the proposal was ultimately turned down. The buildings remained derelict until gentrification hit. They were then bought for a song by condo developers, renovated, and sold to young professionals for more money per apartment than it would have cost six years before to buy up the whole block. Low income people were gradually pushed farther and farther away from the inner city as their old neighborhoods were restored and housing costs soared.) The collective wanted the community group's support for their proposal. The spokesperson for the collective was not Simon but a much wilder looking character: the local poor had been far more frightened than impressed. Then Erika stood up to speak. She was very young then, probably nineteen though she looked younger. She had figured out what was going on and got up to speak to it.

What she talked about that night was the need to look beyond appearances. She understood, she said, that when the city comes to the neighborhood to get approval for housing projects they always wear suits and ties and have slick blueprints and credentials and graphs and for that reason they seem more trustworthy than people who come in looking like ordinary folks. (Though the carpentry collective could only pass for ordinary folks in the San Francisco Bay Area circa 1966.) But she asked them to think about what was really important in a job like this: skill, experience, and good politics, people working for people, not profit, people working for their own community, even if it was their own community only by adoption. She said, Remember that nine times out of ten the men who come into this neighborhood with suits on are here to harm you, to rip you off, to take your kids, to raise your rent, to serve you with summonses or notices to quit. Why, because they come in one time and promise you good, cheap housing, are you going to trust them? What do they have invested in this neighborhood except money? Do they live here? Is this their home?

She was good all right. She almost swayed them. She almost made them see.

And after that, her byline in the underground paper, then organizing the first women's group in the city with Annie Pratt, their push for free daycare, for a women's health clinic, a women's plank at the state Democratic Convention, the rumors about the commune, about Simon and Annie, about Erika and Paul. And then it just all ground to a halt. Annie and Paul went underground; they might as well have taken Erika and Simon along with them.

Silence. And out of the silence Simon emerged as a lawyer and Erika as the apotheosis of married womanhood. As the years went by Simon became more withdrawn and somber and Erika drove her car even faster down the cobblestone streets. Yet there were those who remembered other images, older ones: Erika at a table, a passionate expression lighting her face, her hand sweeping the air in front of her as though in this one gesture she would rid the world of every ill. And Annie sitting across from her, head thrown back, laughing loud and hard. They are there together. Their hair is uncombed and hanging down their backs, their jeans have holes in the knees, their sweaters are shabby and have holes in the elbows. They are fifteen years younger. They are happy and free.

Every choice closes a door.

Their meeting when it finally occurred was awkward. Marc seemed puzzled by her interest; Erika couldn't think of anything to say. Finally he wrote his address and phone number on a matchbook cover and gave it to her. She didn't even know his last name.

She never mentioned this meeting to Simon. She never mentioned Marc at all. But even if she never mentioned him by name or suggestion, she gave Simon warnings. She was willing to put up with anything but living her life with a man who wanted to be dead. It was only when he told her pointblank one night that he had no choices and she was nothing but a romantic to think that she did, it was only then that she chose.

Marc was waiting for her. He assumed that she would come to him, that it was inevitable that she would come. Women did, many women did. Erika was simply another one, another lost soul, another hungry waif he took in and fed and then sent out again. He knew what she wanted and he gave it to her and he thought it was enough. And if it wasn't, well, it was the best he could do. He acquiesced to women, but he could not love them. So he gave Erika his body but withheld his heart and she left him feeling as though she had stolen something, that somehow she had done him an injury, a terrible injury for which she would have to pay a terrible price. Holy and precious, the price of the passing of time.

CHAPTER 3

Time Was Holy,
Days Were Gods

It was time throbbing away in her hands the way she always imagined blood would, throb out of her in a stillness that was like hesitancy, like floating suspended over the brink of sleep and feeling time itself ebb away. Her body seemed paralyzed there in her bed, yet she herself was vibrating as though she was breaking down, her consciousness becoming so acute she could feel the energy in her molecules, the electromagnetism of her own atoms. The buzzing in the air, the graininess of the dark, and time, pulsing, pulsing, and she, Annie, waiting to be awakened from a nightmare. What is the price for delay? The price for self-indulgence? For weakness? For believing yourself immune from catastrophe?

There was no question about it. They would be home by now. Even if the call went wrong, by now they would be home.

But she is asleep. The alarm has gone off and she knows that she has to wake up, that time is passing, that she will be late, and yet she knows it in a place that is so far away, at such a distance, that she can barely feel it. Only the slightest beat of anxiety, at long intervals, breaks through the gauze of sleep.

Somewhere in between she dreams of a woman dressed entirely in black, a young woman with short black hair. Black clothes, white skin, red lipstick. She is standing in front of a class and she is singing. She sings very badly, in a cracked whisper, and as she sings she

51

shrugs her shoulders, plays with her hair. She isn't even trying to sing and yet Annie knows that this woman in black (now adjusting her dress, now smoothing her hair) is a brilliant singer, renowned for her voice. Perhaps she simply hasn't started the performance yet, perhaps she is warming up, waiting for some signal to begin. Then Annie has to change classes. She goes down the hall to the stairs, opens the door, finds herself on a wide curving staircase made, like the walls, of cement, and like the walls, painted light blue. She is going down a curving tunnel of blue steps, the steps so shallow there must be hundreds of them, and the curve seems endless, and she wonders how children can possibly make their way up and down these stairs, how frightening it must be for them to enter this blue cement spiral. She will go and speak to the principal...She dreams of a white cat who leaps onto her bed and licks her face. She dreams she gets up (it feels as though she does get up) and follows it around the house, wondering how it got in. But the house is the house of her childhood, always in dreams the house of her earliest childhood, and she makes her way down the stairs and down the hall, stairwell and hall covered with pictures of her father in uniform, pictures of ships, huge, grey ships, and decks full of young men in white t-shirts and funny round white hats, grinning, pictures of carriers and cruisers, more formal photographs of men in their whites, saluting on another deck, her father among them, (all of the pictures behind glass in black frames that need dusting), and through the kitchen with the blue and white tablecloth and the jar of flowers on the table to the screen door and out the door to the porch where she looks out across fields of low plants dotted with white balls, like tiny puffs of cloud caught in the branches and the white cat chasing the balls and in the sky, white soaring birds.

The gauze of dreams.

Oh, she says, to break through.

Oh! she is crying it out.

Oh! wailing it.

NO.

Awake.

She is awake. Conscious. Focused. She knows who she is and what she has to do.

How much time?

When they question the children, when they say, We'll take you to your mommy...When they say to Emma, You'll be away for awhile. You'll need your dollies...Unless stupidly, ignorantly, or, worse, purposefully, intentionally, like murderers, they had stormed the house, burst in shooting, given no warning...If they had given no warning, if they had attacked, surrounded the house or the van, given Paul no choice...

No, no. They are talking to Emma now. It is a woman. She pretends to be kind. She says, We want to talk to your mommy. Just tell me where she is...

They came bursting in with guns. Surrounded the house. Didn't call them out. Didn't want to alert them. Maybe they'd turn it into a siege. (Oh, yes, with five children inside, of course, what else.) So instead they storm in, bust the windows, bust down the doors. Cocks up and ready to kill, nervous and brutal, and if anyone moved, even a child, if one of the boys made a move, or Emma, terrified, running to her papa...

STOP THIS NOW

Annie runs cold water over her face, over her head. There are certain things she can no longer think. They do not concern her. Nothing hurts anymore. There is no pain. Only purpose. Dresses in black pants, black sweater, dark jacket. In the closet is the emergency pack. Her firearm. Money. In Paul's room too many papers to destroy. The most sensitive, in the cabinet, dumped into a trash can, set ablaze. She tosses in the latest photograph of herself pinned up over his desk. No one was supposed to take their pictures, but sometimes Eli forgot. Everything in the can curls, blackens, the air fills with smoke. The smoke detectors will go on soon. She sprays the blaze with the fire extinguisher, feeling as though she is operating in slow motion, feeling stupid, forgetting something.

At the front door it stops her. It is a wall made up of memories. She cannot make herself walk through that wall, even reach her hand through it, turn the knob, open the door. How can she possibly leave this house? How can she walk outside?

And then she sees what is waiting for her, who is waiting, so many of them, all the other women who have walked through that wall of blood ties and memories before her. The faces rise up in the darkness and they are so beautiful, Black and Native American, Hispanic (all the mothers of the disappeared, the mothers of the plazas, all the brave women of the revolutionary vanguards), and Chinese, Vietnamese, all the women warriors of the African National Congress, they are all there, beyond the door, waiting for her with their arms open in welcome. It is the next step. She is Annie Pratt now. No more masks.

The wall parted. She slipped through the door into the frost-layered night. (She is not thinking of what may be happening anywhere else, not thinking of Paul, not thinking of blood or bodies ripped open, not thinking of her children, of tiny, cold hands.) She takes the path behind the house that goes through the cornfield, intersects later with a dirt road and then another track and another, a zigzag cut through cornfields all the way to the outskirts of town where a bus stopped at 7:30 en route to the city. They might be watching the buses. It would be safer to hitch.

54

Think like a predator. The prey must have the predator's mind: a single mind, yours and his. But yours must have another chamber, a secret door. You can outwit him by knowing him, by becoming him, and then, at the last, just opening up that other door and slipping away.

There was a lightness in the air, an inner glow. Moon full but a cloud cover so the light permeates. A good light for walking through frozen cornfields, for hearing the crunch of boots on crusted soil and the rustling breath of breezes you don't feel but only hear in the dried stalks. Something so eerie about the night, about walking here, the only living thing, the only thing alive, walking blind into whatever comes. Know soon enough, but right now knowing nothing. Is she a mother still? A wife? Is there anything left of her in the world? Does she know her name? Walking in a field of dead corn in a cold milky twilight that could be the color on the moon. Oh, for a color, any color, red or blue, her children's eyes, Emma's new dress.

Annie walks and to keep walking, to keep walking on down the line of dead plants, she fixes on one thing and decides to remember everything about it, to recreate it, word by word, moment by moment, like when she was a kid she would think what would happen if she filmed her whole life, every day, every moment, how it would take as long to see it as it would to live it and how odd that was. Questions that consumed whole periods of her life. Could deaf people think and how if they didn't know any words? How could God know what she was going to do and wasn't there any way to outsmart Him? Now she could see herself walking through the cornfield. It was the last scene of the movie. Her life was exactly half over, it was time to sit back and look at the tape. God would explain why it was impossible to outsmart Him since he had seen the movie once through already. The deaf think in pictures not words. There are many other things you can't figure out because you are stuck in such a little corner of space and the straightjacket of time.

But she defies space and time. Walking in this field she is also back fifteen years, in Erika's kitchen, looking into the face of Paul Rousseau for the first time. And yet it would be hard to say exactly what Annie saw in those hours, carrying her pack through the diaphanous night turning into morning, for like the deaf she was thinking in pictures not words. It is easier to know Erika's version of that scene. Maybe later that same morning as she lay in bed she too was trying to resurrect the past, reassemble it. Maybe she too was trying to remember, paging through her journals from fifteen years before, mingling the scant words on the page with the richness of her memories, letting those ancient days return to her, whole and entire.

But if Erika pored over those notebook pages that Saturday morning, it wasn't to remember the entrance into her life of Paul Rousseau but to conjure up the essence of Simon as he had been, the man who had disappeared, perhaps the man who was truly dead.

March 17, 1972 It must be the weather that's depressing me. I remember St. Patrick's Day when I was a kid. We'd march in the parade, it would be so warm, sixty-two degrees one year, the sky so blue, bagpipes playing in front and behind and our fifes and drums and feeling so good and alive. Up here the winter doesn't break until late April and then it's mud season for a month. And now everything is so ugly, the snow crusted with soot, the streets bedraggled, cluttered with last year's trash, the sky a dirty grey. I would leave but there's nowhere to go. The evil is everywhere, the whole world seeped in soot. The Hopis can't see the rising sun or grow their corn because of the pollution of the air and the rain. All their prophecies (the bad ones) are fulfilled.

56

Simon came home for lunch. I heard him coming up the back stairs, stamping the snow off his boots outside the door. I hadn't even made coffee. I hadn't done anything all morning but think about Black Mesa and our total impotence in the face of corporate greed. So he came in and we had lunch and talked, intensely as usual, about the need to make alternative organizations work, how our resistance is part of an alternative history (the one they don't teach in school) and so we're not as isolated as we might think (historically isolated, that is), things aren't so hopeless, cheer up (Simon's optimism, which I really love in him). Then someone showed up from the Haight, a friend of Ocean's named Annie Pratt. She'll be staying with us for awhile. I like her a lot.

Simon comes into the kitchen and dumps his parka on the chair.

"What's wrong?" He can see into her, instantly, like a palmreader gazing into an open hand.

"Oh, it's just this article I'm trying to write for the paper about Black Mesa. It's so depressing."

"Well, this might cheer you up." He hands her a sheet of paper. The United Working Collectives of this City United in Brotherhood and Organized with the Industrial Workers of the World Present to this State Convention of the Democratic Party the Following Demands. "We met all morning. Everything passed unanimously."

Erika runs her eye down the page. Immediate and total withdrawal from Southeast Asia heads the list. A guaranteed annual income. Repeal of the tax law of 1937. (This is the legalize pot plank, the ganja plank for short.) Worker control of industry. Reading between the lines Erika sees the embryonic public emergence of Simon's major fantasies: corporations owned by the workers, a return to direct democracy, total decentralization of power which meant de facto secession, freaks guarding the state borders (which are

57

no longer state borders but international frontiers), freaks dismembering the mills (shouting the poems of William Blake), opening the prisons, moving the poor into the summer houses of the rich. Simon wrote his doctoral thesis on the French Revolution, but Erika doesn't think the fantasy includes mass decapitations.

Simon rolls a joint and Erika puts up water, heats the pea soup, slices some bread. Simon chooses a record, Alice Coltrane's *Ptah the El Daud,* and lights the joint.

"You seem awful down, Erica." Gently, encouragingly. Tell me, he's saying. Tell me what's. wrong. Down. Yes, she feels down. Up. Down. The lighter your heart, the higher you get. The heavier your heart...But she is heavy-hearted. Her heart feels like a stone.

"I don't understand. It really rains for the Hopis, Simon. When they dance, it rains."

"Yes."

"So they have some power, don't they? Something in the universe responds to them. There is something that responds. Really. So why is evil winning? What happened to those powers? How could they lose?"

"Maybe they didn't lose. Maybe they went underground. Maybe they're still here and we just can't see them. Maybe we're not old enough to see them."

"Old enough?"

"We haven't been around very long. Maybe we just don't know what to look for."

"But, Simon, those bulldozers just go in and level a sacred mountain and nothing happens!"

"Well, what do you expect to happen? Do you expect them to get hit by lightning? That's a Yahweh tactic. That's the kind of god that got us into this mess in the first place. No, if there's a war between good and evil going on, the one thing you can be sure about is that the good powers aren't going to look like the evil ones. They aren't going to come in with Agent Orange and napalm and DDT and bulldozers..."

"But it's that stuff that's killing..."

"Assuming that killing's the worse thing..."

"But if it's all lost..."

"That knowledge, you mean, of..."

"Like the Druids, just gone, all forgotten. What happens to power like that when nobody can remember..."

"Well, nobody we know of anyway. They may be here in disguise, they may keep coming back."

"Assuming people come back."

"It just matters how you die, I think."

"Whether you come back? You mean, whether you're scared or not?"

"Whether you pull back or go forward."

Stoned. The magic weed that clears away everything and lets you see. And they see that they're both wearing the same clothes, blue workshirts and jeans, that their hair is about the same color and the same length, though Simon's is pulled back in a ponytail to keep it out of his face and Erika's hangs loose over her shoulders, that they are both starved. They get up to dish out the pea soup, stand over the iron pot on the stove, both of them the same height, they can look each other directly in the eye. They do, and smile.

"It occurred to me this morning," Simon says, ladling the soup into her bowl first, "that we may really be looking at it backwards. I looked around the building this morning at all these people and I thought, Hell, we *are* Western culture, we're the underground contingent, the old ones. Look," and they move away from the stove to the table where the bread is sliced on the wooden board and the mugs of steaming coffee wait for them, "it was driven underground, the essence of it, when the old deities were pushed out by those tyrannical gods of the Middle East. That's what happened to your Druids and magicians. It was all hidden away. The heretics kept it going, and the witches and the utopians, all the lunatics. All the bad guys are really the good guys, everything we learned in history is upside down. They kept it alive, it kept bursting out, it fought the bastards every step of the way. Men were always jumping up at them and saying, No, you fuckers! It turned into anarchism, rebellion, revolution, and now it's manifesting itself in us. It may be dangerous to idealize other cultures. They all have the same dialectic working itself out in them, the established power elite versus the rebels, the monarchy versus the people, the orthodox versus the free thinkers. It's no different anywhere else. Look at the Chinese with their taoists in the mountains and their boddhisattvas, they didn't pull it off either. Even the Indians. The Aztecs weren't exactly the most humanistic society around. I'm not sure being a woman in Tibet was anything to write home about. So here we are in the perfect spot, the belly of the beast. I wouldn't want to be anywhere else. At least we have a crack at it, from the inside."

Simon stops talking and concentrates on his soup. Erika thinks about the music, how it doesn't try to squeeze itself into the confines of words, how hard it is to have to put one word in front of the other, one idea in front of the other, one fact in front of the other, when everything is at once and flows together like music. Fluid like feelings, but not so vague, not in need of a name. I feel this way or that. Ideas aren't vague, but they shouldn't have to be forced into an order either. They should be like music—five themes at once, five voices, five ideas, all playing with each other, wonderful and true. She wants to turn off Alice Coltrane and put on Bach.

60

"The thing is, Erika, we have to focus on building a new society, not on trying to change theirs. That's the problem with pouring all this energy into the convention. I'm not a Democrat and I don't want to be a Democrat. We have to create counter-parties, counter-industries.You can't wait for it to change, you just have to go around it, make it new, do it yourself."

"You sound like Ben. Whatever you want to do can be done now."

"It can be. We just have to be careful about what we want, see all the dangers before they arise and deal with them."

She gazes out the window at the absolutely colorless sky while Simon pulls off his boots. He will get up then and change the record, change the rhythm of the afternoon. He can switch so easily. But Erika feels like she's all mind, her body is apart from her and strange. She's too high for sex, too light. She wants Beethoven now, not the Cream. She watches him bent over his body, working his boots off, and she feels nothing. But it will pass. It always does. He will touch her and her mind and her body will reunite. And then they hear the sound of feet on the back stairs. The visitor crosses the porch with a heavy, uneven step. Heavy knock on the door. Simon wrinkles his nose and goes to open it and Erika hears a woman's voice. "Simon? Simon and Erika?"

It's a tired voice, soft but weary. Southern accent. Another wanderer. They roll in exhausted, every week or so. It's a long trek up and hard to hitch, not many people on the road this time of year. In the summer it's different and in deep winter people stop, even the natives stop for freaks in winter. But March is a hard traveling month. No one is going to freeze to death on the side of the road in March, they figure, so they just drive by.

She looks tired too and cold. All she's wearing are sweaters, a bunch of sweaters, jeans, a scarf over her head. No gloves. Her hands must be frozen.

"Welcome," Simon says, waving her in and shutting the door. The air is chill, damp. One of the cats slithers in with her, finds a comfortable chair, sprawls on it.

"I'm Annie. I'm a friend of Ocean's."

"So you're from California?"

"No, just lived there for awhile. I came back east for a little reality, you know? Just forgot about the weather."

She laughs. She has a wonderful laugh, the kind of laugh that saves you and everybody around you. She unwinds the scarf from around her head. Blond hair, parted in the middle. Very fair skin, almost pasty white as though she had been ill. Laugh lines around her eyes, a worn but innocent face, burned a lot but still willing.

"Well, sit down and have some soup."

"Best invitation I've had all day. And some of that joint would be real nice."

She puts her pack down and falls into the rocking chair.

"Sorry to bust in on you like this." She takes the joint eagerly. "I haven't been high in two days." She talks about her trip while Erika dishes out some soup: the weirdness in San Francisco, the crash pad in New York, speed freaks and junkies, factory jobs along the way, all the time thinking about this city, Ocean telling her it was paradise, get there and look up Simon and Erika, they're good people, this is where she belonged.

"So what's happening up here? What are you folks into?"

"What do you want?" Simon asks.

"I want the Revolution, brother. I'm looking for it. Seen it lately?" And she laughs again, puts her head

62

back and laughs. Simon and Erika glance at each other and smile. Another one. Oh yes, the resistance is everywhere. Everywhere. We'll do it this time. This time we'll win.

"I'm sure glad I found you folks. Ocean and I were raving one night about psychic negativity, how it just eats at you like battery acid, and then she told me about you two, how tight you were, how right on, and I thought, well, gotta meet these folks sometime. Get to paradise and check it out."

Simon gives her the rundown on alternative goings on in the city. It sounds impressive as he rattles it all off—the collectives, the newspaper, the theatre company.

"Daycare?" she asks. "What about the kids?"

"No kids yet."

"Gotta have kids," she says. "That's where the Shakers went wrong. What about women's groups?"

"Women's groups?"

"Yeah. The women's center, the women's movement. Don't tell me you don't have some strong women's organizations up here."

"I guess it hasn't got here yet."

"Sister, it just walked in your door."

"Well," Erika says, holding out her hand. "How do you do?"

Annie laughs again. "Well, just fine, thank you, darlin', after your good soup." Erika glances at Simon, smiling. It's his good soup. "Now if I can ask you one more favor, I'd sure like to take a hot bath."

Later, over wine, Annie says, "The struggle is necessary, but it pollutes your heart. You have to keep yourself from becoming hard, you have to work all the time at keeping your heart open. Cause I've seen some things, things our own brothers do to us, the same things the man does, you know? Imperialism and racism can't be dealt with separate from sexism. It's all

6 3

the same. But some of our so-called leadership—which I don't believe in myself, but they sure do—they can't see that. You can't attack imperialism in Viet Nam and forget what happens in your own backyard or your own bedroom. Otherwise it's all bullshit and we're just playing games with each other. I'm not interested in playing games."

It is taken for granted by all of them that Annie will crash there for a few nights.

May 25, 1972 Last week Brenda did a reading for me. She looked at the cards spread out on the table in front of her and she said, "I *must* stop doing this. It's so *ridiculous*. These cards are just playing with me because I'm just playing with them." I asked her what was the matter (was I dead?) and she said, "Well, according to this you, my dear, are pregnant. Are you?"

I didn't know for sure at the time, but in fact I was. Am. Officially pregnant.

I was completely freaked out about it at first. I even told Simon I wanted to have an abortion. He was wonderful, of course. He said it was up to me. Just like that. It was up to me.

Give 'em enough rope and they hang themselves.

Because of course once he said that I couldn't possibly do it. Because I love him and I know he wants kids, hundreds of kids. He'll have to have hundreds of wives. But we'll have this baby and see.

Then we told Annie and she got so excited, she was so, so happy. And she'll be here, she'll help. I won't have to do it by myself.

A May night, warm, fragrant. Buds just opening on the branches of the maple trees. The earth beginning to smell like the earth again. A full moon.

Erika is sitting in the swing chair on the back porch feeling as though her life has just ended, her real life, the life she wanted. Now she is going to live someone else's life, her mother's, her grandmother's, the life of all those women she used to watch with pity,

64

women on the beach with little babies, toddlers, women who had no lives of their own. While she would read poetry and contemplate life, they would chase children around. It was a horror she never, never wanted to experience.

Poetry by Sylvia Plath who put her head in an oven after being a mother for awhile.

When Annie comes out, Erika's heart sinks even lower. She wants to be alone, alone, absolutely alone. She doesn't want to be congratulated, she doesn't want any more expressions of joy.

Annie sits across from her, sighs deeply.

"What a beautiful night."

Erika doesn't respond. She wants Annie to go away, everyone to just go away.

"Simon sure seems happy these days. But you, Erika, you're so quiet. Are you feeling all right?"

"Sure, I'm feeling dandy. Kind of like I just got handed a life sentence."

The bitterness takes Annie by suprise. Erika knows it does, can almost feel her recoil from it. You're not supposed to feel this way. No, you're supposed to start knitting or something. But Annie just says,

"It is a big step. I know how you feel."

"You don't know how I feel. I feel like I stepped on a trap and now all I can do is chew my leg off."

"But, Erika, didn't you and Simon..."

"No. No we didn't. I married Simon because I loved him not because I wanted to be somebody else's mother."

"Why are you doing it then? You don't have to. He would understand, wouldn't he?"

But Erika can't answer. He would understand, he wouldn't hate her, but she can't do it to him, so that's all there is to it. It is like being faced with two choices and both of them are equally impossible to choose. Death by fire or death by water. Betray your lover or betray yourself. And she can't answer anyway because her face is trembling too much, because she is going to cry, as though that solved anything, as though it helped.

"Erika," Annie says and gets up and sits beside her, puts her arms around her. The last thing Erika wants is to be mothered. But she can't push Annie away. She isn't able to push anyone away. And it feels good to be held, even isolated as she feels, alien to everyone, even so, like being an animal on a human lap, it feels good.

"You know, Erika, you don't have to change just because you have a kid. You don't have to be any different. You can still do everything you want to do. Who knows, you might even have a kid you like."

"I've never known a kid I liked," Erika says, feeling petulant, feeling precisely like the kind of kid she would never like.

She knows Annie is smiling at her even though she can't see her face.

"Before I met you and Simon, I never knew anyone with a college degree I liked...A kid of Simon's might be pretty far out."

"Yeah. Maybe."

"You'd be a pioneer, Erika, the first one of us to do it."

"Yeah. Then if it's really awful no one else will have to do it. Sort of like the canary they send down the mine shafts."

Now Annie really laughs.

"Erika," she says, "I really love you."

"Why?"

"I don't know. I just do. You're so *honest*."

They swing in the chair, back and forth, Annie's arm still around Erika's shoulders.

"Will you stay with us?"

66

"If you want me to, wild horses couldn't drag me away."

"I want you to. Maybe I'm just scared. In Russian novels women always die having babies."

"You won't die having this baby. This baby is going to be easy. This baby is going to be easy and good and beautiful and you're going to love the shit out of it. You'll see."

"You just reminded me. Oh, Annie, diapers!"

"Oh, God, diapers and shit and spit up and gooey fingers. Oh, no..." And now even Erika finds herself starting to laugh. "Oh Simon will have to do it! That's it, Erika, we'll make Simon do all the yukky stuff. We'll get him drunk and make him sign his life away. He'll have to swear to change all the diapers. Well, it's only fair. You're doing all the hard stuff, trucking her around for nine months. He'll be in charge of all the messy stuff and I'll see that you all eat well. How's that sound?"

"Great. All I have to do is have it and then I can go back to Paris and live in a garret?"

"Then you can go to Paris and live wherever you want."

"Because I don't really want to be a mother, Annie. Everybody thinks it's so great, I think it's a cop out."

"No, it's the opposite of a cop out. All of a sudden you have a bigger stake in it. It's not just you they're fucking over anymore, it's your kid, too. I think it's heavier for parents. I don't think it's a cop out at all. I think it takes guts to have kids in this fucked up country. That's why I didn't do it. I got pregnant in California and I had an abortion because it just scared me too much. But, see, you're in a real lucky place, Erika. You're not alone. And you'll never be alone. You don't have to worry. See, you keep thinking you're going to have a tragic life like those people in Russian novels, but you're not. Not this time around."

"You mean I already threw myself under a train?"

And Annie laughs her great, warm, open laugh.

"Is that what women do in Russian novels? Shit. Well, strong women don't throw themselves under trains and you're a strong woman, Erika. Whether you know it or not...Now what are we going to name this baby?"

So Annie makes everything safe for her, chases the demons away, makes her warmer, closer to herself, closer to other people. Annie pulls her back, always pulls her back into the world, back from that place where mind is separated from body, back to the world of human beings where mind permeates matter, soul and body are one and the same.

They sit in the swing chair and swing and laugh, thinking of names for this baby who is going to come into a world neither one of them trusts but which they are each willing to change for the better, to work on until it's right. They are still, both of them, able to hope.

July ? I am trying to understand. I am trying. I am telling myself that this happens to everybody, that this is just part of the real world, real life. But I hate it. I hate it. I don't accept it. I can't even write down how I feel. It's so big it doesn't have a name. Hurt. That's what it is. Like someone died. And I wonder if this is how it's going to be from now on. Every woman my rival, all my friends my enemies? Well, I won't do it. I'll leave him first. So now we have to talk about love. The nature of love. Revolutionary love. We're just talking about it, he says. Don't get so upset. It's just an idea. *Just an idea!* Like people haven't been killing each other for centuries over ideas. Oh, just a harmless little idea. Open marriage. Not being a tight, closed couple, but a wonderful open loving free dyad floating through the universe, embracing everyone, sharing our love with others. How selfish of me not to have thought of this before! Well, Simon, fuck you. That's what I want to say. Fuck you. But I can't say it because I'm not sure he's not right, I'm not sure I'm not being selfish and horrible. But why now? Why does he have to do it now? And doesn't he see it will change everything, that it won't ever be the same? It was a lie. We are not one person.

Annie is always up first in the morning. Erika wakes up hearing her humming in the kitchen, humming or singing or talking to the cats. Wakes up to the smell of coffee, to the light from the window caressing Simon's head, to the sound of singing.

She jumps out of bed and the first thing she does is feel her belly. Yes, she's still there, the bump in the belly, little Becky Bumpkin. They know she's a girl. Erika dreamt she was a girl. Annie dreamt she was a girl. Brenda read it in the cards—a girl. Conceived so near to the time of Annie's arrival that her middle name is Ann. Annie named her Becky and Simon named her Ann. Erika just trucks her around. And eats.

Simon is snoring so Erika gives him a gentle nudge and a kiss and opens the drapes. Another beautiful day. All of the beautiful days. Summer days. In the kitchen Annie is poaching eggs. She grins at Erika. Erika scowls back.

"I'm not eating any more eggs."

"You'll eat your eggs like a good girl. You want a healthy baby, you eat your eggs. Goddammit."

The goddammit is from Simon. You'll drink this milk, goddammit. Yes, boss. A family joke now. Erika is so well fed she feels like a veal Parmesan on the hoof.

They sound alike. They dress alike. Habits: jeans, workshirts. The kitchen is like a refectory, sun-drenched, smelling of coffee and yeast, the homegrown in pots along the windowsills, some of it hanging upside down to dry along with bundles of basil and thyme. Their days are spent in simplicity and poverty, non-collaboration with capitalism in any of its forms, honest labor, making it all new. How Christian they are in form if not in substance, the same play, different costumes. Erika can't get this out of her head: that they are destined for these roles, that history is replaying the same struggle over and over, that everything they do here and now reverberates throughout time, and that, after all, the women and men who believed in Jesus were revolutionaries, too, had nothing to go on but their instincts, had a friend who was either brilliant or insane, a cause that was either the working out of an ancient prophecy or the highest form of sacrilege and treason, that the choice was never clear cut, there was always doubt, the fear you could be wrong, could be following a lunatic right to the edge of the abyss. And then asked to jump.

Some members of the carpentry collective are lunatics, too, practitioners of crazy wisdom, tellers of tales, anarchists, poets, citizens of the Liberated Zones of Cannabis Consciousness, pot heads par excellence. Meetings take up a great many of their nights. Meanwhile the women meet in the living room. The men talk about jobs and grants and corporate conspiracies; the women talk about organizing a welfare mothers union. The men talk about Blake and Paine and Olsen; the women decide to collect women's poetry and publish it. The men want to smash the state; the women want to find a hot xerox machine. Or even a mimeograph. We need a voice, Annie says. (In the other room, Ben, with his Chinese sage's beard, cries out, There must be justice! Annie says, Let them worry about justice. We have to get these poems on a page.)

Annie is singing "Summertime", bending over a copy of Adelle Davis, preparing Erika's morning

70

potion: brewer's yeast, fruit, yogurt, God knows what else.

"Close the door, will ya?" The blender, the whizz of health. The concoction is yellow today. Bananas.

"I have something to talk to you about," she says. Something hidden in her voice. "I'm going to Miami to check out the Convention. I'll send back something for the paper. I'll be your Miami correspondent."

"How long will you be gone?"

"A couple of weeks. There's an NWRO convention in D.C. I'd like to check out, and then stop to see my folks. I think I have a ride to New York this afternoon. But I have to talk to you before I go. I know Simon will lay this on you. He'll wrap it up in some kind of political bullshit rhetoric and make you deal with it like it was part of the Revolution instead of what it is which is just male ego shit. And I love Simon. I don't want to put him down. He's a good man, but he's just a little blind, Erika. He can't see what exactly he's dealing with, becoming a father, the responsibility of it, all that patriarchal shit coming down on him...Eat your egg."

"What exactly are you talking about? Exactly."

"Simon's got it in his head that marriage is a repressive institution. Revolutionaries shouldn't be bound by bourgeois institutions. Monogamy is bourgeois. This is the new twist. I told him it was a fine revolution that allowed revolutionaries to be so goddam self-serving...Erika, look. Don't get freaked out about this. He loves you. He's just stupid right now. He'll get over it. So he's going to rave for a little while about sexual freedom and open marriages. Just pay him no mind, you hear?" She smiles at Erika. Her smile says, Come on, honey. Smile back. Stupid men. Laugh at them. Just laugh...But Erika feels like a knife has just been slipped into her heart.

There's a long silence. Then Erika says,

"He wants to sleep with you." Her voice sounds faint. Then she hears him moving around in the bedroom, the water running in the bathroom sink, and a strange feeling comes over her. She wants him to vanish, to disappear. She doesn't want him to exist in the same place she does, his existence is an offense to her.

Annie says, "He just wants to have everything."

When Simon opens the door they both turn their eyes to him. Hooded looks. He comes to the table, bends down and kisses Erika's cheek. Maybe he wants to kiss Annie too, but if so, he thinks better of it. Erika wants to take the back of her hand and wipe the kiss off her cheek. His kiss feels like a lie.

She decides the breakfast table is the wrong place to cry so she goes to the bathroom and sits on the edge of the tub. She looks at her face in the glass. So ordinary. Nothing special. What makes her think she should have anything special? Who is she to expect such devotion from anyone, fidelity, loyalty, complete honesty? But that's it, isn't it? She wanted complete honesty and she got it. Truthfulness. Tell me everything you're thinking. And what if what he's thinking is horrible, what if it hurts? He has been protecting her from the truth. For how long? How long has he lied?

What does she want anyway—a romantic lie or an unacceptable truth?

She wants the truth to change. She wants it to never have been. Fidelity is a form of duty. She doesn't want his fidelity. If marriage is that, a duty, a task, then he's right about it. It is repressive. It is bourgeois. It is all of that. She just never saw it before. Open your eyes, Erika. Look!

She turns on the water. Everything will go on as before. Everything will look the same. But inside the plates have shifted. Mountains are islands; valleys are

72

lakes. Where there was once a broad horizon, there is a barrier now, a wall. Where everything was open to him, there is a pass that is closed.

REPORT FROM MIAMI: JULY 1972

Non-delegates to the Covention, we found our way to Flamingo Park to drink some wine and smooth off the rough edges of a long summertime drive. We set up a tent and the most beautiful hand-embroidered Yippie flag and were feeling all right. Up came a brother from the VVAW telling us he'd appreciate it if we would take the flag down. But wait a second, aren't we all Viet Nam Vets? Well, folks, I guess not, due to the great variety of gross realities that face us dear folks these days. The flag couldn't represent the organization called VVAW whose section of the park we had made ourselves at home in and so we had to get a map of the park and figure out who we were.

There were NWRO, NTO, SCLS, VVAW, Farm Workers, Green Power, Women's Coalition, Socialists, Gay Liberation, Yippies, Zippies, Youth for McGovern, People's Party and, of course, the paid agitators, winos, local hippies, and Hare Krishnas. The most bothersome of all the paid agitators were the Jesus Freaks (Graham Crackers). It soon became confusingly clear where energy should be spent. Solidarity, understanding what all these folks were into and why there had to be so many groups. If you think you know your movement, then a refresher will turn your head around and you may begin to know your revolution, baby.

Great people, hard workers, really alive and keeping on in soulful solidarity were National Welfare Rights, National Tenants, Southern Christian Leadership and Farm Workers. Not marching for recognition but telling McGovern and his democrats

73

that he'd better listen to them the same way Nixon listens to General Motors, ITT and the Mafia.

VVAW joined demonstrators in building a dike with sand carried from the beach four blocks away all around the fence that surrounded the convention hall to symbolize the bombing of the dikes in North Viet Nam. That bombing threatened the lives of ten million people due to massive flooding during the monsoons. Repair and evacuation are no salvation in a country whose basic nature, earth and culture are being annihilated by a DICK.

Miami Beach is the home of many old people living on Social Security after working their entire lives. Some folks were wearing Senior Power buttons, so there was no generation gap between the over 65's and the demonstrators. A conversation with an old person revealed alertness and a thirst for news, the ideas and direction of the younger people, and one smile would always beget another.

Allen Ginsberg sang a ballad to Amerika. There was music every day and at nightfall laughter, dancing and just getting on with our brothers and sisters. During the nomination of McGovern there was an LBJ Day March or the Heavy Heart March, trashing all democrats who run as peace candidates—remember LBJ? The Zippies also had a Cadillac they were going to burn, Welfare Cadillac, but the pigs whisked it away one morning. The Zippies are serious/funny good people, part of Youth International, but dead against the exploitation of the revolution and the leadership trip they feel has come from the Yippies.

But speaking of leadership trips and ideology—SDS, Socialists and Communists take the cake. Very polished in their raps, "I will interpret everything for you for I have studied" tone to all they say, never a flash of peoplehood, only their book view of racism, their tape-recorded monologues. The people

74

mean to tell them to blend in to solidarity. Variety is the spice of life. Get out of the structure and live.

The VVAW provided security by watching the gates, Miami Women's Coalition set up a very effective anti-rape squad, and people worked on keeping all downs and heroin (the Man's tool) out of the park. This included an education on how the CIA/government agents passing as one of the folks use hard drugs to weaken and defeat the people.

Well, shut my mouth, it was all pretty interesting, but just a dress rehearsal for the Republican convention. We can't let up the pressure to end the war and we can't miss out on a chance to trash the renomination of Nixon. Old and young, we have inspired each other. But be wise, take care of yourselves, stay in the shade half the time, wear a hat, and bring only healthy things with you. "We will defeat Nixon and serve notice to the Democrats that we are the new hungry majority and we won't be satisfied until we have everything!" By Ann Archy, Special Miami Correspondent.

January 1973 All the simplistic slogans fall away to nothing. Life is the only important thing.

I stare at Becky in her basket, the newspaper on the table. From one to the other. There is no contest.

I feel like my work has been to create anger. My job is to arouse people, get them mad, get them furious. We write the truth in our newspaper, yes, but only part of it, the horrible things, of which there are enough, certainly. But then I look at Becky, the wonderful thing. I look at all of us living happily, without fear. *Without fear.* In fact the government pays us to trash it. The government is our employer! All our energy is absorbed by the government. We feed it. It feeds off us. The most brilliant minds of our generation spend their time fine-tuning the wheels of government. Finetuning the judicial system. Years go into changing one or two sentences in a

75

law book. Meanwhile all our actions are useless because they can never create change. Everything is co-opted, everything is absorbed. What we do is create anti-bodies in the organism. The anti-bodies just make the organism stronger.

We tried to create alternative organizations. The problem is, the other ones work. They are unfair, yes, they are owned by the aristocracy, yes, they rob us, yes, yes. But they work and ours don't, not as well, not as efficiently, and who needs them when the others are so much better? Who cares about what's fair? If it works, there's no pressing need to fix it. The whole society is like that. It works well enough, so why bother fixing it? So no one will.

In only the short month she's been with us Becky has made me feel this way. She was born during the bombing of Hanoi. There were hospitals being bombed. I was in a hospital here filled with joy; mothers there were mourning their dead babies. It is intolerable. Life is the only important thing. How stupid it sounds. Does truth always sound so trite?

There was a big snowstorm yesterday. We sat around all afternoon taking turns holding Becky and people came and left as usual, to talk politics, see the baby, warm up, smoke. I wrote down some remarks:

"The main business is salvation, but we all have to go together." Annie

"Madness is the easy way out." Simon

"What everyone is looking for is depth, but it's also what everyone fears." Zach

"All will occur, but in its own time." Ben

Ben also tells the story of a man whose death was foretold but who lived because by an act of grace he shared his food with a stranger and discovered the snake in his pack.

Everyone was gone by the time it got dark, around five. I was sitting in the rocker nursing Becky, Annie was punching down her bread, Simon was cooking. It was quiet for the first time all day, just the squeak of the rocking chair, the tap of Simon's paring knife on the cutting block, Annie humming as she floured the board and every so often the rattle of the wind at the windows. Then we heard someone coming up the back stairs,

76

heavy-footed, and the knock at the door. The door opened and he came right in, massive and white as a yeti, completely covered with snow. He shook his head and set down his pack.

"I'm Rousseau, from VVAW," he said. "I'm your brother in the struggle. Long live the victory of the people."

Annie looked up at him and said, "There's a little baby in this room, man. Cut the jive and shut the door."

He stayed for dinner and when it turned out he didn't have a place to crash, he stayed the night. Now he and Simon are meeting with some folks from the Bail Project. Paul is an ex-con (and proud of it) and his focus is on prison reform as well as the Revolution. (He did time for possession.) He's tall and imposing, has a powerful presence, black eyes, black hair, bushy eyebrows, something scary and intense about his look. A long scar on his cheek. (A duel perhaps?) Very moralistic, doctrinaire, spouts rhetoric. Talked to Simon exclusively. Big on quoting Mao. All political power grows out of the barrel of a gun. The Revolution is not a dinner party. (I thought it was a tea party.) He and Simon are already deep into ideological struggle. Who *really* started the French Revolution? etc. And here we are, Annie and I, barefoot, if not currently pregnant, and in the kitchen. Where we belong, goddammit! Now at this moment Annie is punching down today's bread dough with more than her usual vengeance, lifts her floured fist over the bowl: Tricky Dick! BAM Westmoreland! BAM All male chauvinist pigs! BAM

May 9, 1973 The seige at Wounded Knee ended yesterday and then last night Annie announced to us that she's moving in with Paul. He's living on the Hill with the working class in an apartment with four other former inmates and Simon's complete works of Karl Marx. I can't imagine how Annie can even think about living there. "They want a political education," she said. "I'll give 'em one. There'll be no chauvinist pigs where I live. If we can't raise our brothers' consciousness, how can we expect anyone else to change? You don't want little Becky to grow up thinking she's half a human being, do you? Well, we've got to start that struggle for her now."

77

But I don't care about raising consciousness. I just don't want her to go.

She left me in my kitchen. Even the pronouns had changed. It hadn't been my kitchen in over a year. It had been ours, everything had been ours. Even Simon, even Becky, everything. Now it was all mine again and I hated it.

Annie leaves with little more than she had come with. A new pair of Frye boots. A few books, poetry mainly. *Monster* by Robin Morgan. Erika and Simon's Billy Holiday records. She didn't want to take them but Erika insisted.

"OK, but it's just a loan. I'll just hold onto them for awhile. If it doesn't work out I'll need them."

"If it doesn't work out, you'll come back here."

"No, Becky needs that room. Every woman needs a room of her own,"

"She doesn't need it yet."

"Anyway, if it doesn't work out, I'll be heading out of here. If I can't make it with Paul, I can't make it with any man, not in this town anyhow."

She picks Becky up and gives her a big kiss.

"So, sugar. Be good, you hear?"

And then to Erika, "Come on, honey. Don't look so down. It's not like I'm moving to Mars. I'll be just a stroll away."

A stroll away. Mars.

May 17, 1973 Simon and I have been fighting ever since Annie left. We fight over nothing. We fight because we're a nuclear family again and Simon hates it and I hate it, but neither one of us knows what to do about it. Annie and I met at Brenda's house, or the house Brenda is staying at. It has a back garden that's all huge lilac bushes and there's a stone table and stone chairs in the midst of the lilacs. We sat there all afternoon and drank wine. Annie misses us, too, but she's in love with

Paul. He has a hard time showing his gentleness, she says. He's been wounded. Everything he's ever loved has betrayed him, even his country betrayed him, everything he's ever believed in or given his devotion to. He has all this love inside, all this devotion, and nowhere to put it, no place for it to go. The Revolution is his love, but we know, you and I, how goddam fickle the Revolution can be. And then there's me, see, and he doesn't know this yet, but I'm going to be the woman who doesn't betray him and who doesn't deceive him and who stays beside him. I am the one who is not going to hurt him, Erika, who is never going to hurt him. That's what she says. I feel so old, so woman-not-in-love. I want to cry when she talks like that. Oh, well.

July 7, 1973   Annie at her new house. I hear a lot of 'trash the man' rhetoric. Landlords are pigs. Simon and I are not politically pure. Poor but not pure. Yet Simon is organizing a lobbying group for the unemployed. He is independent of rhetoric, takes everybody as he is, without labels, gets incredible shit for it.

Now that Annie is gone we think about the future. Join the outwave? Become landed? I shudder to think of it. Stay and struggle here in this tiny part of the cosmos? Annie talks a lot about classes now, but I think all classes are equally oppressed. Except the elite, of course. Everybody else slaves for a system that gives them only *things* in return, things that can't make them happy. Everybody is working for things they don't want. Everybody is affected by things they have no control over. Who has their own real projects that come out of their own innermost heart and gets to see them fulfilled? Who is really happy?

September 18, 1973   A couple of days ago the Allende government was overthrown by a CIA-financed and masterminded coup. Salvador Allende is dead, the fascist military (thanks to the USA) is in control again, a new wave of terror is beginning. Victor Jara was tortured and murdered after the sweep of all Allende's people, killed for singing in the stadium where they were all being held. Simon and I play his records all night. It's impossible to believe that he's dead when his voice is so alive. And his words. And his dream. Meanwhile Simon's new whatever-we-call-it (*it* doesn't quite have a name yet; *her* name is Veronica) seems to be going well, I guess. I am tired of being the hysterical wife, so I just focus on Becky. She is the only important thing, my daughter, my sweet child. The irony is that I still see us bound together. I always see him as forging the path ahead, since he is wiser, more advanced. Every step he takes I have to take eventually, so I learn how from him. Sometimes I forget that he is struggling, too, trying to become perfect. But the dark side of this is that he isn't in love with me anymore. And that he ·was becoming non-sexual with women, because he was trying to be faithful to me. It was horrible for him. It was killing something in him. Once he told me that what he felt most guilty about was that he knew he was shattering my world, which he had also once lived in and loved, a world in which people marry and unite themselves forever and share everything and never part and never grow bored and tired. And what is that world? That is the world of the romantic fallacy. The false world. The lie. It is something that needs shattering. It is a fantasy that enslaves people. (Why do I still believe in it?) And so this is where we are, and I feel more enslaved by the emotions of reacting to this than I ever did by being a romantic dupe. How am I supposed to feel? Maybe someday I'll fall in love with someone else and then I'll understand and believe him when he says he doesn't love me any less than he did before. Somehow it doesn't sound right to me.

I protect myself against him now.

April 2, 1974 Annie and Paul over for dinner last night. We haven't seen them in months. I don't see anybody anymore, wintering with a toddler and hassling with the politics of the paper and Simon's been so depressed about making old buildings beautiful for goddam rich people to live in, the last thing in the world he wants to do, but it's just to survive, everything we do now is just to survive. The last time I saw Annie we had a fight over the Red Guards and she accused me of becoming bourgeois. That's a joke, becoming bourgeois on food stamps. But in my case it's a condition of the mind, an internal bourgeoisness. I can't heroize kids who kill their parents. Sorry.

So last night. Paul was his usual jolly self, like a funeral. The conversation—politics, oppression, corporate barbarism, familiar themes, tried and true. I kept waiting for Annie to laugh, light a joint and say, Well, shut my mouth, but the Revolution is right here at this table, my dears! But she didn't. In fact, I'm afraid their rhetoric is going to lead them to do something and it scares me. Paul is a powerful man and Annie is completely in love with him.

The heaviness at the table is unbearable. Erika feels as though they expect the SS to show up at the door any minute. She feels their paranoia of the system with the same palpability that she had once felt the certainty of imminent victory. (Victory over what? Fear of what?) It has the same vagueness, the same intensity, the same emotional power. After one of Paul's litanies of capitalist myths—the myth of electoral politics, the myth of a free press, the myth of judicial fairness—Simon asks him what he planned to do about it.

"You're being facetious," Paul answers. "I know you don't need me to tell you what we have to do about it."

Erika gets up to put Becky to bed. Annie follows her into the bedroom.

"Need some help with the puddin'?"

It is the first Annie-thing she has said all evening.

"Would you like the puddin'?"

"Sure, I'll take puddin' home. Would you like that, Becky, honey? Like to come live with the cadre up on the hill? Wear red bandanas on your head and eat rice?"

She sits down on Becky's bed with the dollies and the stuffed animals on the quilt she had made out of patches of satin and velvet and embroidery and batik

81

animals they had cooked up one December afternoon in the kitchen, the whole kitchen smelling of wax and fresh bread and Erika bulging with Becky and Annie singing "Summertime". Now she sits there with blond Becky and her dollies and she says,

"Becky, I'm going to tell you a story, OK , honey? Want to hear a story?" Becky snuggles down in her bed and smiles. "I'm going to tell you a story about a woman named Sojourner Truth. She was a great woman, a very brave, strong woman who loved justice more than anything else in the whole world..."

The story of Sojourner, told as though she was a woman Annie knew, an old Black lady who lived down the street and invited Annie and her brothers and sisters in for lemonade on hot summer afternoons.

"And the Black people who had run away from the plantations where bad men treated them worse than you can think, they would show up at her house in the night, scared and hungry and tired and she would take them in and feed them some good hot soup and give them good warm clothes to wear, and she didn't care if she was breaking the law because the law was wrong, the law was a bad law..."

Erika can hear Paul's voice through the door, Paul and Simon struggling about the struggle, while Annie strokes Becky's hair. The little girl is asleep. Annie bends over and kisses her, then glances around the room.

"Don't you buy her trucks, Erika?"

"She doesn't want trucks."

"She's taught not to want trucks. You put her in dresses and tell her not to get dirty."

"She picks out her own clothes and she picks out her own toys."

"And she watches TV and she's taught what to want and how to dress. You just can't be passive and let her be and expect that it won't rub off on her. Sexism's too strong in this society. Besides, you're raising her like she was someone special, like she's the center of the universe. That's how Americans are made, by being raised as though each one of them was the center of the universe. That's why this country's the way it is. Imperialists are made, not born. In China children aren't raised to think like that."

"Well, I'm glad I'm not living in China."

"You've changed a lot, Erika."

"You've changed a lot, too."

"I'm stronger now...Erika, do you remember how we yelled, Smash the state! at the convention? Remember the Ho Chi Minh song? Remember those vets with their red and black armbands? Remember how it felt?"

"Yes, I remember."

"Were you just fucking around then? Was that all bullshit? Or did you just have this baby and decide to start playing it safe?"

"What are you saying, Annie?"

"I just want to know how serious you were. I'm asking you how much you believe in the revolution."

"What revolution?"

There is a long pause. A long sigh. "Oh, Erika," Annie says. And then, "You'll always be my sister, Erika. I'll always love you and your baby girl. But we're moving on now. We're moving ahead."

"You and Paul? You're leaving?"

They aren't looking at each other now but at Becky who is sleeping with her head on the side, her knuckles under her chin, a smile on her face. Babies, toddlers, they smile in their sleep. They smile when they wake up. Little fingers, little hands, soft skin, little soft bodies, a sweetness about them, a sweetness, even their breath is sweet, and their complete trust, their trustfulness, how they slip into sleep trusting the world.

And Erika thinks that it's all true, what Annie says. It is love for this child that has changed her. But it was love that had changed Annie, too.

They leave the room then. Simon and Paul are still at the table, beer cans lined up between them like tin soldiers, like they're playing war, Erika thinks, or chess, which is another version of war. And Paul is saying,

"...and taking it, Simon. We've been letting them fuck us, literally. We've been letting them fuck us up the ass. Think about it."

"I do think about it."

"Well, it's time to stop thinking and do something."

"I keep telling you, you *are* doing something. You're doing the only reasonable thing you can do. You're educating people. You're getting legislation passed..."

"Fuck legislation. By the time they get done with our bills they're only good for wiping your ass with. You try talking to those guys about civil rights, Simon. About who gets busted and why. About who gets probation and who doesn't. About who gets put in solitary and why. I go to that joint, I swear there are more Blacks in there than on the streets. And every goddamn off-reservation Indian in the goddamn state. That's one. Two: you don't change it that way. You don't change it passing laws. How many years since the Civil Rights Act? Go to the South sometime, Simon. Go to New York City, go to Chicago. Three: there's no way to control the conglomerates and that's where the power is — the oil companies, the munitions companies, agribusiness, chemicals, and all their subsidiaries. No law can touch them, and they're the ones running the government, the economy, colonialism inside the country and outside. They own the fucking country. How are you going to touch them?"

"How are *you* going to touch them?"

"The *foco.*"

Simon lets the word settle, lights a cigarette, studies Paul's face.

"Go on."

"A small band of urban guerrillas, well-trained, well-organized, armed. They select targets and then they hit them. Tell people why. Point it out. What this factory is producing--napalm, say. Strike and disappear. Strike again. People see it can be done. People see they're not helpless, they're not hogtied. They can cripple the machine. When a cop kills a Black man on the street, the *foco* avenges. The Panthers were right, Simon. The people must be armed and they must be willing to defend themselves and their communities. The *foco* is the motor for the general upheaval, the catalyst..."

"All you'll see is more repression. More assassinations. More military presence in the ghettos."

"Fine. More repression means more resistance. The more people they repress, the more people are going to resist them. They have a program of repression, it's just hidden. It's invisible. So we make it visible. We make them come out from behind the corporate facade. We make them put their army in the streets where people can see it for what it is."

"Like '68 and '69 all over again. And what did that achieve, Paul? Tell me that. What did it achieve?"

"An awakening."

"A repression. If a general upheaval didn't happen then..."

"It wasn't planned then. It wasn't organized. Spontaneous action turned into riots. Riots are by definition unorganized."

"So what you need to do is organize, not try to start a guerrilla war."

"You have to organize around something. Look at Algeria. The Resistance could have dragged on indefinitely if the National Liberation Front hadn't upped the ante. People get used to a certain level of pain. You have to crank it up so they see their own oppression. Then they have to see that they have the power to attack it and defeat it."

"Algeria was a somewhat different case. Algeria was an occupied colony."

"This country is an occupied colony. The Black communities are occupied colonies. The factories are occupied colonies. This state is an occupied colony. We—you and I, Simon—are occupying this state which in fact belongs to three Indian tribes. But who is really the colonizer? It's a big country, it's a rich country. Why are so many of us desperately poor? Why are there hungry children? Why are there ghettos? Ten percent of the people own ninety percent of the wealth. That sounds like the Third World to me, a little oligarchy and a whole bunch of peons. I don't have to go through this with you, Simon. You're more educated than I am. It's been like this for two hundred years and it's getting worse. Every year it gets worse. Something's got to be done about it. I'm just telling you now so you can think about it. So if you want to join us...Think about it, man. The offer may never come this way again."

He glanced over at Annie, who had sat perfectly still the whole time he talked.

"Ready?"

"Yes," she said and gathered her things together. At the door, she kissed Erika goodbye while Paul and Simon said a few more words to each other in the dining room. As he passed Erika by on his way out, Paul put his hand on her arm. It was a simple enough

86

gesture, except that he didn't look at her when he did it. It was as if he were trying to leave something with her, something even he wouldn't acknowledge, as though he were saying goodbye without saying it, or promising to come back or wishing her well...all that or none of it. Erika could not tell.

Simon lit a joint and opened a beer.

"Simon. Armed struggle? Jesus, what are they going to do?"

"Bring the government down with five guys and a few sticks of dynamite. Like the Weathermen did, remember? He thinks he's in Cuba or in another century. He thinks...God, didn't they wipe the Panthers off the face of the earth for this shit? Oh, I don't know, Erika. God, I just don't know."

He sucked back on the joint and then he said,

"You know, the thing is, a few years ago I might have agreed with him. A few years ago I might just have said yes."

"Yes to what?"

"Yes to anything. Just yes."

May 1978
Dear Annie,

I know you can't write or call or visit. I know it's unlikely you'll ever read this letter. It's unlikely I'll ever send it. Where would I send it to? Your mother? And what would she do with it? Her phone is tapped, her house is watched, they probably open all her mail. So they'll read this. So I won't send it. But, Annie, I can't believe we'll never see you again, that none of us will ever hear from you. It's like you're lost somewhere, but no one knows where...The choice was Paul. I know that. No matter what we say, no matter how strong we think we are, all a man has to do is make love to us with his whole heart and he owns us forever. Politically incorrect, I know, but I'm afraid it's absolutely true.

So writing to you, I'm just writing to myself. And what do I write to myself? You and Paul were right. Yes, you were right. You can't change it from the inside. It changes you. As soon as you get inside it, it just closes its jaws. There's no fifth column, that's bullshit.

So while those comrades of Paul's were blowing up the National Guard Armory, Simon was taking the LSATs and while one of them was singing Paul's name out in interrogation, Simon was deciding on what law school to go to; while you were living in disguise, having a baby underground, trying to survive, he was becoming a lawyer, and now he is a lawyer and I don't even know him anymore. He can't see me and I can't see him. I lie to defend myself against him, against his idea of me. I'm afraid if the revolution happened tomorrow, Annie, Simon would be on the other side of the barricades.

June 1979
Dear Annie,

I saw you today. I walked into the post office and there you were on the wall. You and Paul. New pictures. You look thinner, but just as beautiful. Odd to get news of you from the wanted posters. You have another child now, two little boys, each with half a dozen names. Their pictures are up too. It made me so angry I wanted to rip them right off the wall.

We have a son, too. Noah, who we hope will survive the flood.

December 1983
Dear Annie,

I dreamt about you last night. We were walking down a street together, a slum street in a big city. It was night. You were carrying a shopping bag and were wearing a shawl over your coat. Men were walking in pairs down the street, but I felt perfectly safe with you. We went into a concert hall, but it was like a stadium filled with people. Simon was there and Paul and we waved to them but didn't try to make our way over to where they were sitting. Instead we decided to go outside again. At the entrance there was a guard who said, "You can only leave if you agree to bring a can of gasoline back with you." We promised and he let us out. Then we saw that

88

all the cars on the street were cannibalized wrecks and all the men were carrying cans and looking for gas. And you said, "It's happened already. Look around. It's finally happened." And we kept walking through the rubble, seeing abandoned machines everywhere, vacuum cleaners, hair dryers, washing machines, all our old devices, all useless. "There's no point waiting around for them. Sooner or later they'll get out and find us." So we kept walking, laughing together like two kids, laughing at the end of the world.

This morning there was a story in the paper about the bombing in New York. This makes the fifteenth in the past year, they said. No one was hurt. No one is ever hurt. They're very careful, whoever's doing it. Very smart and very careful. No one in the building, not even a janitor, not even a cleaning lady, not a single Black cleaning lady, cleaning the offices of one of the biggest investors in one of the most racist countries on the face of the earth. No. Even at the military bases and the reserve centers, even at the armaments factories, no one is hurt. Whoever they are, they are careful not to become killers, not to become as bad as the enemy they fight.

Last night Becky and Noah and I were looking through our photograph albums and we came to a series of pictures of you in the rocking chair in the kitchen of the old apartment holding Becky when she was a few months old. She asked me who you were and I told her, Annie. I said, Becky, I'll tell you the story of Annie Pratt, a brave and strong woman who loved you very much, but loved justice more than anything else in the world.

Spring 1984 Memorable Conversations with Simon
Isn't it odd, we have a house, two cars, a nice garden, of course one of the cars doesn't run...
I never wanted any of it.
What did you want?
I can't remember.
You mean you don't want to remember.
Why should I? So everything will hurt more?

I don't make you happy, Simon.
I'm happier with you than I'd be without you.

89

What's less than zero?
No response.

Where's the money you took out of the bank today?
Oh, I forgot.
What do you mean, you forgot?
What do you mean 'what do you *mean*, you forgot?' I just forgot.
You indicated to me on the phone...
Oh, shit, Simon, I didn't *indicate*, I said. I said, Simon, I'll go to the bank. Then I forgot, that's all.
Great. So what do I do for money tomorrow?
We'll stop at the bank.
I have to be in court by nine.
The bank opens at eight.
Did you remember to buy gas?
Yes, I remembered to buy gas.
What did you use for money?
I had some money.
Do you still have some money?
I have five dollars.
Give it to me. Then we won't have to stop tomorrow.
Fine. It's in my pack which is in the car. I'll give it to you in the morning.
No, give it to me now before you forget.
Can I put my shoes on first or do you want me to go out barefoot?

As though death had just lumbered by.

And Erika, reading through these entries, articles, letters that were never sent, records of conversations, thought maybe everything had been written, there were no choices anymore.

And then, flipping through the pages, she came upon a photograph of Marc. It took her by surprise, his dark handsomeness, his smile, the exuberance of him, the vitality of him in bright glossy color in the bitter pages of this book. It shocked her to find him there, to come face to face with him. All that had happened, all those words, those ideals and acts, chaotic, yes, naive,

90

done without any idea of the magnitude of the power blocking every move, but innocent and new, difficult and free, all those years of struggling and struggling, leading to this, the oldest act in the world, the most commonplace, worn and tired, and sad. Just very, very sad.

By midmorning Annie has hitched into a large Midwestern city and made her way to a safe house where, since the news has already broken over the local station, she is able to rest rather than mourn. A few hours later, while Erika is making grilled cheese sandwiches for Noah and Becky's lunch, slicing up the pickles with a deft hand, pouring the milk, the phone rings.

"I have a collect call for Simon Donnis from Paul Rousseau. Will you accept the charges?"

CHAPTER 4

The Fruits of the Poisonous Tree

I

"Will you accept?"

Erika stood holding the receiver in one hand, a pickle in the other, feeling as mute as a tree. When the word finally came, it came in a rasp. "Yes." Then she yelled hard for Simon. But before he arrived to relieve her of the weight of the phone, another voice, slurred and faint, came to her through the line.

"That you, Erika? You two still together after all these years? That's good, that's good news."

"Paul!"

"Listen, I got to talk to Simon right now, if he's around. But I want to talk to you, too. Soon. Guess I'll be having plenty of time to talk to everybody. First we got to see what kind of legal genius that husband of yours is. How's Becky?"

She said, "Fine. Everyone's fine. Here he is," and passed the receiver to Simon quickly, as though it had been scorching her hand.

They talked for forty minutes while Erika fed the kids and bribed Becky into taking Noah outside for a little while. She was in the process of pushing them both out the door when Simon appeared in the living room. He chose an album at random, took his box of grass from the piano, sank into the rocker with the album and box on his lap. Slowly, meticulously, he sifted the grass through the tea strainer to separate out the seeds and began rolling the joint. She waited.

"The last of the dope," he said. "About three joints left."

"*Simon.*"

He looked across at her and she looked back at him. A look devoid of content, like a pause in a conversation or between movements of a symphony, a pause that indicates the subject is about to change.

"Maybe there was a good reason why I went to law school after all," he said. "Funny, that's what Paul said to me. He's got a sense of humor now, sounds like he mellowed a bit. Made a joke about the lawyers' role in the French Revolution. We used to argue about it, remember? But it was hard to understand him. Guess they beat him up pretty bad. Broke Bobby's nose, he said. Just working them over a little. Bastards."

"So they busted him? Simon, tell me. I don't know anything. Where's Annie?"

"Annie escaped. She's the only one. They got Bobby and Marlene and all the kids. Annie wasn't there and they don't know where she is now. The Feds have a dragnet out, but maybe she'll slip through. Maybe she'll give herself up. They don't have much on her or Marlene either. Not yet anyway."

"Are the kids all right?"

"Yeah. Yeah, they're fine."

"And?"

"And?"

"Why did he call you?"

"Oh. Well, the only warrant they've got on him is for that action here ten years ago. So they'll try him here first unless some bigger indictments come down in New York. There's a grand jury meeting there now, has been for the past six months or so. They're looking for a conspiracy indictment out of that, RICO, big time. Then there's stuff in Boston and D.C. and God knows

94

what else. Paul's going to spend the next ten years just going around the country from courthouse to courthouse, retracing his steps. Unless of course they get him on one big one and don't bother after that. You can only give a man so many years. After the first hundred it gets a little redundant."

"So he needs a lawyer."

"Yes."

"And he asked you."

"Yes."

"And you said?"

"I said I'd think about it."

"Simon, you didn't!"

"No, I didn't. I said yes."

Erika smiled at him. "Shit," she said.

"Listen to this. I told him I'd never done a criminal case in Federal court before. He said, 'We know that. We know everything you've done. We know all about you.'"

"Jesus."

"Yeah, it's pretty weird. And he does, too. 'You did a hell of a job with that Perkins case.' That's what he said."

"Your murderer?"

"My man-slaughterer. Now, I'll tell you, that little back alley stabbing did not get picked up by the wire services. Another thing, Erika. I mean it about this being the last of the grass. We have to start being really careful. The armed resistance isn't the only bunch that's going to know all about us now."

"What do you mean?"

"I mean once the Feds know I'm representing Paul they're going to zero in on us. Don't talk about anything on the phone. Don't mention dope or the case or anything important. Start telling people, OK? We assume the phone's going to be bugged. Then we'll just have to keep our eyes open. They've infiltrated

95

lawyers' offices before and defense committees. And with me, once they find out I knew Paul before, they could try anything, even subpoenaing me for one of their star chamber grand juries. There are all kinds of ploys..."

"But, Simon, you're his lawyer!"

"Sure I am. And do you know how many lawyers are in prison right now for non-collaboration?"

"Non-collaboration with what?"

"Grand juries. Refusing to testify. Refusing to appear. Eighteen months for contempt. Then they're subpoenaed again. They refuse to appear again. Back in the slammer for another eighteen months."

"How do you know all this?"

"I keep my ears open. You'd be surprised what I know."

"I would?"

"Yes. I have my spies."

"Simon, don't get weird on me."

"I'm just warning you, Erika. You have no idea what these people are like or what they are capable of. Anyway right now we've got to get lawyers for the kids lined up out there and get them away from the Feds. I've got to make some calls."

He was on the phone most of the day. Through legal contacts in New York he found several lawyers in the state where the children were being held who had the politics to step into the breach in the custody case. Annie's sister and Marlene's mother were already on their way out to get the children, to meet them for the first time. Erika could imagine such a meeting. She could imagine everything: the children seeing their parents being seized by men with guns in their hands, being forcibly separated from them, being taken to a strange place and questioned, wanting their mothers and not being able to see them, and now having more strangers appear and tell them, I am your grandmother,

96

I am your real aunt. You're going to come with us. Say goodbye, goodbye, your whole life is going to change forever...Oh, yes, Erika could see all that in detail. She had trained herself to be able to envision the incomprehensible.

Later that evening after the children were in bed (her own children, safe in their own beds with their stuffed animals, everything dependable, secure, while Annie's children were somewhere lost and confused, sobbing for their mother or maybe even for each other, maybe they were separated, maybe they were entirely alone. And Erika kissed her children again and Noah wrinkled his nose and wiped the kiss off his cheek.), Simon gave her a report on the day's work. He had talked with some of the more famous radical lawyers in the country, the big guns. They had called him. News travels fast. It seemed that Paul Rousseau had no sooner laid down the receiver that morning than every resistance law firm in the country knew that some totally unknown small town criminal lawyer in northern New England had just landed one of the most important political cases of the decade, and they all wanted to check it out. But Simon, as always, was playing it close to the vest. He wasn't saying anything to anybody, but he was listening hard. He had talked with a lot of other people, too, old friends and former comrades of Paul's who were apparently still loyal.

"Loyal to Paul?" Erika asked.

"Loyal to Paul. Loyal to the struggle."

"Are you saying that in quotes?"

"No. That's what they call it. That's what we called it. That's its name."

"Why did you say 'apparently'?"

"Like I said earlier, we have to be careful. The consensus is that there's a snitch somewhere. There have been three major political busts in the past four months. Some of these people have been underground for fifteen years. Now how did the Feds all of a sudden get so smart?"

"Somebody underground is doing it, you think?"

"Got to be. Who else knows what's going on? But they need spies and rats above ground too, people to get close to the case and report on strategy, fuck things up. So they find someone they have something on and they deal. Or they just buy somebody. And all those old friends of Paul's are sitting ducks for deals. They all have colorful pasts and they're all broke and down and out and fucked up, most of them. We just have to be careful."

"You'd think he was a mass murderer."

"He's worse than a mass murderer. He's a revolutionary."

"A revolutionary without a revolution. One man against the United States Government."

"One man and a handful more kicked our ass out of Cuba. One man and a handful more started the FSLN and kicked our ass out of Nicaragua. Sometimes all you need is one man. And they hate him. They hate him because he outsmarted them for ten years and made them look like fools. And they hate him because he stands for something they fear."

"He probably stands for everything they fear. The big fear. They'd be the first to go."

"And they deserve to be. The only thing that keeps them from turning into a national death squad is a very old piece of paper with some powerful words written on it and a pretty rag-tag collection of watchdogs, and even so they get around it as much as they can whenever they can. And you know that piece of paper may turn out to be the only thing that will keep Paul from spending the rest of his life buried inside Marion."

"You think there's a chance?"

"Of course there's a chance. I haven't seen anything yet, I haven't even looked at the indictment. But, generally speaking, whatever they've got for the case here is ten years old. And that's pretty old stuff, Erika. And they're sloppy and arrogant. We'll see. For the other cases, the ones they really want to nail him for, my guess is they'll wind up relying on whatever they got out of the house, and unless they were really careful, they fucked up the search. Of course, I could be wrong. They could have a snitch, they could have tapes, they could have Paul's fingerprints all over that bomb that didn't go off in D.C. last year, and they could wind up crucifying him. If they do have a snitch, it's probably over. All they need is a credible quisling."

"Sounds like an oxymoron to me. A credible quisling, a truthful liar..."

"A faithful spouse," he said, absently, as though thinking of something else.

So Paul Rousseau, until that weekend the most wanted man in America, became overnight its most feared prisoner, reputed to be able to kill by an act of will while shackled and chained to a wall, and Simon Donnis, until that weekend one of the most cynical and jaded lawyers in America, became his champion. Paul was right when he said that Simon was the only lawyer in the state with the politics to defend him. He might have said the wits or the balls, but politics to Paul Rousseau meant all that and more—the purity of heart, the idealism, the vision. And it was true. Simon had all that still, though he had tried valiantly to bury it. And Erika smiled and said, "It just shows you. Your destiny will find you even if you're hiding under a rock. It will lift up the rock and say, 'Hi, there. I'm your destiny'."

He laughed at that. He laughed and dug his old Frye boots out from the depths of the closet. They made him look taller, his step developed a certain bounce.

The next morning she heard him whistling to himself as he was getting dressed. She was so amazed she burnt the toast, but instead of yelling at her ("Goddammit, Erika, can't you pay attention to anything?") he ate Cheerios for breakfast and then put the bowl down for the cats. He had turned the calendar back as easily as turning back a sheet.

Erika's house was filled with people again: middle aged freaks with braids down their backs; women in ratty sweaters and long skirts who, in between recounting stories of FBI harrassment, talked about the size of their looms or the best way to get decent cheese from goats; old time radicals who had spent the last ten years holed up in the Vermont woods cranking out political broadsides on decrepit mimeographs; young wide-eyed Green Party people; burnt out vets; ex-cons. All of them had known Paul Rousseau in one capacity or another—or if they were too young, wished they had—and all of them wanted to help. They came in flurries all through November for Sunday afternoon meetings. There wasn't a whole lot they could do except drink beer and swap stories and make up lists of potential donors to a legal defense fund and then fold letters and address envelopes, but their presence changed the energy of the house. Erika found herself in the kitchen cooking up iron kettles of soup again, drinking wine in the afternoon, talking about government conspiracies, tales of the empire. Noah learned the soul brother handshake; Becky got one of the long-skirted women to teach her how to crochet.

Before the month was over a similar Defense Committee had been formed in New York and some money was being raised primarily for the custody fight going on between the state and the relatives of the children. The state had put them all in foster homes and was refusing to let any relatives see them prior to

100

the custody hearing. No such rule applied to the FBI, however, who were permitted to see them at any time and ask them questions. The theme of the fund drive was Free the Children.

Then in early December, Paul arrived back in his home state for trial and a new wave of visitors began arriving at the house—the resistance lawyers.

A December night. They are sitting around the dining room table, Simon and two other men. One is Jon Golden, a lank, scholarly-looking young man, bearded and balding. The other, Golden's opposite number, is Dan Weinberg, rugged and burly with long grey hair and a weathered face. They are poring over some documents, half a dozen government affidavits, the draft of a defense motion. The government has collected six thousand pages of evidence from the two houses, Paul's and Bobby's, but not one of the lawyers has bothered to drive over to the Federal Building to look at them.

Erika has put Noah to bed and opened a beer. Now she is ready for her nightly update. She knows by this time they are worn out, need an excuse to sit back and see what they've done. Talk it through again, in English, for her benefit.

"So, what's up, team?'

Dan smiles at her. He looks hard, almost frightening, until he smiles. Then he looks like a man you would willingly follow on your pony with your bow and arrow against the amassed artillery of the United States Army. His voice is resonant and full. He speaks slowly. He's been through all this before. He has very few illusions left.

"We have discovered the fruits of the poisonous tree."

"Amazing. And here all this time I thought you were doing law."

101

"It is law. Even the law can become poetic sometimes. Poetic justice, my favorite kind. Let me get myself another Coke and I'll spin it out for you."

"I'll get the Coke, you start spinning. What about this fruit?"

"If the tree is poisoned, so are the fruits. If the warrant is bad, so is the evidence. Illegal warrant, inadmissable evidence."

"And the warrant is illegal?"

"We sure have a good Fourth Amendment argument here. Now whether the court is going to have the balls to throw this case out on the basis of an improperly issued warrant..."

"Wait...Fourth Amendment...It's right on the tip of my American History memory bank."

"You are at this moment sitting at the table with three of the most knowledgeable Fourth Amendment scholars in the country, as of this afternoon anyway, so forget your American History memory bank, it's probably all wrong anyway. Jon, do you want to..."

"No, I gotta write all this down before I forget it."

So Dan continues: "The government is not permitted to search your home and seize your property without a warrant stating exactly what they want and exactly why they want it. And they must have probable cause, that is they must have a sworn statement or affidavit to present to the judge explaining why they think a search warrant should be issued. Historically this amendment was created specifically to protect your right to privacy and to be secure in your possessions, and more specifically your political writings. It was to prevent the government from walking into your house and nosing around in your stuff, your correspondence, your books and papers. It was a measure designed to keep the new government from engaging in the same political repression practiced by the old.

"Now let's say the cops hear from one of their sources that you have stolen goods in your house. A stolen TV let's say. They make out a statement and bring it before a judge and the judge is convinced on the basis of the affidavit that it's probable that you do indeed have stolen TVs in your house. He issues a search warrant stating specifically that the cops can go into your house and look for TVs. So far, so good. Now say the cops come in with the warrant to search for TVs and they decide to go through your desk drawers while they're at it and there, eureka!, they find a gram of cocaine. Can they bust you for possession? Sure they can. Can they seize the cocaine? Sure they can. They're cops, they can do whatever they damn well please. But will they get a conviction? N-O, if your lawyer's worth the time of day, because their warrant was to search for TVs and reasonable search for TVs does not take you to somebody's desk drawer..."

"Of course, if they really wanted to bust you, they'd say the stuff was lying out in plain view..."

"If they wanted you bad enough to perjure themselves, sure. But this is theory we're talking here. So the warrant has to be specific. General warrants are illegal. Period."

"And this warrant?"

"This warrant is pretty damn general and the affidavits are pretty damn sloppy. In fact, worse than sloppy. I'd go so far as to say that the agent whose affidavit this is lied, deliberately and recklessly."

"And," Jon says, still scribbling hard on his pad, hard and fast, even while he talks," what they don't do is state probable cause. There's nothing in this affidavit to convince an objective person—notice my choice of word, objective—that what the Feds wanted would in fact be found in the place to be searched." He picks up one of the documents from the pile and reads: "'Political writings seized in the house are similar in

103

style and content to communiques left by the August 7th Brigade at bombing sites: like the August 7th's, the communiques are numbered consecutively.' Brilliant, huh? This is the genius of federal law enforcement condensed into a nutshell: What does Paul Rousseau have in common with the members of the August 7th Brigade? They all think the U.S. government sucks and they can count."

"But that's what they said after the fact. The affidavit itself says essentially: We are the FBI. We think Paul Rousseau is a terrorist. We think he has committed a variety of crimes, though we offer no proof of that, and we want to search his house and afterwards we will tell you what we were looking for...Logically there isn't a shred of purported fact to link any criminal activity with this house. It's an absurdity. There was no surveillance, there was no phone tap, there is no informant..."

"I mean," Jon says, warming to his subject, "you know, what does 'similar language' even mean, anyway? That they were written in English? I mean, several million other Americans can write English, and count, too..."

"The house was over six hundred miles away from the site of the last bombing. The whole thing is completely speculative."

"And the irony of it! The irony, you know?" Jon stops to slurp a mouthful of beer off the rim of his glass. "Irony transcended! You know what they took from that house, besides everything but the kitchen sink? Besides Paul's love letters to Annie? Besides her poems and journals? You know what else? A copy of the Bill of Rights and *1984*! Well, what do you expect? The warrant says they can seize 'books, documents, and other papers tending to show motive and intent'. I mean, it sounds like a writ of assistance, you know? Like, the reason we had a revolution in the first place

104

was because of the writs of assistance, and here we are two hundred years later. The Framers are probably rolling in their graves."

"So what you're saying is, all those thousands of pages..."

"The urban guerrilla tracts, the essay on the Foco, the blueprints, the drawings, the diaries, the letters..."

"The man sure wrote his life story. Some good friend of his should have done him a big favor and cut his right hand off..."

"None of it should be admissable."

"That's wonderful."

"Yes. Wonderful. Now all we have to do is convince a federal judge of it."

Jon is scribbling again on his yellow pad. Erika glances over at it. Scrawled across the top: Defendant's Motion to Suppress, page 18. He stops and pours his beer into his glass. He watches it come to a head and keep rising. He doesn't sip it down. He just watches as it spills over leaving little beads of beer on the yellow pad. Then he starts to talk, his voice getting progressively louder and higher pitched.

"You know the worst thing about all this? The worst thing is, like, it doesn't matter that we're absolutely right. I mean, this motion is gonna be faultless, our argument is faultless, we have every case cited on point and they all agree with us and we are goddam fucking right, but it fucking doesn't matter. They don't even have to read the case law, they don't even have to address the arguments. That judge denies us this motion and they know and we know that we won't take it up because we don't have a prayer higher up, not with the Burger court, not a fucking prayer. Plus we'd wind up making bad case law in the bargain, give them a chance to attack all the Fourth Amendment cases and wipe them out in one decision. Jesus. And they'll wind up getting away with this *shit*,

105

Simon, and what the fuck can we do about it? Jesus. The man's never gonna get out, that's the truth. He's never gonna sit around like this and drink a beer with his friends, he's never gonna see a fucking tree again or make love to his wife. We create all this paper, you know, but they're never gonna let him out."

Erika listens. She closes her eyes and listens and he sounds like a precocious adolescent instead of a brilliant paper man. The paper man, they called him before he arrived, and Noah, hearing them, had thought Jon was made of paper. (Like the time he asked Erika for his book's coat and it took her a few minutes to figure out he meant jacket. And records have sleeves, clocks have hands, to get busted also means to get broken, there's a prison called The Tombs, and yes, it would surely take more than paper to bring Paul Rousseau back from the dead.) And Erika listens and now she hears Simon's voice, calming, encouraging.

"One step at a time, Jon. We have to take it one step at a time. Anything can happen." And Erika smiles into her glass and tries to remember the man Simon had been not two months before, the man who believed nothing could happen, who believed everything was already written.

"No word about Annie?" she asks.

Dan shakes his head and lights another cigarette. Smoke wafts around him. "Nothing. She's OK. There's a network and she's plugged into it. But still it must be hell for her, being separated from those kids. She's a strong woman."

"And what good does it do to be strong?" Erika asks. She wants to know. She wants his answer. He studies her face and knows she wants it, not being glib but wanting the truth.

"Because we have to be strong like any people must be who are trying to fight an empire with pencils and rocks. The unarmed resistance have the pencils,

106

the armed resistance have the rocks. It's not much, but it's been known to work."

"Yeah," Jon says, "look how scared they are of Paul even now."

It's true, Erika thinks. She remembers standing in the cold watching the convoy that accompanied Paul Rousseau to the Federal Courthouse for his arraignment, the SWAT team, the U.S. Army bomb demolition unit, the squads of state and city police, a dozen U.S. marshalls. She remembers him getting out of the armored truck which had been used to transport him from the prison. She remembers the drawn guns, the tension, the small band of supporters gathered around the barricades at the far end of the street in front of the little shops with their Christmas decorations, the TV cameras, police with sniper rifles on the rooftops, the sound of the chopper hovering overhead. And Paul stepping out of the armored car. Yes, they were afraid of him all right.

They had brought Paul Rousseau back to the city in chains.

A December morning. Erika wakes with a start even before the first of the alarms goes off. She wakes up and the first thing she thinks about is Paul. (He had written her a letter. Why her? He had written it the day after he saw her standing in the crowd outside the courthouse and blown her a kiss, hard to do with hands chained, but he had managed. He had written to her about love, armed love, love for the people, love for the oppressed. The revolutionary picks up a gun with one hand, reaches out to embrace the people with the other. Armed love is deep and everlasting, he had written. And I will take it to the wall and beyond.) She wakes up in the thin winter light under a warm quilt, the day open in front of her like a door, Simon beside her, so close, sometimes touching, the children asleep

107

in their beds just a wall a way, and she thinks about Paul and about Annie and about walls. She imagines Annie somewhere watching Paul on the news, watching him in chains, chains on his wrists and ankles, being hustled from armored truck to courthouse, surrounded by his enemies, at the mercy of his enemies. She imagines Annie seeing him being pushed along the sidewalk by those men, his fist raised in greeting, looking straight into the camera, shouting, "Annie! I love you!"

It is easier for Simon, she thinks. Strategy is, after all, a kind of emotional defense. You can't think too much about individual prisoners of war when your job is to position your guerrillas around the POW camp and liberate it. The first day the defense team visited Paul in prison, Dan came to the house in jeans and a fatigue jacket. Simon and Jon were wearing suits. Don't worry, he said, I have a suit in the car in case they hassle me about the way I'm dressed. Yes, Erika said, you look like the liberation army. He gave her a beatific smile. I am, he said.

So she thinks of all this as the wind roars and tiny pebbles of ice are blown up against the glass, of the children being taken to a small town in the South, raised from now on by born-again Christians (Annie's sister, who found Jesus), and of Annie and her helplessness, and of walls.

At seven Becky's clock radio comes on. "We are living in a material world and I am a material girl." Erika cringes and thinks about getting out of bed.

At seven-fifteen Jon's buzzer goes off, like an early warning device at some nuclear power plant. But Erika knows he's already up, decked out in his magenta running suit, watch cap in place over his tonsured head, on his way out for a thirty minute run. She checks the thermometer. Shivers. Wraps herself in her robe, goes to head him off at the front door.

108

"Jon, it's only eight degrees."

"It's OK. Have to clear my head. It's sleeping in Noah's room. I wake up and think I'm six years old."

She watches him from the window. The snow plows that came through during the night left a pretty clear track up the street. Still it's slippery under foot and the wind is harsh. But she knows Jon, she feels that she knows him. For one thing they like the same books. For another, well, like her, like everyone, he does things for a complex of reasons, one interwoven with another, no one easily separated from its fellows, not even the most fragile, the hardest to articulate, the belief that this act, this quiet, insignificant, mundane act, if done with the proper intention, can somehow escape its own limits, become bigger, mean more. The day before, during the snowstorm, she caught him at the door. You're nuts, she said. You're a lunatic. No, he said, pulling on his mittens. I'm running for Paul.

Now she hears her own alarm ring and sees Noah, pillow tucked under his arm, blanket trailing behind him, still half asleep, making his way to the TV to watch *He Man and the Masters of the Universe*, the old Manichean cosmos, good and evil locked in eternal embrace, brought to you by Mattel Toy Corporation. She goes back to her room, shakes Simon awake, turns up the heat, goes into the kitchen, feeds the cats, puts up the coffee, all the usual morning rituals, but in her mind the image of Paul in his six by six cell, his windowless room, merges with the quick-fading images of her dream, the coded messages of the night which she must decipher as though they were the innards of a sacred bird laid out for inspection on a plate.

The code is not too hard to break: her unconscious is an open book. Involuntarily, even against her will, something calls up the picture of Marc as she sleeps. Now as she turns on the tap and watches water rush

109

into the sink, she remembers what it was that woke her. It comes back to her with the clarity of a motion picture: she dreamt that she had fallen asleep in the wrong bed.

And Simon passes her on his way to the bathroom, Becky scurries by looking for her homework and thirty cents for milk, Noah dashes through the kitchen to grab his sword before the commercial ends, the water boils, she pours it into the filter, watches the water turn into coffee, the phone begins to ring, and yet in the midst of all this action, in the very heart of it (for she feels herself to be the heart of it) there is something gnawing, something torn, there is a tear and something tearing it more, it is her heart and it aches, sometimes in great waves of ache, sometimes in little spasms, sometimes sneaking up on her when she least expects it, slicing vegetables, stirring oatmeal, suddenly there is the ache, or sometimes when she makes love to Simon the ache is so great she cries, she doesn't want to but tears roll down her cheeks and yet what Annie wouldn't give to be where Erika is now, Annie who will probably never hold Paul again, never make love to him, and it's too much, all of it is too much. She could stop it now, stop it for Annie, the way Jon runs for Paul. Stop it now, heal herself, which would mean building another wall to keep out his face, the memory of him, his body, his voice, even the way he smells, everything of his that she has grafted onto herself. How stupid.

The telephone call is for Simon, a reporter from Channel 13. Erika passes the phone to Simon who is still in the bathroom.

"Get me a tie so I can talk like a lawyer," he says. All he's wearing is shaving cream.

Erika likes it. He's getting his sense of humor back. She hands him a cup of coffee and a cigarette, hears something about pre-trial detention. She knows

110

the rap by heart now; it's horrible, but she's almost used to it. Paul Rousseau, despite what the Feds may think of him or suspect or profess they know, has only one indictment pending against him: two counts of malicious damage to government property and one count of conspiracy to commit malicious damage. Hardly a capital offense. But will the government grant Paul Rousseau a bail hearing, set bail for him and allow someone to post it so he can be free until his trial? Not on your life. Paul Rousseau is a dangerous terrorist and therefore must be held in preventive detention, another gift of the Reagan Administration. Preventive detention in solitary confinement. No visitors. No exercise. And he hasn't even been convicted of a crime.

It's seven-forty-five. Jon comes in from his run, mills around the bathroom door. His beard is frozen, his cheeks, naturally sallow, are unnaturally rosy. Simon comes out with the phone, Jon goes in. Becky leaves for school but comes back for her gym clothes. Noah says he wants raisin bran, Capt'n Crunch and an egg in the shell. Not runny. A cat cries to go out. Simon is talking into the phone about appealing Paul's civil rights case to the First Circuit. Now he is wearing a towel.

By eight everyone is dressed and sitting around the table, except for Noah who eats in front of the TV. Jon is suited and tied, poring over the newspaper like a bearded prophet of the apocalypse in corporate disguise.

"Look at this," he says, shaking his head, "I just can't believe they keep doing this. 'Suspected anti-U.S. terrorist, Paul Rousseau...'. Like, why don't they just say, 'untried but convicted terrorist'. Like, this is a total outrage, you know? '...who has been linked by the FBI to a string of political bombings including the bombing of the Capitol...' Sure, and you know what the FBI knows about those bombings? The same thing that everybody else knows, that they happened. Big fucking

111

deal. You know what they have to link him to those bombings? It's right in the affidavits. They were all detonated by the same timing device they found plans for in that car ten years ago. And do you know where the design came from? *The Anarchist Cookbook*. You know how many people own a copy of *The Anarchist Cookbook*? Or *The Blaster's Handbook*, for that matter, published by Dupont? It's like the government's saying, Well, Paul Rousseau had a recipe for apple pie in his kitchen, therefore he made every apple pie in America. Well, goddammit, Simon, if they keep this up we'll have a great argument for a polluted jury pool, whatever that's worth."

Erika peers over his shoulder at the article in question. ROUSSEAU SUES STATE FOR SIX MILLION.

"See, look at this. I mean, every time we walk into that courthouse some asshole reporter grabs us. And every time they print his name they stick 'terrorist' or 'revolutionary' in front of it. Why not 'father of three'? Why not 'Viet Nam veteran'? Why not 'prison reform advocate'? Oh, no. You'd think they were writing their copy in the U.S. District Attorney's office."

"Oh, but this is a great quote, Jon. 'Responding to questions regarding the government's claim that tightened security at the prison was essential due to remarks made by Rousseau to the effect that he had a duty to escape, defense attorney Golden replied, 'If Mr. Rousseau had said, Tomorrow I'm going to fly to the moon, would the government have ordered cordons placed around the Apollo capsule? Or if Mr. Rousseau had said, I'm going to change the warden into a piece of green cheese, would the government assume by virtue of that statement that the defendant had not only the intention but the means?' Local attorney Donnis, also representing Rousseau, added, 'Federal agents terrorize his children in front of him, beat him, shoot him with

112

a stun gun, keep him chained and shackled, won't allow him to receive visitors or books—under the circumstances Mr. Rousseau's remarks are the epitome of rationality.' This is terrific. What are you complaining about?"

Jon scowls, Simon swallows his toast. "Channel 13 wants to interview us."

"Good. I think we should do it."

"I told them we were going to be at the prison most of the day. They're bringing the cameras up."

"They won't get in."

"I told them that. Daniel's meeting us up there, too."

Erika leaves the table and finds Noah's shoes. He tells her he needs ten cents for the African Relief box. "Go ask your father. He's finally got his pants on."

And she thinks, Innocent until proven guilty. Such a noble idea. The kind of idea that might make you weep for joy. Like the brotherhood of man. Like animal heaven.

By eight-thirty they are ready to leave. Heat down, lights off, cats kissed—they are off.

They laugh in the car. Noah, as usual, has snuck a few of his toys into Simon's briefcase. He does this surreptitiously, by night. One morning Simon opened his briefcase at the office and found a G.I. Joe machine gun. Now, and especially on the mornings when he's going to see Paul, he examines his briefcase with extreme care. He calls it 'sending out the ferrets'. Noah thinks it's the greatest joke in the world.

This morning the ferrets discover an uzi, a beretta, and three sticks of dynamite cleverly disguised as Lincoln Logs.

"We were almost dead meat today," Jon says. "Come on, Noah, 'fess up. What else did you plant on us?"

Noah laughs. His laughter reminds Erika of Annie's, the way he gives himself completely to it, the way the laughter itself runs up and down some musical scale, the way she might describe it as 'a peal of laughter', the way a bell sounds, and only for Annie and Noah would she ever use such a pat phrase, only for them would it be nearly true.

She brings Noah into his daycare center still laughing at the great joke. Then she drives to Simon's office.

"What are you doing today, Erika?"

"Oh, I don't know. I thought I might just off a few pigs."

Jon grins and shakes his head. He has a scholar's face, the moist brown eyes and tonsured head of a desert monk. Erika can see him in a black hat and ringlets with a copy of the Talmud under his arm instead of the *Federal Rules of Evidence* and LaFave's *Treatise on the Fourth Amendment*.

"Sometimes this gets so futile, you know. I mean, it's debatable whether that's really not the best idea, given the current state of the legal system."

Simon leans over and kisses Erika goodbye. His hair is stuck under his shirt collar, he has a toast crumb in the corner of his mouth and circles under his eyes.

"Don't get busted today, will ya?" he says.

"I'll try not to. Keep your nose clean, honey."

They take their briefcases out of the back seat, one on the right, the other on the left, slam the doors in unison, cross the icy street, Jon, tall and lanky in his long black overcoat, Simon, short and compact in his grey. A rather unlikely pair, Erika thinks, this latest model Quixote and Panza, off to fight windmills. But this time around the windmills are armed and dangerous.

114

Ordinarily Erika would have stopped at Marc's, but today when she gets to his corner she resists the tug. She wants to see him, but she has decided to wait until she misses him not like a man misses water on a desert, but the way a woman misses the comfort of an old and worn, but fleecy and soft robe. It takes a great act of will. She is coming to know what will is, where it abides in the body and what it is that it struggles against. She manages to turn the car the other way and drives toward the beach to visit her friend Brenda.

BUILD TRUST, scrawls the Night Writer, NOT CONDOS

Brenda is already up and dressed when Erika arrives at her house. Her table is set for one, but beautifully with her Harlequin service, plate, cup and saucer, coffee pot, sugar and creamer, salt and pepper shakers, every color of the rainbow there on the wooden table by the windows overlooking the beach. Cold winter sunlight streams through the blinds making stripes on the rug and over the gold brocade cushions on the crimson velvet chairs. The room is like a painting, has the texture of a painting: stylized, anachronistic, every space filled with something and every single thing precious, chosen, redeemed. Erika loves to be here, inside Brenda's painting, its old hats with their veils and feathers hanging on the wall, its salt and pepper shaker collection under glass, its Egyptian princesses and medieval knights in ornate gilded frames, its shelves of knick-knacks, its black Spanish shawl thrown over the back of an overstuffed chaise lounge, its lace curtains and antimacassars, fringed lampshades and brass clock, its canary in his copper cage singing his heart out. It is a time-haven, Brenda's house, and yet there are compromises even

115

here: the stereo and TV, a copy of *The Village Voice*, a carton filled with leaflets from the city's branch of Solidarity with the People of Central America (SOPCA) that say NO CONTRA AID, tokens, all of them, of the century Brenda inhabits through a mere accident of birth.

She is a big woman, generously built. This morning she is wearing, for her own amusement, a black lace blouse and a long dark red satin skirt, red embroidered slippers (Persian, without the point, her harem slippers, she calls them), an arm's length of silver bangle bracelets that clank when she moves, and long silver earrings. Six immense rings on her fingers and a heavy silver necklace: Brenda believes in dressing for breakfast. Her hair is night black, kinky, rather wild. Her eyes are china blue lined with kohl. For a living she sings with a local jazz band and draws up astrological charts; for her friends she reads cards and bakes pastries.

"Erika! How amazing that you've come!" Brenda is effusive as ever, kissing Erika at the door. "I just tried to do a reading for myself and your card came up."

"My card comes up a lot. I think you must stack the deck."

Brenda shakes her head and her earrings jangle. "No stacking the Tarot, or you pay, believe me. I made muffins this morning. I was feeling creative. Want some, and a cup of coffee?"

Assuming the answer, she goes into the kitchen. Erika hangs her jacket on the coat tree and lowers herself into a chair. She feels weighed down, heavy like the ocean which is darkening even as she watches it, turning the color of slate. And she thinks how he has actually made it easy for her. Another man might have lied, or told her the truth. With Marc, she doesn't know what he has told her. A lie is having one thing on your lips, another in your mind. But when the

116

thing resides in the heart, a dark and secret place, the mind has no access to it. Perhaps he doesn't know his own heart. Perhaps it is just as well that he doesn't. Perhaps she is preparing him somehow, perhaps the next woman will reap something from what she has so patiently sown. But the truth is he will let her go with the same ease that he had taken her in, like a pool that opens to you when you enter it and then closes again after you leave, unmarked by the dive, as still again as though you had never plunged into its depths.

"So, Erika." Brenda sweeps up to the table, an orange plate of muffins in one hand, a yellow coffee pot in the other. "I'm so glad to see you. This is such a wonderful surprise."

Erika is suddenly struck with guilt. How she uses her friends for comfort. How little she thinks of them anymore. How she has let him absorb her attention entirely. No, how she has simply given it to him, unasked.

She smiles at Brenda and tries to look like a person who might be worthy of the appellation Wonderful Surprise.

"You look superb. Do you have a breakfast date?"

"No. I've just been depressed. I thought I'd dress myself out of it."

"I've been a little depressed, too."

"Oh, of course you have! It's so terrible about Annie and Paul. Poor Annie. I think of her so much. I feel so awful for her. I want to hear all about it, Erika. How is Paul? How is he doing?"

"OK, considering. I think he's preparing himself for Marion."

"Oh, God. How can he do that?"

"By facing it. By seeing that there's no hope. By killing hope. By facing it."

Erika stares at the muffin on her blue plate, the butter, the jam. She can't eat anything.

"Surely there's hope. What does Simon say?"

"I think Simon's hopeful, about these charges. But this is nothing, really. They're going to try to pin every explosion that happened east of the Mississippi over the last ten years on him. They want him bad."

"I wish I knew him better. I didn't even *like* him, though. I remember thinking Annie was out of her *mind*. Arrogant. Well."

"Simon says he's mellowed out. I don't know, I haven't talked to him except on the phone. They're strip searching visitors. Not that he can't *have* visitors, you understand, but they just make it damn uncomfortable. So he's refusing to see anybody. It's part of that suit Simon's bringing against the state. They're really treating him like he's Jack the Ripper or something. No, they're treating him like *they're* working for the Gulag, like *they're* subhuman."

She is thinking, What is the difference between the two?...How a society treats its dissidents...puts them into a zone of silence and isolation, outside the ken of ordinary people, invisible, like the inside of a mind. Perhaps they are the inside of society's mind, the ideas and feelings that the superego wants repressed. And that's where Paul is now and he is beyond reach and he will be beyond reach forever. And why? For greed? For hatred? No, they would understand that. They share that. But for love. Armed love. By comparison, what was her love for Marc, what was it after all, what did it look like, what would it be called?

But Brenda is saying, "I wonder if Simon would be willing to come to a SOPCA meeting and talk about him. I think we need to know what Paul was doing and why, even if we don't agree with his tactics. After all, Somoza would still be in power today if the FSLN didn't blow up a few buildings and fire a few guns. And it was all centered on Central America and South Africa, wasn't it? I mean, the bombings."

118

"Yes, but Paul isn't admitting being involved in those bombings. His position is that he's in complete agreement with the aims of the group, the August 7th People's Resistance Brigade, but that he himself is guilty of no crimes. The wording is important," Erika says, smiling at Brenda.

"Ah."

"But I'll ask Simon."

"Great. Sometimes I think SOPCA's just wonderful. The people *are* wonderful, and the spirit of non-violence is the only way to create real change, etc. etc. And then at other times, I just get so *angry*."

"You're leaving for Nicaragua soon, aren't you?"

"*Si, compañera,* exactly one month from today, and I am tickled pink about it, too, I'll tell you."

"You're such an unlikely *brigadista*," Erika smiles.

"Oh, Mother! I can pick coffee for three weeks, it won't kill me. Sing the blues up there in the mountains, sing to the little red beans. But then I'm going to Leon for the Ruben Dario Festival and listen to poetry for three days straight. Ecstasy! Such wonderful poetry, Erika, you would *love* it. And women poets, Erika! I have to meet some of those women. They all fought in the Revolution, too. I would just be in paradise if I could meet my heroine, Nora Astorga. You know the story about her, Erika, you must. She was an attorney at the time of the Revolution, still working in the system, but secretly a member of the Frente. There was a general of Somoza's, a real pig, known as The Dog, who was also a skirt-chaser, to put it politely, and he was chasing her. So she invited him home one night, disarmed him, and then, just as he was about to pounce, out from the closets stepped her *compañeros* and took him out, the bastard. Now she's Ambassador to the United Nations. Isn't that a great story? *And,* I don't know if this was accidental or not—but, of course, *what's* accidental?—The Dog got his on International Women's Day, March 8, 1978!"

"Wonderful!" Wonderful. Another strong woman. Why isn't she strong? Why is it that she can't bear to give him up?

"Erika," Brenda says gently, "you look so sad."

"It's nothing," she lies. "Did my card really come up?"

"Yes."

"Or what you think is my card. It's such a joke; you know."

"The reader chooses the card. You have to trust your reader to perceive that much at least."

Erika's card is Strength, the beautiful woman in white with garlands of flowers around her waist bending down to caress a lion whose head rests in her hand. Now she can't even think of this card without thinking of Marc, whose sign is Leo.

"I feel so weak."

"Do you want a reading?"

"Yes....No....Yes....God! See, I know what it would say. The covering card, Sorrow, the heart pierced by three swords. Crossed by Justice. There is a choice. There are two men, one a Page, one a King. There is much at risk, the future is murky. The Judgement card shows up, perhaps, or the Hanged Man, a good card, yes, but ambiguous, leaves you somewhat up in the air."

"So it's that, is it? *Plaisir d'amour*. And, God, what hell we go through for it. You don't want your muffin? Give it here. I have to eat when I'm under stress."

Erika turns her head and watches the waves, the line of waves, the rise and fall. And listens to Brenda's voice, with its own rise and fall, which, even now seems to have a full octave range, starting high, lowering, rising again. Everything she already knows but has to hear again.

"Women and love, such a messy business. And when you think, there was a time when we were *adored*, for big breasts, big hips, big bellies, worshipped for giving birth, think of it. Now, my God, it's worth your entire spiritual equilibrium to sleep with a man. It takes so much *out* of you, it's so draining, and for *what*? This is what I think. Every time a woman mates successfully with a man, in orgasm, you understand, she conceives a creature called woman-in-love. The more she sleeps with him, the more it grows until finally she's so big with it—the goddam man doesn't want her anymore. The goddam man says, 'How *dare* you be in love with me! What's *wrong* with you? I thought we agreed this was just fun. We've just been playing and here you are big with love!' Oh, yes, he's outraged all right. He threatens to leave her if she doesn't abort woman-in-love pronto, that very day, *cut it out!* Don't you say that nasty word *anymore!* Of course, she does cut it out, but then she doesn't want *him* anymore, the shit, who'd blame her? Either way we wind up mourning for them, those little creatures we've lost....So, it's him. Erika, do you really think this one's worth it? Throw him back, he's too small for you. Oh, yes, he's exciting and on all the time, but there's more to life than good sex."

Erika's beginning to smile, just a little. "There is?"

"Oh, I agree, it's something when you get it, it's the perfect high, to find a man who just—fits you." Now Erika laughs, hoots with glee, because Brenda's delivery is so perfect, so flamboyantly dramatic. It is high drama, all right. Or melodrama anyway. "But," and she makes a sweep of the air with her bracelet-covered arm, "attentive and energetic as they may be, one can tire of them."

"I'd like the chance. I'd like to tire of him."

121

"I'd give you a week, max. Oh, with your tolerance level, maybe ten days. Then, ho-hum....Simon still doesn't know?"

"Actually I'm thinking of telling him."

Brenda makes a sucking sound through her teeth. "Ouch," she says.

"Maybe you should get the cards."

"Let's get high first and think about it."

They smoke from Brenda's little brass pipe, not with any serious intent, but as a sort of gesture to the higher powers, and to the past. Then Brenda begins to probe, explore. She has met Marc, she is the only one of Erika's friends who has been formally introduced. Though Brenda is a notorious source of information, Erika trusts her since she understands what passion can do. Brenda is Erika's cover with Simon, her show-and-tell with Marc, proving to him that she is a real person with friends and a life, not just a wife and mother, not just that. Marc invited them to brunch one Sunday morning. Brenda went in her gypsy disguise. "Some VIP's travel with their own shrinks," she said to him. "Erika travels with her fortune teller." Brenda's opinion was succinct: He's a good host. He should own a restaurant. But her heart ached for Erika who was, she thought, playing the role of the Little Prince to Marc's flower, thinking him unique when any experienced woman might have told her in an instant that he was a rather common garden-variety rose. Brenda, with an experience of men and women which she often thinks should be catalogued for the long-range good of womankind, has to bite her tongue now as Erika says,

"He gets up in the morning and there's no cloud over his head. He isn't dragging the last twenty years around with him."

"What's wrong with him? Does he have amnesia?"

122

"He thinks Voltaire is *serious* about this being the best of all possible worlds. He believes it." And she thinks about what it's like talking about politics to Marc, looking at him over the gulf of years, a decade. How he pontificates about the power women have over men, yin over yang, water over rock. He's read Lao Tzu all right, but he's never been a secretary. Injustice? Unhappiness? Well, no one gets everything they want. Except him. Everything that happens to him happens for the best. Voltaire was right, see? It is the best of all possible worlds....Maybe I should read some feminist stuff, he says. I've never come across any of this before. And Erika beside him feels the wrinkles spring into her face.

"But the thing is," she says finally, "he's the only man I've ever desired." She says the word "desire" with amazement, a kind of wonder, as though she has waited her whole life to feel this particular form of human anguish.

"So why do you want to tell Simon?"

"I don't want to lie anymore."

"There's a lie right there. What you really want, *think*, is for it to stop. Because you'll have to stop it, you know. You can't tell Simon you're sleeping with someone else and then keep doing it."

"I can if he doesn't mind."

"Oh. And you think he won't mind?"

"He's done it."

"Oh, yes, a hundred years ago, sandwiched in between long hours of self-criticism, with signed permission slips and equal time provisos....Yes, yes, I remember. I remember how you flipped out about it, too. I remember months of bonafide hysteria...."

"OK, OK. I'm just thinking about it."

"Why not ask Marc what he thinks?"

"About telling Simon?"

"Yes."

"I know what he'll say."

"So do I. DON'T DO IT!"

"He wouldn't want the responsibility."

"Of course not. So he'll tell you not to say anything to Simon. And then what will he say?"

"Then? I don't know."

"Think, Erika. You know what he'll say."

"You mean if I insist on telling Simon anyway?"

"No, no. Just as a tag-on to the 'Don't do it, Erika'. The next line."

"The next line? I don't know. What will he say?"

Brenda feels ridiculous, like she's stumbled on an alchemist and is trying to explain to him why he can't make gold.

"Are you going to do this or not?"

"I don't know yet. Why?"

"Because I can predict what he'll say and you have to be ready for it. Don't start unless you're ready for it. He'll say that you shouldn't tell Simon and destroy your marriage—he will assume that it will destroy your marriage, it wouldn't occur to him that Simon might be broad-minded about these things—and the reason you shouldn't is because he, Marc that is, doesn't love you....And, Erika, it won't be a lie. Because even though he loves you now, and he does love you, in his own way, the minute you talk about Simon, the minute you introduce reality into it—and I have to give you credit, you've managed to keep reality out of this relationship for, what?, a year or more, which has got to be a record of some kind—anyway, as soon as you do that, he's going to stop loving you and he's going to forget that he ever did."

Erika's gaze is fixed on the shoreline.

"But don't worry," Brenda says, cheerily, "if you like the type, there are a million of them out there. A million. As common as rocks. And we've been breaking our little hearts on those rocks time out of

124

mind. It's an incurable disease. They got it, we feed it. I've had my share of them, too, cute little narcissists, magnetic, charming, beautiful narcissists. They come in both sexes, and, God, the female versions are just as bad. But there's something irresistible about a human being with that degree of self-love, like a gravitational pull. They're so outrageous, it's spellbinding."

"Maybe you're wrong."

"Maybe I am. What's the other scenario? You tell him you're going to tell Simon. He throws himself at your feet, says he's been waiting a year for you to say those words—he being far too chivalrous to bring up the subject himself—and where do you want to go for your honeymoon?"

Erika is laughing now. "No. My scenario is that Marc and Simon decide to meet, not to duel, you understand, but to become acquainted." Brenda chuckles into her cup of coffee. "Afterwards Marc says, 'Simon's not such a bad guy.' But Simon says, 'Erika, for God's sakes, that Marc's a complete asshole.'"

"They'd both be right."

"Simon *is* a pretty nice guy."

"He is."

"Why don't you tell me how nice he is?"

"Erika, you are blind in one eye and can't see out of the other. You have the perfect man in your own bed. In fact, I personally know three women who are waiting in line for him, breathlessly in the wings."

"Really? Who?"

"Let me make some more coffee. Then we should take a nice healthy walk on the beach."

"You're not serious, are you?"

"Of course not. Are you crazy?"

And in this way Brenda, who used her cards, her ears and her wits to meditate on the future, to see destinies coming, and to stave off the worst, tried to guide Erika away from the edge of the abyss. But

125

although the domino theory has been held up to ridicule as a political metaphor, it has never been disproved in personal relationships. Every action has its reaction. In this respect Erika was like the Queen Elizabeth: she displaced a lot of water; she could not move in any direction without leaving behind her a rather forbidding wake.

That same day Simon was in the maximum security wing of the state prison arguing with Paul Rousseau about his stance of 'politics in command'. The aim of the endeavor was not necessarily to win, Paul said. In fact, given the reality of the situation—the corruption of the judicial system, how it was hand-in-glove with the enemies of the people, a tool of the ruling class, the legal arm attached to the FBI's fist—it was sheer nonsense to think he had a fair shot at an acquittal and any member of the defense team who thought otherwise was in need of a little political education and a large dose of self-criticism. The object was not to play the game, to manipulate a set of bullshit rules in a bullshit system, but to resist it, defy it, expose it to the people's view, to use the trial as a public forum to denounce the imperialistic policies of the government.

They tried to dissuade him. Week after week, as the strategy of the case developed, as the arguments emerged, as the idea of winning this one fast, invoking the Speedy Trial Act and winning it before any new indictments came down, getting Paul out of prison and then out of the country, as that dream grew in strength, their pleas against politics in command grew in intensity. But Paul would not budge. In fact, now he was saying that he wanted to declare himself a prisoner of war under the Geneva Convention. Insane as it seemed to Simon, the last thing Paul Rousseau wanted was to see his political writings suppressed because of a bad warrant.

Finally, while Erika and Brenda were sitting around a wooden table talking about love, Simon lost his patience.

"This strategy would be fine, Paul, if you really expected the Revolution to happen within the next twenty years, if there was any hope that you wouldn't die in Marion. But look around you, man. This isn't South Africa. They'll put you away and you'll stay there for your whole life. The Revolution isn't coming. There's no Liberation Army. There's nobody else out there."

Paul just looked at him and smiled.

For Simon, it was that smile that changed the tenor of the case.

For the truth was that Simon wasn't used to playing the role of retainer for any of his clients. He didn't serve the rich, big business, corporations. He was never told by anybody what to do. Most of his clients were poor and scared and they looked up to him and trusted him to do what was best. But Paul Rousseau was not poor and scared and didn't look up to anybody. Just as he was the general of the people's army, he was chief counsel of the case. He permitted the lawyers to do certain things, forbade them from doing others. Nothing happened without his approval and he would think nothing of firing any or all of them for insubordination with the arrogance of a czar dismissing a member of the imperial staff. As delusional as Simon might sometimes think he was, there was no question that the man was strong, his inner strength was enormous, his presence powerful. He was hard to resist, his vision was hard to resist (since it was Simon's vision as well) and he was courageous, nothing intimidated him. And Simon understood why security was so tight, why the guards and the marshalls and the

Feds were so frightened of him, had to compensate for their fear by beating him, chaining him, keeping him shackled even on the twenty foot walk down the corridor to the showers: he was a man other men desired to serve.

And yet there was something in Simon that held back, that calibrated the effect Paul had on him, but recognized every source from which it sprung. Simon hated surprises. He thought, he *knew*, he was in control of the case and of his client, that he was indulging Paul the way he indulged some of his Social Security clients—in this way he kept an emotional distance. He had to, or he would be overwhelmed by anger, anger at the waste, the terrible waste, the mistake in judgement that had led to this, a mistake, however, for which he refused to allocate blame.

Then there was that smile.

"By the way," Paul said as they were leaving, "I'm going on a fast starting tomorrow. I'm a vegetarian and they're not giving me vegetarian meals. Since I'm not eating much anyway, I might as well stop altogether and see if we can't get some attention put on the situation here. I'm sure I'm not the only vegetarian in this joint."

They came home that night thoughtful, puzzled. They sat around the dining room table and studied each other's faces. Wondering.

"It isn't possible," one of them says. It's what each one of them is thinking.

"But so what if there is a bigger organization?" Simon asks, lighting a cigarette, grabbing for the nearest pack on the table, Dan's Marlboros. "So they are organized into *foco* units, so there is a network of urban guerrillas, so they have a hundred or two hundred, or

128

five hundred, or a thousand, even if there were five thousand, what of it? They're a front without any backing. There is no *cause*."

"And yet," says Dan, lighting a match, squinting into it, "look around. At any moment on any street in any city you can see a dissident. You can pick them out. And every dissident is a potential revolutionary. So if you scratched every surface, planted a seed here and a seed there, and you were clever and patient and you could tap into all that discontent, if you could unify all the oppressed classes in this society...." He takes a long drag of his cigarette and sighs out a stream of smoke. He leans back in his chair and the chair creaks. He is a big man, his face all hollows and bones, framed by silver hair that hangs to his shoulders. There are not many lawyers like him, more like a tribal elder than an attorney at law. He has seen it all many times over and there are many things that he knows but will not speak of, for it is not wise, he says, for anyone to know more than he must to do the job he has to do. He has his own brand of moral authority which Simon knows comes from dedicating your life to noble but hopeless causes. Rousseau touches a nerve in him. Maybe he longs for a victory, too, a single triumph, something once, just once, to pan out. It's one thing to sit in front of your TV and watch the Sandinistas liberate Managua. It's another thing to dream about liberating New York. But Dan says,

"I'll tell you the truth, it scares me to death to think about what would happen in this country if a revolution actually took place here. If they fucked it up, and chances are they would. If they tried it and lost, the repression afterwards would be incredible. You see the kind of knee-jerk reaction this government gets into, concentration camps for Japanese-Americans during the war is the most blatant example I can think of. Try to imagine the response to real insurrection. And what

129

if the insurrectionists won, what then? You see how hard it is to maintain a revolutionary government, warriors being notoriously bad at running bureaucracies, and think of trying to run this one and think of who'd be doing it. And then if something went wrong, if it got worse than this, and it could, too, easily, there would be no hope for a counterrevolution, there would be no making it right again, no second crack at it. You don't get a second crack at it. And, frankly, I don't see any leadership anywhere in this country that I'd stake so much on. I'd rather deal with the devil I know...."

And in the silence they all think for a moment a single thought, a kind of treason or heresy, though they immediately retract those words, for Paul Rousseau is neither their king nor their god. It is a thought that rises from a part of each of them which is not "movement lawyer" or "political radical", but from a more primitive part, younger, the part that is half anarchist, half stubborn yankee, the part that would live free or die. From that region comes the thought they each recognize and acknowledge and it is this: I would not want to see a revolution led by a man like Paul Rousseau.

Simon gets up and disappears into the bedroom. A few minutes later he emerges with two joints. Dan raises an eyebrow.

"I see not even the threat of FBI harrassment can keep a true pot head straight for long. Well, pass it right over here, Simon. Maybe it will inspire us on our next move."

"I think," Jon says, scratching his beard, "that our next move should be to send a personal invitation to this elusive *foco* to demolish the state prison and get Paul out. As far as I can see, that is the only circumstance under which he will agree to leave."

130

They each acknowledge the rueful humor in this while Erika, who is wearing a silk blouse and deep purple linen skirt, moves around them, leaning over them, setting plates at the table. Each of them watches her, each of them thinks of touching her, but only one does. As she passes by him, Dan pulls himself up and puts his arms around her.

"Ah, lady," he says, stroking her back, "give me a hug."

When Erika repeated this conversation to Marc the next morning, he rolled over onto his back, tucked two pillows under his head, and squinted up at her.

"But don't you see, hon? We've already won the Revolution. We just don't all know it yet. We haven't all realized it. But it's true."

"What are you talking about?"

"The war, hon. We won the war. Or we didn't really win it. We just danced around it. We just danced through it."

"Marc, will you speak English please?"

"Oh, *mon petit chou*, come and lie down next to me and I'll speak English to you." He lifts the cover, she slips in beside him, snuggling against him, feeling how taut he is, his arm going around her, strong. "It helps if you take your clothes off first."

"I understand English better with my clothes on."

"Ah, now you tell me. And all this time I've been saying the most profound things to you in bed and you haven't understood any of them."

"The most profound things you say to me in bed aren't in English."

He holds her tighter. "It's the only real battlefield, you know."

"Where ignorant armies clash by night."

131

"But you get smarter. You clash by night enough, you learn."

"You can afford to be flip about it, if you don't mind my saying so, because you're not oppressed. You're a white American male."

"Last time I looked I was, yeah. But there are a lot of oppressed white American males, if you don't mind me saying so. My town was full of 'em. The mill was full of 'em. Even the high school. I could have grown up feeling oppressed, I just didn't. My father wouldn't let me. He'd say, Marc, if I catch you feeling oppressed I'm going to beat the shit out of you." He smiles at her. "I was lucky. I got oppression beat out of me."

"So you think you can beat oppression out of people? I thought oppression was beat in."

"Look, Erika, life can yield to you. It's like sex, OK? You can't demand it. You can't force it. You can't take it. You got to seduce it, flirt with it, sweet talk it. If you love it, it loves you back. If you make war on it, man, it's a lot stronger than you are, and you're gonna get crushed. So you sweet talk. We're all people, all of us. Even the assholes, even the pigs."

"But oppression can be organized. You've never been up against organized oppression."

"Honey, I live in America, too. I'm not extra-terrestrial. I worked in the mill. I know about institutionalized oppression. I went to public school. You can walk away from it. You can just say, Fuck it, and walk away from it. And if I walk away and you walk away, if enough of us walk away, if we just don't play anymore, we just say, Hell no, you know, then it's all over. The mill doesn't run if people don't work in it. The war doesn't go on if people don't fight in it. The fucking school system can't get us if we drop out of it. And if there are a million of us, all not playing their game with them, what are they gonna do? *That's* the

132

revolution. Saying, Man, the insides of me is mine. I'm not hating people because you tell me to, and I'm not gonna feel oppressed because you tell me to, and I'm not fucking carrying war around with me. I don't make war on anybody. Remember how you used to yell, ' Hell No, We Won't Go.' Remember that? I watched you on TV. I was in the third grade, but I saw you. You were there. I don't know, Erika. You convinced me. It's all true."

"I wonder."

"Act as though it's true and it becomes true. You taught me that. You and William James."

Erika thinks again how very young he is. How old she is. Jaded, cynical and old. And yet she would forget everything for him, all she wants is to forget everything, her history, her life, just to laugh with him, just to be lighthearted with him, to believe with that innocence that it really is going to be all right.

The best of all possible worlds.

"Or, you know, there's a psycho-killer in the middle of the street, you can either keep going and get blown away or you can take a little detour around the block."

"What if there's a psycho-killer on every block?"

"Oh, honey, then you wait for somebody to pinch you and wake you up."

"If you were a Black in South Africa..."

"But I'm not a Black in South Africa. Do *you* know what it's like to be Black in South Africa? Or Puerto Rican in New York City? Or a Franco a little upcountry? That's what I know. I know what I know, I don't know anything else and I wouldn't presume to know anything else. So, yeah, I know what it's like to get beaten up in an alley because you speak the wrong language or you have the wrong last name or you go to the wrong church. And I know what it's like to be in a

133

gang and beat up kids who are in a different gang and know there are people who want to kill you. I don't think there's a kid alive who doesn't know that. But if you have any sense you get out of it, you figure a way to get out of it. Or you figure out how to control it. Or you die."

"What did you do?"

"Well, I didn't die. I cut out. It's not my idea of a good time, getting sliced up in an alley. Now look at me. I own a bar with four other guys. I'm the Franco. There's a Puerto Rican, a Vietnamese and two gays. We're all of us refugees. We have a great time together, we have fun. And it's our place, see. We don't have to take shit from anybody. A guy comes in and starts acting like a jerk, we very politely ask him to leave. And people know that about the Front. They know how to behave. We kick you out for homophobia, we kick you out for racism. You don't like Asians? Bye-bye. Ask for Coors, you don't get it. Now one night about a month ago I was working the bar by myself and this guy was drunk and hassling people and I told him he had to leave. The fucker took a swing at me. All of a sudden five guys, regulars, picked the asshole up and threw him out. I didn't have to do a thing. It was real nice. People protect each other. There's a brotherhood in the world, even in a two-bit beer joint...Now isn't that the most profound thing I've ever said to you in bed?"

"In English, yes."

There is a pause, a long pause. She wonders if he's talked himself back to sleep.

"Marc?"

"I was just wondering."

"What?"

"I was wondering if there was a way I could tell you I love you in English so you'll believe me. Because I haven't known how to tell you—in English."

"And is there a way?"

134

"Maybe. What if I said this: Erika, I love you as much as a man can love another man's wife. Not divorced wife, not estranged wife, but wife, who goes home to him every night except once a year or so when we sneak out of town together like fugitives."

"Like that night it was so hot?"

"There was nothing cold to drink."

"We woke everyone up."

"They banged on the walls."

"Where *were* we anyway?"

"Out of town. That's what I mean. We're only OK together out of town."

"So why don't we leave the country?"

"You can't do that."

"You're right. I can't."

"And see, Erika, I'm a pragmatist in everything, even in love. I don't want any of us to get hurt."

He turns to her and kisses her. His kiss is gentle, undemanding. He is like water, clear, a mirror. He will be whatever she wants, friend, confidant, lover, but reluctant lover. Reluctant because there is always something in the way. Simon has always been more real a presence to him than to her. Now he's real to her, too. Now it's as though he's sitting in the next room. She had ignored his presence here for so long. She had felt no guilt at all. But there is brotherhood in the world. Marc was aware of it even if she wasn't.

She senses his relief—or maybe she simply imagines it—when she stops kissing him and asks him if he wants coffee.

"I'd love coffee. Let me jump in the shower and then we'll go out for breakfast. I'm out of everything God made. All I have in the house is toothpaste."

She watches him pad into the bathroom, listens for the sound of the shower. She could go in with him, wrap her arms around him. Maybe he is waiting for her to do that, passively, submissively, almost as though by

135

never initiating anything himself, by only responding to her, he avoids complicity.

Because she is another man's wife.

Because you can't have everything, certainly not two of everything. That's one of the rules.

And because you reap what you sow.

Especially because you reap what you sow.

That's one of the rules, too.

The defense team split up for Christmas week. Jon went home to New York where he would spend most of the week at the Metropolitan Correctional Center visiting Bobby and Marlene; Dan had Christmas visits to make at prisons in Massachusetts and the Midwest. For the first time in two months the Donnises were a nuclear family again. But it was Christmas, it wasn't like real time at all. And then Erika found Simon on the floor playing with Noah, in the kitchen baking cookies with Becky, at the door with arms full of presents and bags of brandy cakes for the guests he had invited over. And people arrived whom she hadn't seen in years and Simon prepared food and punch and engaged in conversation. But the conversation was always the same—the case—and the questions were ones he couldn't answer, chief among them, Where was Annie?

Where was Annie? Erika sat in front of the Christmas tree night after night, after everything was quiet, dishes washed, children bathed and put to bed, and asked herself that question. She would curl up in an armchair, turn on the stereo, set the needle down on the same record—side two of the Fauré Requiem (for a darker image, alternating it with side two of the Mozart)—stare at the lights and the decorations and the wild living/dying tree on which they hung, and she would think about Annie. Annie in hiding somewhere

136

(yes, but where?), Annie watching it all, or imagining what they didn't show on TV, Annie in pain. Erika could almost feel the pain. It came to her through the air, she was a receptor for it. For Annie it was (must be) as though everyone had died.

And yet Erika knew something, something important, something that Annie couldn't possibly know. A gift from Simon, who because he treated everyone humanely was treated humanely in return. Simon had been given the unofficial word from the enemy camp: if he happened to hear from Annie, if she happened to contact him about a deal (Simon just nodded, thoughtfully, never even tempted to say, "Annie Rousseau is not going to collaborate with you. She is not going to cop a plea," since it was his job to listen, not to judge) he could tell her this....What it came down to after all the talk was a simple admission that they didn't have much on her after all, that they could make life tough for her or they could let her slide through with a count of harboring a fugitive and a count of conspiracy, worth about five years each. If the judge ran them concurrently, with good time, Annie could be out in under four years. And all she had to do was say she was sorry. Cross her fingers and say uncle.

Four years, five max. It was a long time to be in prison, but wasn't she in prison already, locked away from everyone she loved? And so the idea was born, to Mozart, to Fauré, to find Annie, to bring her back from the dead. Yes, saving Annie, that was everything.

She didn't say anything about this to Simon. She watched him, she smiled at him, after an hour or two of requiems she was ready to snuggle up beside him on the couch and watch old movies on TV with him, but she resisted opening her heart. She thought about it, she was always on the verge of doing it, but something always held her back. Maybe she didn't entirely trust this rebirth of his, maybe she was suspicious of it.

Unconsciously she kept her guard up, unconsciously she was steeled for his rage whenever it should surface again, for the harsh word, the condescending remark. His gentleness kept surprising her, but she refused to trust it. She watched him carefully, but from a distance. The distance was important. She was beginning to love him again, maybe she even wanted to love him again. She couldn't lie to him, he wasn't her enemy anymore. But if she couldn't lie to him, she couldn't make love to him, either. It was too much, too soon. So she waited, doing nothing at all, poised at the edge of something, holding quite still, waiting for time, that old devil, to tell.

There were actually several things she did do, though. She wrote to Marlene at M.C.C. and asked to be put on her visitors list, and when the form came from the prison she filled it out and returned it. And she sent gifts down to Annie's children with a letter asking Annie's sister if she could come sometime to visit. She had called first to ask about the sort of presents they would like. It tickled her to hear what they wanted: Eli and George asked for anything from the G.I. Joe collection; Emma wanted a Barbie doll.

III

Annie took the rainbow colored ribbon in her hand, slipped it around the big teddy bear's neck and tied it in a bow.

"She'll love this," she said.

"You think so?"

"Oh, yes. This bear is perfect. You are perfect," Annie said to the bear. She picked it up and hugged it. It felt good, big enough and soft, something a five year old could give a good squeeze to and still feel that there was a lot more of it there, that there was something

138

solid inside the squeeze. Emma had a bear like it. It had cost so much money. Annie remembered while she was buying it that there had been a time in her life when seventy-five dollars was her weekly take-home pay. The fish factory. She'd come home every afternoon stinking of fish and Erika would hand her a joint and push her into a tub. Don't dare come out until you're high and smell human.

She had been thinking about Erika so much these past weeks, fitting into people's lives again the way she had fit into Erika's, coming from nowhere, the friend of a friend, being accepted, taken in and cared for. But the difference now, leaving soon, a few days, a week, leaving before she could begin to feel at home, to love or be loved.

To love or be loved. She stares at the bear and pictures a little girl holding it, a girl with Emma's face. But they were safe, all together at least. Paul had got that message to her, buying the *Voice* every week, reading through the classifieds until she found it, finding it and feeling as though he had whispered the words in her ear, as though his voice were speaking to her from the page.

"You're sure you don't want to come?"

"No. You go and enjoy yourself with your family, Eileen. I'll stay right here. Thank your sister for me, though. I appreciate the invitation."

The woman sat down across from her at the table. She was in her forties, Annie thought, though her face was almost unlined, unlined and plain and at this moment filled with sincerity and concern. Sincerity and concern were wearing on Annie. She had had sincerity and concern for ten days now and she was almost suffocating on it. It was time to move on.

"I hate to leave you here alone on Christmas. You'd be so welcome at their house. My sister knows I work for the shelter and she'd be so happy to have you come."

"Please, Eileen. I'd really rather be here alone. I don't think I could handle it, really. Thank you, though."

"You're not going to call him, are you?"

"No, I'm not."

"Sometimes on holidays...Well, it is a time for forgiveness, isn't it? And it's only natural to want to forgive. But you know, Judith, if he abused you before, he'll do it again."

"I know that. I'm not going to call him. Don't worry."

Eileen bent over and kissed Annie's cheek. "All right, then. I'll be home about six."

"And I'll be here. Don't forget to give that sweet little niece of yours a big kiss for me, OK?"

Finally Eileen put on her coat, put the bear in a bag, and left Annie in peace.

No, she thought bitterly, I'm not going to call him. I'm not going to call anyone.

She sat in Eileen's living room and looked at the little Christmas tree with the manger nestled underneath. Such a little tree. They always had big ones when they could, when they were in the country and Paul could cut one himself. Never a manger underneath, though. Never that.

She pulled herself away from the tree and memories of other Christmases and for what seemed like the hundreth time, checked out the bookshelf. What you can tell about people by looking at their books. How you should check a boy's bookshelf before going out with him. Her eighth grade nun's advice. As though thirteen year old boys read books. But it was advice that stuck. She had checked out Paul's books all

140

right the first time she went to his apartment. A lot looked very familiar since they were Simon's. Simon and Erika had a lot of books, all kinds, novels and poetry, history and anthropology and books about people she'd never even heard of before, writers and artists and revolutionaries. Paul always stuck to politics, wasn't big on poetry, never touched fiction. The world was too serious a place for fiction. Reality was enough, good enough or bad enough, just enough. It was frivolous to make up things or to spend time reading things that were made up, to waste your time like that when there was so much work to be done.

From the look of her bookshelf, Eileen had that attitude, too. She was into theology, though, which was a kind of fiction, and pop psychology, not reflective of reality either. Why people were unhappy. Why people didn't feel good about themselves. Well, how could they, living under such a fucked up social and economic system? How on earth could they be expected to? And then there was Mary Daly on the superiority of women. Separatist stuff. Books on lesbianism. Lesbian nuns. Where Eileen was coming from.

She was a good woman, Eileen, doing good work, taking strangers into her home, harboring them. Dangerous work, too. There was nothing to keep one of these women from going back to her man, telling him where she'd been. If the Man were crazy enough—and some of them probably were—he could come here and harass her, threaten her, make her life miserable. That the women were all carefully screened first, that they were all desperate and on the run, that they were never going back—well.

She wondered what Eileen would think if she knew that the screener this time had knowingly and deliberately sent her a woman who was on the run not from her own man but from the Man himself.

141

She was only supposed to stay here a week but she had stayed longer. She was at the end of the line now. She had waited two months, she had done everything she was supposed to do, set herself adrift away from the squads, followed the rules, gone through complete submersion. There had been no more busts. It had been a paper chase all the way and the Feds had won, finally tracked them down with paper, a vehicle, a registration, probably Bobby's or Marlene's since it was their house that had been hit. But there was no snitch. No snitch, only paper.

But how smart Paul was, what a genius at what he did. Every contingency covered, because it was their duty to survive. Like other families practiced fire drills, they drilled themselves on escapes. Like other families, but not like other families. Practicing, drilling, memorizing things, demolition techniques, building plans, maps, how everything worked down to the last detail, every weapon, every tool, and codes, how to send messages and how to read them, and first aid, and locksmithing and electronics, but especially the proper use of explosives, pages, chapters, whole books committed to memory, taped into their minds, taped and recited at sets, so there would be no mistake, never be a mistake, and the various squads and people and code names, safe houses, drops, meeting places, and if you didn't know them, if you didn't study, then there was punishment, symbolic but necessary, extra workouts, like the army.

After all, they were an army.

But she has memorized other things as well, phone numbers that no one else knew, addresses of safe houses, codes, drops. There were people whose names appeared nowhere else except in his mind and hers, that not even Marlene and Bobby knew about, in case this happened, in case this very thing happened, that, like death, they dreaded but had to discuss.

142

So she had followed the rules again. There were choices along the way and yet even with the choices she knew that Paul was tracking her, that he always knew where she was, whether she had initially contacted A or B, taken route X or Y, in either case he knew the options, he knew she was either in one place or the other, and so it would be for these months until the time came for her to enter into the loop again, to rejoin the squads. Until it was safe. And now it seemed clear enough. A paper chase. The squads were still intact. There had been no domino effect, no break, no betrayal.

It cheered her to know this. There were worse things than capture. The destruction of a man's life's work, that was worse. But his work hadn't been destroyed, it would continue. The clandestine movement would continue even without him. No, with him. With him, because even prison couldn't hold him. In fact now, in prison, he was more powerful than before.

And safe.

And Annie looked at this, this thought that had been growing in her, that she kept pushing aside because there was so much else to think about and because there was something terrible about it. But it had occurred to her over and over again and now she had to look at it square in the face.

It was about how much he loved her and how much he had sacrificed for her.

His life.

Annie sat down crosslegged on the floor. The room smelt of pine. The manger under the tree. Mary and Joseph. She had never appreciated Joseph. She had never even liked him.

And now it comes keenly, a stabbing pain. She wants to cry out to him. She wants to tell him that she knows now, she sees, it's so clear to her. She wants to thank him. How can she ever thank him?

143

He had never planned on taking her with him underground. But when Frankie DeRose was busted after the armory bombing ten years before, she and Paul were together. She had never liked DeRose, never trusted him. Paul hadn't trusted him, either. DeRose was a creep, crazy, a hanger-on. A snitch. They never knew why he planted that bomb at the armory, though Paul believed he'd been paid to do it by the Feds, that the whole thing was a set-up from the word go, except that Frankie went nuts in the car, ran the road block, killed his buddy, Ouellette. Then they had a body to deal with. Manslaughter, reckless homicide. Then they had him. It wasn't a question of paying him then; he had to sing and he had to sing long and hard.

Even then Paul was prepared. He was already a marked man; word on the street was the city cops wanted him and wanted him bad. So he got himself a safe house out of state, made contacts in the underground, was ready to slip away and disappear. Slip away from Annie, too. Kiss her goodbye and slip away. But Annie wasn't prepared for that number at all. She wasn't going to let him go alone. She loved him.

And now she wipes tears off her cheek. The tree and its ornaments have become a blur of color. Her whole face is trembling, her throat aches. Straighten your back. Think this through, Annie. Think!

What does it mean to love someone so much that you tie him to you when being tied is the last thing he wants?

But I am a revolutionary too, she says out loud.

Now you are, she answers herself. Then you were just in love.

She was pregnant, too. On top of everything else. And she wouldn't have an abortion. She wanted his children. She wanted everything of his. Some feminist, huh? Shit.

So against his better judgement and every rule he had made for himself to survive, he took her with him. Instead of travelling light, he went underground with a woman and child. Instead of being free, he was weighed down and everything that could have been easy became hard and harder still as Eli got older and then George came and Emma. They could melt into communities with the children, yes. They had an almost perfect cover. But wherever they were, they were only a few steps ahead of the Man, and the children were a liability, too: their pictures up everywhere, the Feds questioning daycare directors, school teachers, pediatricians. Worry, constant worry. Paul, who had no fear for himself, lived in constant fear for them. They were hostages to his care, his constant, unending care.

Every time he asked her to surface with the children she refused. She thought that refusing told him how much she loved him.

And yet in all those years he had never once said it. He had never said, You are making it impossible for me to live the way I need to live. You are chaining me when I need to be free.

Never.

Now, Annie thinks, now it is I who am free.

What it feels like: lightness. Walking down a street: lightness. Going into a library to read the out of town newspapers (to see photographs of Paul, always looking for photographs of Paul): lightness. Making a call, hearing a voice, going to an address, meeting a stranger: lightness. It amazed her how light she felt. At first she thought it was shock or that she was losing her mind. But all she had lost was the weight of fear. The weight, the terrible weight, the burden: where is Paul? where are the children? why is Eli late from school? who is Emma talking to over there? why hasn't Paul called?

145

Now in the homes of strangers he chose for her (and how did he do it, find these directors of battered women's shelters, these households of ex-nuns, these sanctuary workers skilled at harboring fugitives, all these women with gentle voices, how did he find them for her, and for the children, yes for all of them, for when she agreed to surface, so it would all be prepared for her before she had a chance to change her mind?), now she can feel what his life would have been like without her. Now she can feel what his love for her felt like, the weight of it, the seriousness of it. How, even now, mingled with the pain of loss, even she feels the relief from that weight.

And if she had surfaced? Last year or the year before? Five years ago when Emma was about to be born and Paul knew he had been spotted and they had to pick up and leave again? If she had just done it, isn't it likely, isn't it more than likely, that Paul would still be free?

Now she wants to go to her bed and lie down and she wants to think about him. She wants to think about his hands and his body. She wants to summon him back to her, she wants her hands to become his hands, the image of his face and his body fixed in her mind, fixed there always, her hands becoming his as perhaps his hands become hers, every day of her life so she will never forget him.

But she doesn't do this. It is a weakness: she will never forget him. She doesn't need this to bring him back to her. She has something else. His work.

The people are the sea. The revolutionary is the fish who swims in the sea. A fighting fish. A fish who strikes.

When Eileen returns home at six, Annie is in the kitchen. She has made cupcakes and is decorating them with red and green icing. She has also washed the kitchen floor and vacuumed the rugs, scrubbed the bathroom, scoured the stove and the kitchen sink, not that the house wasn't nearly spotless to begin with. Eileen kept a clean house.

"Merry Christmas," Annie says.

"Oh, Judith, you didn't have to do all this." Eileen notices everything.

"An idle mind is the devil's workshop," Annie says, laughing. "Anyway I think best when I'm doing something."

"And what do you think?"

"That it's time for me to be moving on. You gave me the space I needed. The peace and the quiet and the support. I can't thank you enough."

"You're not going back to him?"

"No."

They take cupcakes and coffee into the living room and turn on the TV. Christmas night movies. *It's a Wonderful Life*. They watch it and at the end, when Jimmy Stewart finally goes back home after seeing what would have happened if he'd never lived, and all his friends are there and his wife and his kids, and it's Christmas and they're all so happy to see him, Annie finds herself crying, crying....

"It's only the movie," she says to an anxious Eileen between sobs. "It's just that it's so sad."

The next morning Eileen called the director of the shelter, talked to her for a little while, and then put Annie on the line.

"So, Judith," the voice said, "Eileen tells me you're ready to leave us."

This woman, like most of her other contacts, had only been a voice over the phone, a voice that, like the others, had responded to certain words, that, like the others, had given out other numbers, numbers of people who were so completely removed from the clandestine movement that there would be no way to trace them to her, people, like Eileen, who didn't even know a clandestine movement existed or what it could possibly exist for. Even the contacts themselves might know nothing, might be merely friends of friends.

But this voice reminds her of someone and now Annie has figured it out, where this network came from, how she got plugged into it, what it is. An older woman had befriended Paul eleven years ago, maybe twelve, while Annie was still living with Erika, a lesbian, very political, a woman Paul often mentioned with great respect, a woman he claimed taught him what feminism was all about. This was her network, the lesbian underground, for women coming out the hard way, from convents and fucked up marriages, from hateful families, drugs, alcohol, from courts that wanted to take away their kids, husbands who claimed they were unfit mothers. The softness of the voice; inside the softness, a strength. The teddy bear you could hug and hug and yet it was big enough to still feel solid inside the hug.

"Yes," Annie said, pulling herself back. Paul had friends everywhere. She wasn't the only one who loved him, she had never been the only one. "Yes, I'm ready now. I want to thank you so much."

"We're always here for you if you ever need us again."

"Thank you," she said.

"Take care, Judith," said the voice. "God bless you."

Did the voice know who she was or not?

148

Yes, the voice knew.

"God bless you, too, sister," Annie answered, meaning every word.

IV

In some respects Simon was now like a man waking up from a coma or recovering from a long drunk. He had vague memories of what he had done and he was told (by Erika mainly) what he had said, but it was hard for him to grasp that it had been himself who had acted or spoken in the manner alleged. Had he really, for example, called the people at SOPCA (Brenda included) airheads and granolas? Had he really shown no interest in Becky's life? ("What?" she had said in mock surprised when he asked about her next school concert, "You mean you *know* I'm in the orchestra?") Was it true he yelled about money? Was it the case that he and Erika never went out anymore? What had he been so worried about? He couldn't figure it out, he couldn't remember. He had been feeling trapped and defeated and old, but they were just words now and nothing to do with him.

Now he felt other things. It was like riding a bike, he thought with amazement, you never forgot how. Yes, it amazed him that he found enjoyment and pleasure in the simplest things. Stopping to talk to someone he knew on the street. The most commonplace exchanges. Happy New Year. Yes, it sure is cold. Expecting a big storm near the end of the week? Where are we going to put it all? Time honored phrases he would otherwise have scorned as he would specious arguments in conversation or blandishments in personal relationships. But now they were no longer contemptible to him. Odd. Leaving the office in the middle of the morning with Dan and Jon, walking to

149

the coffee shop, drinking a cup of coffee, paging through the *Times*. Then returning to the war room, plotting strategies, sorting through the Rousseau Archives, thousands of pages of it, everything saved for history—and the prosecution—piecing it together, finding the government's blind spots, the flaws. He thought he had forgotten—he *had* forgotten—what it was like, this feeling. He was having fun.

And then, of course, being awake now, finally paying attention, being in the present, he began to notice that certain things were different than he had thought. Erika had been right. He could let go of his cases a little and the world wouldn't come to an end. He had let go and the world was still in one piece. He didn't malpractice, his secretary covered his calls, he ad-libbed successfully, his clients still loved him. He spent money and nothing bounced at the bank, and if it did, it did. So what. He bought presents, he bought records, he bought himself some new clothes and he enjoyed it. But the more he paid attention the more he saw and the more he saw the more he came to realize that while he had perhaps been overscrupulous about his practice, about money, things that didn't matter (from his new perspective didn't matter) in one very important sphere he had been negligent and here in this one part of his life he may have made mistakes that were beyond curing.

He felt he should apologize to Erika for something he had done or not done. He wanted her to know he was sorry, that she had been right (yes, that much he remembered, that she had pressed him to stop worrying—nagged him, he had called it at the time—to have fun, and that he, self-righteously, had pushed her away), but something stopped him. It seemed ridiculous to apologize. They were still together, nothing had changed. Everything would get better from now on, evolve naturally into something wonderful.

After the trial was over, they would take a vacation, go to some exotic place, dance every night, have fun.

He said all this to himself, but he only half-believed it.

Sometimes he'd look up at her from the newspaper or glance at her across the table and catch her staring at him. For a split second, before she could adjust her face, something was exposed there, but he couldn't read it, couldn't tell what it was, pity or contempt or sadness, or whether it was just that he hadn't really looked at her in so long, that she had grown older and he hadn't noticed.

It made him want her more.

And when had she started wearing make-up? When had she bought perfume, patterned nylons, high heels? When did she abandon denim for silk?

And he watched her wait for Dan to light her cigarette. When they met for lunch or after work for a drink, he watched her watch the men in the bar. Sometimes he would call her in the morning, but she wasn't home.

He became alert around her. He didn't know what he was looking for, he didn't know who he was looking at. He was feeling around in the dark for a familiar object, but he had been in the dark for so long he may have forgotten what exactly the object was he was searching for.

And at night in the dark he would reach out for her but somehow she always slipped through his grasp. Always good reasons. People in the house. Jon right in Noah's room. Then a cold. He was in a hall of mirrors. He would see her and reach out, but his fingers touched something smooth and cold: her reflection everywhere, nowhere her warmth.

Then one night he couldn't accept the no. He wanted her, he wouldn't let her slip away. He felt her body tense. As much as he kissed her, caressed her, he knew she was submitting herself to him, knew she was gritting her teeth, hating it, wanting to escape. He wanted to believe it wasn't so—how could it be?—but she didn't want him, and how long had it been like this, that she didn't want him at all?

Kissing her face, finding it wet. "Why are you crying?"

"I'm not crying," she said.

With the same strategic brilliance that he used to plot out the various steps in a legal chess game, Simon doggedly pursued Erika's lie. He was willing to accept the fact that whatever the problem was he was to blame for it. But part of him was well-schooled in self-punishment and it was this part that picked up the trail and followed it and wouldn't give up or let go. It was this part that was out for blood, not Erika's but his own.

And it began innocently enough—as most things do—with a simple question. "Who do we know who smokes Camels?" He had been cleaning out the car and found half a pack under the seat.

Erika shrugged. "Daniel, doesn't he?"

"Well, they're no good now," and he tossed them into the trash.

It was stupid of Erika. Very stupid. Simon had been bumming cigarettes from Dan for a month. They both knew damn well that Dan didn't smoke Camels.

But he remembered seeing unfiltered butts in the ashtrays before. He remembered seeing them and wondering and then shrugging it off. One of Erika's friends. Someone of no consequence to him.

The arrogance of it. Now he realized the arrogance of it.

The Defense Team went out to lunch every day, Simon's old habit of eating at his desk having been abandoned in the interests of sanity. Every so often he would call home in the middle of the morning to invite Erika to join them. Some mornings she wasn't home. This morning she was and wanted to talk to them. The SOPCA meeting was at eight; Dan had offered to talk to them sometime; she needed the particulars from him so she could offer dates if the group was interested.

It was nothing really. A rational man, a purely rational man, might have dismissed it. Two or three months ago Simon himself would have dismissed it if, as he had to admit to himself, he had been aware enough to have noticed it at all. But he was remembering how to trust his instincts again, how to trust his sense of things, especially in regard to Erika, around whom he was more alert now than he had been in years. So when Jon said he had a taste for chili and suggested going to The Second Front for lunch and Erika adamantly refused to go, the bloodhound in Simon perked up its ears. Oh, she had good reasons of course: it was too loud in there, too crowded, they'd have to wait forever, the service was so slow. But it wasn't like Erika to worry about noise levels or seating arrangements. And Simon remembered there was a time—last year, wasn't it?—when he couldn't keep her away from the Front.

Now Simon was like a man at a poker table, picking up his cards one by one, studying each of them in turn, gauging which one was going to give him his pair.

"What time do you expect the meeting to end tonight?"

They are standing on a corner near Simon's office. The corner itself is iced over and treacherous. Long icicles hang from the eaves overhead. It is a mean day and people who pass are wrapped up tight against the weather. The corner is like a wind tunnel, words are lost there, they must yell at each other to be heard. Around them store windows announce sales, 25% off all merchandise. The Night Writer has left his mark, too, on the brick wall over their heads.

LIBYA IS NOT THE ENEMY
  BOYCOTT SOUTH AFRICA NOT NICARAGUA
    U.S. OUT OF NORTH AMERICA

"I have no idea."

"Will you be coming home right after?"

"Unless Brenda wants to go out."

"Give me a call. If you're going out, I'd like to come."

"It might be late."

"Jon will be home with the kids. Unless you'd rather I didn't."

"What?"

"Unless you don't want me to come."

"Of course I want you to come. If we go. We may not."

"What?"

"I said we might not go anywhere."

"Call me anyway. I'm going to feel like a beer after working on this brief all night. I'll meet you."

She kisses his cheek but the pressure of her lips makes him feel ruthless.

"You don't mind the Front at night, do you?"

"We'll see what happens," she says.

The weekly meetings of Solidarity with the People of Central America took place in a church basement. Ten, fifteen years ago, when Erika was politically active,

154

nothing took place in church basements. What could this new partnership signify? The politicalization of the church or the de-radicalization of the left? Simon, of course, thought the whole concept of non-violent revolution was a co-option by the right wing, or that's what he had thought a year or so ago. Erika had no idea what he thought about anything anymore.

It was a small but colorful group that gathered in the church basement that night. She was expecting small—it was a dark night in January, windy, five below—but not colorful: the brightly woven bags, the orange, red and blue woven bracelets, the red and black FSLN pins, the embroidered shirts. And the people themselves were unlike radicals of her past. Five were distinctly elderly, one was a nun, one group looked more like pig farmers than politicos, another few were members of the *contra Contra contradancers*, the remaining dozen or so were city folk like herself, a few of whom she knew by name, the others by sight, from film festivals, ERA and gay rights benefits, anti-nuke rallies. By and large, not a group likely to go ga-ga over Paul Rousseau's *foco* theory of armed resistance.

She listens to them, though, as they discuss the upcoming visit of Salvadoran refugees, the press conference they will hold condemning the air war in El Salvador, the plans for Central America week, the fundraiser for the city's delegation to Nicaragua for the coffee brigade, she studies the movements of their faces and their hands (these things are important to her), absorbs the gentle rise and fall of their voices, the laughter, the ease with which they come to agreement (someone asking if there is consensus, someone else voicing a concern, the concern responded to, an agreement reached, a task delegated, someone offering to take responsibility) and she wonders what makes these people care so much about all this, what motivates them. Guilt, perhaps. Trying to forgive

155

themselves for having this undeserved good fortune, to have been born white in America, somehow lucking out, waking up and finding themselves among the chosen, the world's elite, living in safety from bullets and betrayals, able to raise their children, put dinner on their tables, go to the movies, go to the Mall, write a letter to the editor, demonstrate on the streets, having everything, in short, except a clear conscience. And yet, why these people and not others? Why these people and not herself?

Because, she thinks, they have something she doesn't have anymore—hope.

They finish their business and Erika is introduced. She takes a deep breath, looking at these faces, feeling that no matter what she says about Paul Rousseau, his presence in this room will be jarring, violent, somehow unacceptable. But she begins, she says everything she feels she needs to say, she finishes. Silence.

It is a thoughtful silence. Erika studies the colors in one of the shoulder bags on the table, wonders if she can buy one here or if Brenda would bring one back for her. Finally an older man begins to speak. He remembers Rousseau from the old prison reform group. He remembers him as a good man, though impatient and very angry. He adds that although Rousseau is not admitting participation in the bombings, the group should know anyway that whoever was responsible was careful to avoid any loss of life or injury.

A woman adds that learning about the judicial process especially in respect to political issues would be useful since so many of the members of the sanctuary movement were under indictment and who could say when one of their own members might engage in some act of civil disobedience and find herself or himself in need of a lawyer with a conscience.

Now other people add concerns and ideas. There seems to be a consensus that the lawyers should be invited to speak. Someone states this as a proposal; it is accepted unanimously. Two possible dates are agreed upon, Erika is thanked, the meeting ends.

Erika watches Brenda, who has been uncharacteristically quiet all evening, talking with one of the grey haired women. What she sees in Brenda's face, what she has sensed at the table, the ambiance of the meeting, is new to her. The process is new, the tone, without urgency, tension, without the pressure of time. An image comes to mind of elders sitting around a fire. A nice image: she thinks of Dan. Equality at the table. Mutual respect. A noticeable lack of overt leadership. Patience.

They are talking about Brenda's trip to Nicaragua. Several other women are going too. They are leaving quite soon, in a matter of days.

"Have you been there before?" Erika asks one of the women, Nina. It is her bag that Erika has been eyeing.

"Yes, in fact several times. The first time I went I couldn't wait to leave—the heat, the poverty, and I didn't know any Spanish then. But as soon as I got home I realized I'd left something behind. They say, the Nicaraguans, that you can't visit their country without leaving part of your heart there. Maybe that was it."

"And are they all very heroic in Nicaragua?" Erika asks. She detects the sardonic tone in her voice; she hopes no one else does. "Are they all very strong?"

"Oh, there's heroism all right," Nina replies. Her voice has a distant quality to it, as though she is speaking from a distance or into one. "Mundane heroism, everyday heroism. The kind that either grinds you down or makes you so strong you will never, never break. Invulnerable, like a god."

"And what's heroism for us, do you think?"

157

"Eating dinner."

Erika smiles. "Well, that's easy. I eat dinner every night."

"Eating dinner with your family."

"I do that too."

"Eating a peaceful dinner with your family."

"If you keep adding conditions to it..."

"All right. Here then: it is heroic to eat a peaceful dinner with your family—and by family you know I mean not necessarily a nuclear family, but a community family, a group of friends, or whoever it may be you usually eat dinner with—conversing honestly with them, opening your mind to them and listening in turn to what they say."

"A little nourishment, a little truth?"

"And a little justice. Yes. And it's hard, it takes courage. At the same time it's a sort of drudgery, very mundane, nobody notices it, you might as well be doing nothing at all."

"Does the word heroism still mean something if you use it for something like that? I'm just curious."

"Let me ask you this: how do we know that it isn't just people sitting around eating dinner together that is the one thing that's keeping the bomb from dropping?" She smiles at Erika, who can't tell if Nina is putting her on or not. Her guess is not. Her guess is that this woman is absolutely serious.

"It sounds mystical to me."

"Yes. But isn't that why people fast for peace? Why else do it? You know, it has always struck me that those little heroisms are far harder than the big ones. The little acts of justice, the daily routines, raising children, every day the sacrifices parents make, the justice they dispense, the generosity they find in themselves, that to me is heroism. Not throwing yourself in front of a tank. All that is is one single, momentary act of will. Even a narcissist could do that."

158

The word rings in Erika's ears. Narcissist, yes. She tries to imagine Marc throwing himself in front of a tank, a molotov cocktail in his hand, that one moment, then his body, broken, blown to bits—isn't that the phrase—nothing left of him but bits of scorched flesh, muscle, gore. She remembers then and goes to the hallway phone to call Simon.

Dan was in the car with Simon and that cheered her up, but she didn't understand why Simon was suddenly so unyielding about where they were going. It was almost as though he were enacting a text, he was that intractable (a text by Sophocles). Marched to the Front, to the door, the door opening, it was like a dream, a nightmare, The Meeting, followed by The Duel.

"Oh, Simon," she said, "I hate this place. Please let's go somewhere else."

"Who's in there you don't want me to see?" she thought she heard him say. But between the wind outside and the noise from within, she couldn't be certain. And, no, he couldn't have said that, though she did notice that he was studying her face.

But inside the madness of the place worked to her advantage. The Second Front was packed. If they could find a few seats, they could drink for an hour and leave and Marc, in his usual frenzy behind the bar, wouldn't even know they'd been there. If they couldn't get seats, they'd leave even sooner, which wouldn't be too soon for Erika. Scenes in bars never appealed to her, except in movies.

They forced their way in under the ceiling fans through the smoke which hung in the room like veils, diaphanous, the smell of it along with beer and bodies and leather and wet wool almost dear to her by now because it was Marc's smell, too. They pushed on past

159

the brick archways and the brick pillars, Erika in the lead, planning to veer off, to squeeze them into a corner farthest from the bar. And then she looked ahead and saw him, not behind the bar but coming right toward her, directly in front of her with a smile on his face and she knew he would come right to her and kiss her, never looking any further, never suspecting that one of the men behind her might be her husband, especially not the one directly behind her, towering behind her with the craggy face and grey hair flowing to his shoulders wearing a fatigue jacket, surely *that* could not be Simon.

But he wouldn't look anyway. It wouldn't occur to him to look.

She had to stop him, she had to make this stop. She dropped back, let Dan pass her, took Simon's arm, whispered something in his ear, putting her mouth very close to his ear so Marc would see.

And it was all transmitted. Marc stopped in his tracks at a table a few feet ahead of her, felt in his pocket for his cigarettes, took out the pack of Camels. And first Dan and then Simon squeezed by him, then Erika, so close, brushing against him. They sat down, he lit his cigarette, she looked at him and he nodded back to her as though he knew her vaguely, though not by name, then turned and made his way back to the bar.

Simon said, "What's that bartender's name again, Erika?"

"I don't know," Erika said. "I don't remember."

Simon couldn't look at her. He'd finally come up with his pair, he'd finally got just what he wanted with a wild card and a jack of hearts.

But Erika, Erika saw in Marc's nod, in that vague nod (as though he knew her vaguely, as though he couldn't quite place her), not a disguise, no, but reality itself. True, he had done just what she wanted him to do. True. And that was the point, exactly the point. She

160

would have loathed anything else, any gesture, any acknowledgement, and that loathing, that was real. It was as real as anything in her life. It revealed everything to her. She turned back to Simon, talking now to Dan, and in him she saw what she had always loved, but, just like a latent child, had simply forgotten.

Simon goes into the bedroom. He carries his new knowledge like a stone, like a weight in his gut. If it is knowledge. Knowledge or fantasy. Knowledge or fear. Erika is so far from him, so far away. He doesn't know if he can reach her or even if he can make the attempt. Part of him wants to confront her, part of him shrinks away. When he tries to grasp hold of what he feels, he finds it disappears in his hand. Anger, rage, these he could hold onto. But it isn't anger, it isn't any kind of passion at all. It is desolation, that he could even think this and believe it and still feel nothing, meet in himself only an absence.

He goes into the bedroom. Erika is sitting in bed reading. She looks up from the page and smiles at him.

"It's about time," she says.

"Time for what?"

"Time you came to bed. Look what I pinched for you." She holds up a joint.

"Where d'you get that?"

"Brenda. I inherited her stash. This is it." She lights the joint and passes it to him. "It's to break the impasse, Simon."

"What impasse is that?"

"Our impasse. Come on, Simon. You know what I mean. Passing the peace pipe...sharing oysters...the ritualistic fertility dance, I don't know. Let's just get stoned and fuck our brains out."

"Fuck our brains out. God, Erika, you're such a romantic! And here I thought you'd taken a vow or something."

She leans over and switches off the overhead light so that only a small lamp remains on, a light that is soft and intimate. She reaches down beside the bed. He hears the sound of liquid spilling into a glass.

"The longer you wait, the better it is, I hear. Want some five hundred year old bourbon?"

"No, I don't want any bourbon now."

She slides across the bed and wraps her arms around him, her skin against his clothes.

"I'm sorry, Simon. I was just afraid you weren't really you."

"And am I really me?"

"Yes. You really are."

He holds her in one arm, raises the joint to his mouth with the other. The room seems vast, his mind reaches out into the vastness. Whatever he wants to know he will learn from her body. Whatever is real in the present. Forget about the past—yesterday, this morning, even this evening, even a moment before.

He puts the joint out in the ashtray, brushes her hair back from her face, kisses her.

"Are you really you?" he whispers.

"Come and see."

CHAPTER 5

The Thing Itself
is Deeply Veiled

I

"Simon, I've been thinking."

"Uh-oh. What?"

"I've been thinking about Annie."

"Join the club. What about Annie?"

"I wonder where she is. I wonder about her kids. I wonder about Marlene. I'd like to go to New York and visit Marlene. I feel like I should be doing something."

Simon studied her across the table. They were sitting alone at a table in a restaurant for the first time in so long that neither one of them could remember precisely when the last time had been. It seemed like a great indulgence, a fitting one to celebrate the occasion of rediscovering they really were who they were. But who Erika really was remained a mystery to him still. His wife. His lover. Still mysterious.

"I'm sure Marlene would like to see you. But I'm also sure that she won't tell you where Annie is, assuming she knows, which I doubt. Even if she does, Erika, I don't want to know and I don't want you to know. You don't want to ever have to be in a position of having to lie to a grand jury. In a situation like this, ignorance is bliss. In many situations, ignorance is bliss."

"And what you don't know won't hurt you. Want to keep bouncing cliches across the table?"

163

"There's some truth to cliches. That's why they've lasted so long."

"Like us? Are we a cliche, Simon?" Smiling at him over her glass, skillful and dangerous.

"Drink your wine, Erika. *In vino veritas.*"

"Anyway, what do you think? Could you live without me for a week or so?"

"I feel like I've been living without you for a couple of years."

"I'm back."

"And you want to leave again."

"I can get a ride down with Brenda."

"That bartender's not going down with you, is he? *In vino veritas*, Erika. Is he?"

They stare at each other across the table, Erika feeling everything go soft inside her as though she has been hit by a great weight, crushed beneath it, something falling from the sky, the card of judgement in the form of a ton of granite, and Simon, lightheaded, brazen, feeling the liberation of those words shake everything from him—his blindness and his rage and all the years during which he denied the best part of himself, the part he could only now see returning to him. It was no one's fault that it had gone, and now it came back to him with such a pang, a pleasure mixed intimately with pain, that he could take it back so easily into himself and it could fill him and yet it had been there all along and he had simply refused it. And then he saw her face and he reached his hand across the table and took hers.

"It's all right, Erika. You should go if you want."

"It's not that I want to *go*, Simon. If I'd just wanted to *go*..."

"...you would have gone a long time ago. Yes, I know. I know. I told you, I have spies everywhere." His smile to her was warm, like his hand. "Don't worry. I'll take care of him while you're gone. A lot of people owe

164

me favors, a lot of bad motherfuckers. I'm not a criminal lawyer for nothing."

"Simon, sometimes I just don't know about you."

"Good," he says, lighting a cigarette, grinning at her like the Cheshire cat through the smoke. "That's just the way I like it."

Erika called Brenda later that night and arranged to ride down to New York with her and Nina. They would catch a flight from there to Miami on the first leg of their journey to Managua. She would stay with friends in Manhattan on the first leg of her journey to Annie.

Erika, already thoroughly scanned by a hand-held cylindrical device that reminded her of a curling iron, moves through the metal detector and reaches a glass door. She puts her hand on it, half expecting a siren or a shock. A click instead. "Push it!" An angry voice. All the voices are angry here. She pushes on the door, feels it open, and suddenly dread is there waiting for her: beyond this door, another and then another, one locked door after another, the farther in she goes the more doors will shut and lock behind her. She must tell herself that she is not in their power, not as Annie would be. She must repeat to herself, "My husband is a lawyer, my husband is a lawyer," over and over like a mantra or the little prayers called ejaculations that at the moment of death are said to save even the worst sinners from damnation.

My husband is a lawyer. They can't keep me here.

A few steps now to the elevator, already crowded with other women, children, babies, already programmed to take them somewhere. They wait. The doors close. They wait. The doors open. A baby begins to whimper. They have all of them already waited for hours in rooms that are stuffy, filled with air that is stale. And now another hallway, another glass door, another click. Inside this glass anteroom the heat is intolerable. There is a desk, a guard, a coke machine. On either side, glass doors lead into larger rooms crowded with people. She waits again while one by one they hand over a piece of paper to the guard, have the stamps on their hands checked. Then a click, a door opens into one of these rooms which are more like pens, windowless boxes of cement, and she enters. The noise greets her like a physical presence, the sound of sixty voices trying to make themselves heard inside a box of stone.

It is altogether an ugly, mean place. Against the ugliness and the meanness, there is counterpoised in this room a liveliness and an energy that defies the place, defies the existence of the place. That's what Erika sees here, defiance that takes the shape of laughter and kisses and hugs.

Erika knows who many of these women in blue smocks are. Not criminals but political prisoners, grand jury resisters most of them, women who will not collaborate with government attempts to break the New Afrika Movement or the Puerto Rican Independence Movement, the FALN. They sit on folding chairs in a cement room and hold their children on their laps. They are wives and mothers, women with doctorates and law degrees, faces that smile and laugh now, but that could close up at any moment and become like stone.

Erika waits for the far door to open (constantly, jarringly, doors are opening and closing, CLICK! SLAM! CLICK! SLAM!) and for someone to enter whom she doesn't even know, the friend of her friend. While she waits she watches carefully. Like the vestibule of death, this place is somewhere to stay awake in. The women across from her are sitting in a bunch, chairs turned to make a circle. The visitor, a girl maybe sixteen, sitting

166

with her back to the glass wall and the guard sitting behind it, whips out of her pocket a bottle of nail polish. Expertly, without even looking down, she paints her mother's nails bright red. Further down the row another young girl is passing around a package of gum, but this time the guard, from his perch outside the door, notices. He bangs the door open, marches in, snatches the package of gum away, orders them all to spit it out. No nail polish, no gum. (A few months later the Correctional Center will issue another rule: no one will be permitted to move the chairs away from the walls, visitors will have to crane their necks down the rows of chairs to see each other and converse, children will not be permitted to sit on detainees' laps.)

The far door opens and Erika recognizes Marlene. She is the only other white woman in the room.

Not close enough to embrace—they have never met before—they shake hands awkwardly and awkwardly sit side by side.

Marlene is younger and taller than Erika. She has dark hair, shorter on the top than in the back, a sort of modified punk cut. She is very pretty, or would be if she weren't so pale. Her eyes follow the line of chairs: she nods hello, waves, smiles at women with their kids, but sadly, every movement has a sadness to it. Her own kids, Jesse and Winnie, are with her mother in Vermont, too far away to come often to visit, though she did see them on Christmas. And she wants to talk about them. Sensing this, Erika asks the right questions until soon Marlene's face relaxes and some color returns to it. She almost looks healthy when she talks about her kids, she even laughs.

Erika turns the conversation to Annie's children. ("The boys are strong, that's the way Paul raised them," —Erika winces— "but Emma was so attached to Annie.") And from the kids to Annie herself. She is tempted to come right out with it, lay her cards down

167

on the table, but it doesn't seem fair. Marlene is too vulnerable and she has no reason to trust Erika. And Erika isn't ready for a flat No.

Instead she tells Marlene that she intends to visit Annie's children and bring them up to visit their father. Marlene asks if she could stop back in New York on her way home and bring them in to visit her. They are like her own, they are so dear to her, and she may never see them again. So long as they are in Jesusville, she will never see them.

"I've called them there," she says. "I have to call collect. Those damn people won't accept the charges. I can hear Eli saying, Please, please...He thinks it's Paul calling, I guess."

"I'll fill in the application for them today," Erika says quickly. "I'll be happy to bring them in for you."

The hour is up. This time they hug each other. Marlene is so thin, there's nothing to her. Erika is afraid for her. A female guard comes and takes her by the arm.

But then across the room someone's child refuses to let go. She clutches onto her mother, screaming, screaming, "Don't take my mommy away!" A sudden rush of energy swells in the room; something fragile, some web of lies, breaks. The air turns electric, heat lightning. People move closer together, cluster.

"We got a situation here," says the guard into her walkie-talkie.

CLICK! SLAM! Two big male guards, billy clubs hanging threateningly off their belts, guns there as well, strut into the room. The grandmother tries to take the struggling child into her arms. "Let's go now, honey. Let's go." But the child screams again, now picking up on other fears, and all through the suddenly silent room children cling to the nearest adult, every child's ears pricked up, every adult wishing for a weapon. ("Touch that child, bastard, and we'll rip you apart." Wishes.)

They are all frozen. There is nothing they can do but watch the guards draw nearer, the child cling tighter. Then from the diorama someone moves forward. A man, an old Black man, white-haired, frail. The grandfather. He moves slowly, arthritically, a brown stain, gravy perhaps, on his white shirt. He moves so that he is between the guards and his wife, his daughter and his daughter's child, who has arms and legs wrapped around its mother, nothing can pry this child loose. He raises his voice, though it trembles. He says, *Don't touch this woman. Don't you touch her!* Such a frail man, a single shout might bowl him over, a push. But everyone in the room recognizes him. Everyone knows what he's made of, what lives in him, what pulses through his body like blood. One guard looks down at him. "Visiting time is over for you people," he says. "Now you have to leave or you won't never come back again."

The grandmother helps the mother unpeel the child from her body, the mother allows herself to be led away, the child screams more, wailing, crooning, as though someone has died.

"It happens to someone every time," Marlene says. "Oh, God, maybe you shouldn't."

"They'll be all right," Erika says quickly, wondering for the first time if they will.

Erika settles in at the apartment of her friend, Denora, and Denora's lover, Mike. Mike is a poet and puppeteer and has the sharp, pointed face of a pan, even his hair, a reddish orange, spikes up at odd angles. Denora, in all ways his opposite, is a small, dark haired woman, a doctor. Mike has been to Central America,

169

touring with a North American puppet theatre group, performing in refugee camps in El Salvador and in hospitals, prisons and old age homes in Nicaragua. Denora met him there while she was working at a clinic in Managua. They both intend to go back, knew they had to go back the minute they stepped off the plane in Miami.

"While you're there," Denora said the first night over dinner, "you think you're only putting bandaids on and that the real job is back in the States, somehow opening people's eyes, making all that pain stop here, at the source. But the minute you get back you realize how impossible it is to stop it, how the only thing that could stop it would have to be something so dramatic, so intense, that it would galvanize the American people into action. And I can't make that happen, no matter how many letters I write or slides I show. All I can do is train midwives to deliver healthy babies and then teach medics how to remove bullets from them and sew up little bayoneted bodies and amputate little blown-up legs...."

"Stop, Denora," Mike said. "Please, please stop."

One wall of the living room is covered with puppets, faces in all colors, magical creatures, too, animals, exotic birds. Against another wall, a bookcase containing medical texts in Spanish, books of poetry, Russian novels, several volumes of testimony from the Permanent People's Tribunal, *Tyranny on Trial: Guatemala.*

Erika spends the next few days reading Dostoyevsky and talking on the phone with people she has never met: Annie's sister, Marlene's lawyer, the warden at MCC. Finally everything is arranged. Marlene herself calls, collect. She is so happy and thankful Erika can't bear it. And she feels the stirrings of rage, such rage. Why is Marlene in preventive detention? Why isn't she out on bail? What has she done? Where do they think she would go?

She walks around the apartment, picking things up, putting them down. A photograph of Mike grinning from ear to ear, his arm around a young Sandinista soldier, also grinning, both of them standing in front of a graffiti covered wall, the only thing she can read on it, the letters FSLN. A small elephant carved out of ivory. A music box that plays Strauss waltzes. Another photograph of a dark young man who could be Denora's brother. She pulls books down at random, reads a few paragraphs, puts them back. ("*Being conscious* is in the first place a purely descriptive term...a state of consciousness is characteristically very transitory; an idea that is conscious now is no longer so a moment later...". "And that people/ who rescue physicists, lawyers and poets/ lie in their beds at night with reports/ of mice introduced into women, of men/whose testicles are crushed like eggs...imagining bracelets affixing/ their wrists to a wall where the naked/ are pinned, where the naked are tied open/ and left to the hands of those who erase/ what they touch...") She takes a bath. Washes dishes. Writes on a yellow pad: Dear Simon, Becky and Noah.

Simon, Becky and Noah.

At night it was different. The apartment came to life. Denora cooked what to Erika were gourmet meals, no macaroni casseroles, no pea soup. Mike had stories to tell of his day at the school where he was giving a poetry workshop. Sometimes they went to the movies after dinner, sometimes they stayed home. She had told them about the prison visit. Now every day they wanted an update, wanted to know what she had heard from Annie's sister, what the plans were, how she felt about going down.

171

"Well, we won't send you down there alone," Mike said, as though she were going into the Amazon. "We'll take Denora's car. It doesn't have a hole in the gas tank like mine does."

"And you'll bring the children here," Denora had added. "I want to meet them. We'll put them in our room."

They had compromised on the guest room for the children and Erika sleeping on the couch in Denora's study. Erika looked around the apartment carefully. It was big, but three children took up a lot of space.

"Maybe I should put some of these breakable things away," she said.

"Don't worry," Denora said, pouring the wine. "I know about children. I'll take care of it."

One night Marlene's lawyer, who made her living defending radicals, phoned with an invitation to lunch. It was unexpected, but Erika agreed.

"When are you going down for the children?"

"Saturday morning."

"You know we got the warden to agree to a joint meeting. It's quite unusual, since they aren't family."

"Yes, I know," Erika said, wondering where this was leading.

"I've been in touch with Paul, you know."

"Oh?"

"While the children are here he'd like them to come to a meeting of other children of political prisoners. Unfortunately we're having one Thursday night and then not another until a week from Sunday. I wonder if you'd be willing to go down a few days early."

"I don't know if I can do that. I'm borrowing a car."

"Well, we can discuss it over lunch," Gert said.

172

So that was it. Erika put down the phone, feeling too wary for her own good.

Over lunch Erika thought with a certain grim amusement that talking to Gert Kidd was like having your brain picked with a steamroller. As subtle as that. Gert was possibly the most formidable looking woman Erika had ever met, even in sweats, even with glasses that kept sliding down the bridge of her nose, even eating a Reuben. Formidable. Not someone you'd want to tangle with. Not someone you'd want to offend. Good thing they were on the same side. If they were on the same side.

Same side of what? Other side of what?

"Of course," Gert said, finishing up a long analysis of the case, or the politics of the case, all of which was so familiar that Erika didn't even have to listen to it anymore, "the government sees Marlene as the weak link and they know how to play on the thing with her kids. That's why I would have advised against bringing Paul's kids here for a visit now, if you had asked me." (And Erika glances up at her and thinks, Oh, honey, I wouldn't ask you for the time of day. And then bites back on the thought, feeling so angry again, feeling so angry all the time.) "They're offering her a reasonable plea bargain and we were afraid that if she saw them she might consider it. But she's going to hang in, I don't doubt it. The struggle isn't clandestine anymore, it's public and political, but it's the same struggle. She knows that. They're willing to engage in a full-blown political trial down here. Bobby and Marlene recognize that they're political prisoners, that they're prisoners of war. And we have a duty to provide that forum for them. It's difficult to make these decisions without Paul down here and it seems as though his lawyers are working against him in this respect. Your husband is somewhat inexperienced in this area of law. He may

173

still be idealistic. But I can tell you, the system isn't going to work for Paul or anybody like him."

"Maybe you don't give it a chance."

"I think that's a rather naive view, frankly."

"My husband seems to think he has a crack at an acquittal."

"Then your husband is being naive, too."

"Or maybe our courts up north are a little less political than yours down here."

"Maybe. Then again it depends on how you present yourself. Paul Rousseau is a combatant in a war against capitalism and imperialism. If he presents himself in an American courtroom as he is, he can't help but make it a political forum. Does your husband expect to try Paul for a political bombing without talking about his politics?"

"I think you should talk to Simon about what he intends to do, not me."

There was an abrupt and elongated pause. Then Gert said,

"So what are your plans now? You're going down to get Paul's kids, bring them for a visit here, and then up to see him?"

"Yes."

"Paul would like them to meet the other children of political prisoners."

"So you said on the phone. I don't think it's possible for me to get them before Thursday night. I have to go on Saturday. But it might be helpful if I went to the meeting Thursday. Then I could get an idea what it's like and tell them about it. For the next time."

It was a lie, of course. Erika had no intention of bringing Annie's children anywhere near a group of Gert Kidds. She would take them to see their father and then she would keep them...if only they had more money to keep them, all of them, Eli and Emma and George and Jesse and Winnie. Live in a big house, have

174

the biggest family, five new children and Becky and Noah and dogs and cats and gerbils, a whole garage full of bikes, life with a purpose, sinking herself into motherhood for millions, no more twenty-five year old lovers, no more mistakes, no more desire.

Gert told her the address, but didn't write it down.

That night Marlene called, collect from two miles away. The plea bargain. She couldn't accept it. It would mean pleading guilty and the party line was that they were guilty of no crimes. But she wanted to accept it. It would mean getting out before her kids were grown. There was no one she could talk to but Erika, but Erika didn't know what to tell her to do. Call Simon, she said. Simon will know. Simon will tell the truth. Simon believed in beating the system, getting people back on the streets. Simon believed his duty was outsmarting the other side, not turning his clients into martyrs. Get a second opinion, Erika told her. Pretend it's a tumor.

As though in preparation for some major quizzing she expects at any moment, Erika spends a day in the public library brushing up on her revolutionary rhetoric. This combined with what she remembers of her readings of The Complete Revolutionary Tracts of Paul Rousseau, the subject of Simon's suppression motion, makes her feel confident that she has her rap down solid.

Perfect love. Perfect hate. That's the insides of me. Erika agrees with George Jackson on this completely. Sometimes it feels like the insides of her, too. Maybe it's the insides of everybody.

Armed revolutionary struggle finds its expression in armed attacks against the enemy ruling class and their agents. City structures will hide the guerrilla as well as the forest.

Two, three, many Viet Nams.

175

The duty of the revolutionary is to make the revolution.

Revolutionary justice: After an attack upon the people, there must be funerals on both sides.

An oppressed class which does not learn to use arms, to acquire arms, only deserves to be treated like slaves. Lenin. Always was a hard-ass, Erika thinks.

A revolutionary is not necessarily a Marxist-Leninist. A revolutionary is necessarily someone who fights. Thank you, Fidel.

The Foco is a small band of guerrillas acting as the motor to a general upheaval that would trigger a revolution, a mobile force capable of moving quickly, striking an enemy target and executing a well-covered retreat. The Foco is supported by above ground contacts and recruits into its ranks only those comrades who will maintain the most rigid security and who do not fear the inevitability of imprisonment and death which is part of guerrilla life.

It is the use of the word "inevitability" that strikes Erika here. It is the presence of *thanatos*, it is death calling, death, like a beloved, waiting for the guerrilla, calling him back, calling him home.

The support group. Part of the network. Overt but careful. Above ground and under surveillance. Erika becomes suspect simply by walking in the door. The Feds will check her out. Well, what of it? The wife of Paul Rousseau's attorney takes tea with his soon-to-be co-defendants' attorneys at the home of the ex-wife of another anti-U.S. terrorist, now safely incarcerated for life, the ex-wife, of course, still on tea-taking terms with her ex-husband's ex-attorneys. Reasonable.

Inside the apartment—a long corridor with bedrooms off it and a kitchen, the hall ending in a living room with windows onto the street—the

176

predictable posters of Che, copies of radical newspapers, the less predictable Steinway piano, class schedule for one of the city's most prestigious and expensive private schools, Perrier. A yuppie revolutionary cell.

There were four children, all white, all with parents in prison. One lived in the house, the others were visiting for the brigade meeting. The oldest child was ten, the youngest three. This Thursday evening they were going to be discussing the real map of the United States. The real map is considerably different from the unreal map with which most people are familiar. On the real map the United States is substantially smaller and is bordered by new and different sovereign states. The entire South is a separate country called New Africa. Texas no longer exists at all, but has been reabsorbed into Mexico. The Southwest is the United Federation of Tribes. Puerto Rico is independent. Sadly she notices that the Northeast hasn't been liberated; the cartographer evidently had not spoken to her local secessionist group. And she wants to listen in, to hear what these children have to say about the real map of the United States (she likes it; Simon would like it, too), but Gert caught her in the kitchen.

"It's unfortunate," Gert says, "Mandy's grandparents start a scene every time they come. They undermine everything we do here. They have custody, despite their own daughter's wishes. We try to teach her to be proud of her mother, but they make her think it's a tragedy."

Mandy's mother is a revolutionary, captured, tried and sentenced to more years than any human being could be expected to live. Mandy's father was shot dead in a gun battle over an armored car. Someday she might be proud of them, but it's a little hard for her now. She's three and a half.

177

But Erika recognizes this as a cautionary tale. She is being told the correct way to handle Paul's children; she is being told what is expected of her. And so she shakes her head sympathetically, doesn't balk at contradictions, drinks Perrier (without gagging), agrees it's a shame Mandy's grandparents are confusing her so much she still poops in her pants, smiles valiantly while her host's daughter plays a little Bach on the Steinway. When she knew Paul back in the '70s was he already a committed revolutionary? Oh, yes, absolutely, a man among men. (And she remembers with a shock—she had forgotten about it completely—facing him one night in the kitchen of the apartment he and Annie shared with what was to become the first *foco* cell, five petty criminals and ex-inmates Paul was whipping into shape. Facing him in the kitchen, stoned, so much tension in the room the pots shook on the stove, holding her face, kissing her hard, saying, Don't worry, you won't get your hands dirty, or am I just the sort of man you won't fuck on principle?)

Night. Erika is going to leave very soon. She has to face the fact that she cannot trust these women with the truth, and not the whole truth, either, not why she wants to find Annie, but even that she wants to find her. She will never find her without them (she believes they know where she is) and yet she cannot bring herself to ask them, to be vulnerable to them in any way. ("Or am I just the sort of man you won't fuck on principle?" How could she have forgotten that moment and why did she remember it tonight?)

She picks at the quiche in that smoke-free kitchen, Malcolm X's bearded, bespectacled intellectual's face staring down on her from over the stove, and wonders to what part of these women she could appeal, who don't understand tragedy the way she does, or admit to contradiction or irony. And she thinks of Simon and his appreciation of ironies, how much he would enjoy the irony here (enjoy it and yet refuse to judge it, unlike herself, who judged everything), how she could always trust him to know what was real and what wasn't. How he knew—but how could he know?—about Marc, and yet refused to judge. Thinking of him here in this kitchen while feeling all around her a sense of something pernicious, cold-blooded, a lack of passion, a complete void where passion should be. And yet she tries to resist it, to withhold judgement. She wants to like them, Gert who intimidates her, and her host who quizzes the children after their meeting and keeps no alcohol, caffeine, nicotine or men in her house, all four of which Erika requires for basic sanity, and her host's friend or lover or roommate who hovers around saying nasty things about straights. She wants to like them, but she can't. They are alien to her, they would seem alien to Annie, too. She can't ask them to contact Annie for her, and she knows they would refuse to do it anyway. They live in fear, have to be suspicious of strangers, emotionally cold. They are probably warm to their own, but she is not one of them.

Now if she wants to find Annie, Marlene is her only hope.

And thinking of Annie she tries to imagine for the first time the three children she is going to meet in a few days. Annie's children. Will they be like these children, who look normal enough, who play like normal kids, but who are always watchful?

Mandy's grandmother comes to pick her up and Erika decides to take the opportunity to make her own exit. She overhears her host telling the grandmother that it isn't necessary for Mandy to wear a dress, in fact she would prefer her to wear pants. Erika, slipping on her coat, can't hold her tongue any longer, says to Gert,

179

"Maybe somebody should thank this woman for bringing Mandy here for the brigade meeting in the first place. Not everyone would."

"It's what her mother wants," Gert says sharply.

"Yes, but her mother isn't in a position to do what she wants, is she?"

"Mandy is her child."

"What does that mean to Mandy, do you think?" Erika asks. "It looks to me like Mandy's being raised by somebody else now." The words make her feel harsh and cold, but they sound true.

Marlene is surprised that she's been called down for a visit. Her first reaction is fear.

"Has something gone wrong? You're not going tomorrow?"

"No, everything's still on. Everything's OK. The visit with you and Bobby is all set for Sunday afternoon. I just came to see you. There's something I want to ask you."

They sit down next to each other on the hard chairs. Friday night visiting hours, they must crank up the heat. Sleet outside, but inside beads of sweat cling to women's skin. Marlene fans herself with her hand.

"Marlene," Erika says, "I want to see Annie."

The silence is awkward. Marlene won't make eye contact, instead stares down the row of women prisoners and their families and friends. It occurs to Erika that perhaps they are being watched. Paranoia. But still, who on the outside knows how the inside of this world works, what pressures are exerted and by whom? The plea bargain is still in the works. Marlene hasn't decided, has another week to make up her mind. She is being lobbied hard not to plead, to hang tough, to be strong. Stand by your man. Go the distance. Go to the wall. In this scenario Erika may be perceived as the

180

outside agitator, the bleeding heart: Think of your children, think of your babies. And this room is filled with women who have chosen not to think of their children and their babies, who have chosen instead to think of their men and their people and their children's future. At that moment it seemed to Erika to be altogether too much, being the vanguard, having nothing to rely on, nothing but hope, empty faith in something that may never be, that probably would never be. If they are banking on the Revolution to open up the Bastille again and set them free, if they are banking on that, she can only pity them.

"I just want to talk to her."

"A lot of people just want to talk to her. The Feds want to talk to her, too."

Erika waits. Marlene is right, of course. She is right to be firm. She is doing the best thing for her friend.

"You want to tell her she can cop a plea? Don't bother. Annie won't cop a plea. She's a strong woman."

"It's not a question of strength," Erika says, thinking that if one more person says "strong woman" to her she's going to scream. "Nobody doubts that she's strong or that you're strong. You've been underground for ten years. Jesus, that takes enormous strength. But it's a question of priorities. What's more important, making a political statement that nobody much cares about or raising your children to be the kind of people you want them to be, not what your mother or Annie's sister want them to be? Isn't that why you did everything in the first place? For your children?"

"Yes," Marlene says, "and nobody understands. They say, like my mother, my brother, they say, How could you have kids? How could you do this to your kids? But we say, I say, How could you do *that* to your kids? How can you raise them to be murderers or slaves? How can you stand to turn them into cannon

181

fodder for the fucking rich, the fucking rich motherfuckers? God, if I didn't have kids I wouldn't be a revolutionary. I'd just be a dilettante."

Erika is sure she hasn't heard anyone use the word dilettante in twenty years.

"So what would you say to Annie? You'd try to convince her to surface. She won't do it. I know her. She won't."

She has to believe that. Erika knows she does. But what a conflict of loves: husband on one side, children on the other, the judgement of history and personal honor set against the happiness of a little boy, a little girl. Erika can't bear it that anyone should have to make such a choice.

"I'm not going to try to convince her of anything," she says. "I just want to see her."

"Why?"

The noise level in the room has reached a din. Kids are crying in every corner, from every corner there is wailing, screaming, laughter, she can't tell which. Doors slam open and shut, chair legs scrape, echoing off the stone floor, stone walls, and all around her women in blue smocks with strained faces sit and wait, doing time, wasting time, ill, malnourished, bored, deadened, nothing to do all day, one day after another, days wasted, lives wasted. Erika couldn't bear to have someone she loved in this place, this place or a worse one, for this isn't prison but detention, this isn't maximum security, this isn't the hole. How could she bear to see Annie here? Maybe all she wants really is to tell Annie she loves her. A stupid reason for the risk. Selfish. Something to do so she wouldn't have to think about who else she loved and why.

Why.

"Why, Erika?"

"You're right," Erika says quickly. "It's a dumb idea."

182

"Just tell me why."

"Because we were friends. Then we stopped being friends. And I still miss her. I can't stand the idea that I'll never see her again. I can't bear it. It's like she's dead." She didn't want that crack to open up in her voice. She could be strong, too. But it cracked anyway, though quietly. Maybe so quietly that in this racket nobody, not even Marlene right beside her, would hear.

"Let's talk about something else," Marlene says.

"I think I'm going to head out."

"No, please, talk to me. Tell me about the kids. Have you talked to them on the phone? How are they doing?"

So Erika talks. She tells Marlene that Annie's sister won't let her speak to them, so it's odd that she's letting Erika take them away. Evidently no one has spoken to them on the phone, not even Paul. But Erika was getting them and they would be here soon.

Thankfully it is almost time to go.

"There's some feeling among our supporters," Marlene says in a new, quiet, firm voice, "that your politics aren't correct. That's what you and Annie broke up about, isn't it? Politics?"

"That's right. It was over the Red Guard. We fought over the Red Guard."

"You don't believe America is an imperialist state?"

"I don't have to believe it, I know it. And I'm not a big fan of apartheid either. I'm not a Republican, Marlene."

"You're not a socialist, either."

"No, I'm not. I mean, maybe I am. I just don't think..." she sighs deeply. In the sigh is everything she doesn't think about, that she can't sort out into slogans or words. "I don't think it's that simple, that's all. That if you just replace capitalism with socialism, say, you'd have a better model human being. It might help some

183

things, sure, but the economy's not the disease. I don't think it's the disease. I think it's a symptom. And I don't think bombing buildings is going to change the disease or the symptoms."

"So you think our whole lives, everything we've done, is bullshit, right?"

"No, not bullshit. I don't think that at all. You believed something and you acted on it. That's admirable. I believe all sorts of things I don't act on. But I hate to think...I hate to see you here. Don't think I'd tell Annie to turn herself in. I just want to know what she wants for her kids. I'd offer to take them if that's what she wanted."

Erika stops herself, hears what she's just said. Did she really say that? Is she crazy?

"So what do you think the disease is?"

"The disease?" She has to pull herself back. The entire philosophical rap of The Brothers Karamazov runs through her head. But she can't start talking about original sin here. Instead she translates it. "Greed," she says, smiling at Marlene, hoping she will understand and smile back. Then she remembers another conversation, about justice at the dinner table, and thinks about Jon running in the snow for Paul. "But you see if I really believed that, if I acted on it, I'd be...."

"A Christian."

"Or a Buddhist. Or something. But I'm not. I just talk, Marlene. And talk is cheap."

Marlene smiles at her, for the first time a real, open smile. "I haven't talked to anyone like this in a long time," she says. "Will you write to me?"

Erika feels her eyes begin to ache. She holds Marlene tightly and kisses her goodbye. "See you Sunday," she says.

She waits until she's out of the building before she lets herself cry.

184

II

The car passes silently through flat, frozen country. If there is life here in the barren stretches between one industrial wasteland and another, it is in hiding. Erika, driving with Mike in Denora's car, driving south to meet the children of her friend, Erika feels as though she is in hiding, too. Something is hiding inside her: love, warmth, selflessness, the ability to nurture these three children she has never seen before. She hopes it is there, anyway, waiting to emerge. She doesn't feel it. She doesn't know where it would come from. The outside world, the January world—that flat, frozen, barren country—that is the way she feels inside. Whenever she thinks of the children, she imagines something inside her is dead.

But Mike cheers her up. He is, after all, a storyteller by trade, an actor, and he is looking forward to this adventure. He talks through two states, makes her laugh...until she asks about Central America (thinking of Brenda, wondering how she is). His stories of El Salvador bring them back to the present, the reason they are driving along frozen roads under a frozen sky.

Children named for a dead soldier, a dead revolutionary and Emma Goldman.

And Mike asks about them and Erika answers as best she can.

"Until two months ago they lived their lives thinking they were just regular kids in a regular family, except they moved a lot and had to keep changing their names. I don't know how Annie explained that to them. And I don't know how anyone explained to them why it was that in the middle of Jesse's birthday party a virtual army surrounded their house, burst into

185

the living room with guns drawn and took away their father and two other adults they loved, why they were taken away from everyone they loved, why they couldn't take anything with them, why they were handed over to strangers. Marlene told me that they stood there that night looking down at the ground, eyes fixed on the ground. They couldn't even say goodbye."

"They were in shock."

"That happened to all the kids except Eli. Eli must have known more all along than he let on. When they were taking Paul away he said to Eli, Take care of your brother and sister. Eli looked right into his face and said he would, but with such an expression on his face, of horror, like, How could you let this happen to us?, that even Paul recoiled. Marlene told me that. She said Paul recoiled."

"What gets me is that they're working class people making a working class revolution, and yet they live such middle class lives. Of course you can't talk to your kids about Daniel Ortega and Nelson Mandela if you're trying to pass for middle Americans. And the money they ripped off was for the cause, I take it. What do you think they did with it?"

"I don't know. There's no legal defense fund, I'll tell you that much."

"I don't know the man, but just from what I hear, Rousseau sounds like a pretty scrappy guy. Blowing things up, it doesn't make for the best karma in the world. It's like picking a fight, you know? Why do it? What did he hope to gain?"

"He says he wants a world in which no child will ever have to suffer."

Mike cocks an eyebrow at her. "Hits pretty close to home, doesn't it? Well, you can't accuse the man of unbridled self-interest, that's for sure. What did your friend Annie see in him? I assume there must be something lovable about him."

186

"You think being a revolutionary makes a man unlovable?"

"Not at all. I know, or I've met, very lovable revolutionaries. But they were driven to violence as a last resort. They hated war, they hated destruction, they held life to be precious and they never risked theirs or anybody else's without being forced into it, without feeling that they simply had no choice. They didn't *luxuriate* in it."

"I don't know that he was as self-indulgent as that."

"No? What do you call it then? What was the point of it? What kind of sense did it make? Was he responding in solidarity with a Third World struggle, was he making his actions count in any kind of broader context? When the *contra* hit a cooperative farm, did Rousseau hit a National Guard Armory? No. He hit banks when he felt like it and he hit military targets when he felt like it and he never gave a real good reason why. And he could have. If he was willing to take that step in the first place, he could have focused it and used it, but he didn't. So what it looks like to me is just somebody using power for no reason except to use it. The power of life and death—pretty heady stuff. And then, you know, you stick up a bank, it's not a plain old bank robbery, it's a political expropriation...", Mike chuckled a little, "...not a bad racket."

Erika thinks about this, about the old Paul and the new one, about sitting with Annie in a lilac garden, drinking wine, talking about love.

"Annie told me once," she says, "that Paul was wounded, that was the word she used. That everything in his life had betrayed him. She loved the child in him, the wounded child."

"Ah, but Erika," Mike says, "we're all wounded, each one of us. It's the human condition. She could as easily have fallen in love with a gas station attendant

187

or a garbage man if all she was looking for was a wounded child—or with you or with me. Jesus, show me a human being who isn't carrying a wounded child around inside and I'll show you a monster, or a god. Something that's only pretending to be human anyway. The legitimate article is always a little battered inside. How else do you explain how we live in this fucking beautiful world and are still so goddam miserable?"

As they drove farther south the day turned rainy and grim. Mike began reciting poetry to her. He had come to learn of the power of poets in Central America where, among the illiterate, poets are considered magicians and priests, and among the ruling class, subversives. Poets were hounded by the dictatorships; when captured they were thrown into volcanoes, like human sacrifices.

"Or look at Victor Jara. They cut off his fingers before they killed him because his fingers had such power in them, to play music, to sing. Poets—they cut out their tongues."

And then he recited:

> I, like you,
> love love, life, the sweet delight
> of things, the blue
> landscape of January days.
> Also my blood bubbles over
> laughing through my eyes
> which have known the rush of tears.
> I believe the world is beautiful
> that poetry is, like bread, for everyone.
> And that my veins don't end in me
> but in the unanimous blood
> of those who struggle for life,
> love,
> things,

    countryside and bread,
    poetry for everyone.

"That's Roque Dalton. His photograph is on the piano, maybe you noticed it. Beautiful man. The Victor Jara of El Salvador. Except instead of being tortured and killed by the right wing militarists, he was tortured and killed by the left wing militarists, his own side. It's so ironic, Erika. Because Dalton was one of the authors of *the* urban guerrilla handbook, he and Debray. They developed the idea of the *foco.* Plus he's descended from the Daltons, from the Old West bankrobbing days. He and Rousseau have a lot in common. But Dalton changed his mind about strategy, decided El Salvador wasn't ready for a vanguard. It needed a mass movement, not a party coup. He alienated the militarists, so they sliced him up into little pieces, slowly, amusing themselves. May 10, 1975."

"You remember the date."

"It's not hard. It was my eighteenth birthday."

"Funny about dates. They were bombing Hanoi when my daughter was born."

" *We* were bombing Hanoi," Mike said.

She never could get those pronouns straight.

It was afternoon before they arrived at the little trailer park on the outskirts of a small Southern town not far from the place where Annie had spent a good chunk of her childhood. Three battered valises stood outside the door under a plastic awning that only just protected them from the drips of rain coming down off the roof. Three valises, no bags of toys. An image of all the stuff Noah and Becky brought with them on overnights flashed through Erika's mind long enough to make her feel the weight of those three little suitcases, the lightness of them and the weight. The Feds had all the children's toys, or the IRS. They were in vaults somewhere or just abandoned. Lost one way or the other. But then the most important things had been lost first, nothing else really mattered. When Annie's brother-in-law asked Emma what she wanted from the old house (he went out to sell off whatever the Feds had left), she just said, "My Mommy."

Mike and Erika stood under the dripping awning next to the three little bags. She couldn't knock. He did it for her.

It was worse than she had imagined: the anemic young blond woman in fluffy pink slippers and a pink duster, the baby in the playpen, the counter with its array of dirty plastic dishes, the immense picture of Jesus done in black velvet and lurid blues and greens, the stuffiness and the heat, the column of smoke from the cigarette left burning in the ashtray, the magnetic rectangle of moving color and the demanding voices issuing from it ("And what category, Bill?" "TV personalities." "TV personalities. Good. Now for your first question....") And the three children, like refugees from the city after the bomb dropped, incredulous, confused, just wanting to go home, not being able to believe there was no home left to go home to.

Mike and Erika filled up the dining room/kitchen, squeezed themselves in between the TV and the playpen, brought with them a rush of damp, fresh air, the smell of rain, the outdoors. The children looked like they hadn't been outdoors in a long, long time.

Annie's sister had sandwiches waiting for them, white bread and Spam, instant coffee. The children, she said, had already eaten. They expected them several hours ago. They had begun to think they were never going to come.

And Erika thought, Yes, you probably told them we were never going to come. But she smiled and said they had to drive slowly because of the rain. And then she introduced herself and Mike to the children, Eli and George, whose hair had been long in all the photographs she had ever seen of them, but who now had buzz cuts and looked like little Marines, and Emma, whose hair was still long and pulled back with pink barrettes. She was wearing a frilly pink dress and looked uncomfortable. The boys looked wary, scared. But maybe they were just all dying to get outside.

They stood while Erika and Mike sat at the table and forced down the sandwiches and coffee. Erika noticed that all the children wore crosses around their necks, that the only book in the room was the Bible. She noticed the tension, the suspicion, the oppressiveness, the heat. Mike noticed something else.

"Hey, George, is that a Donkey Kong I see peeking out of your pocket? Boy, I haven't had my hands on one of those in a month of Sundays. Can I give it a try?"

Before Erika had finished her coffee, Emma was sitting on Mike's lap, Eli and George were peering over his hands, cheering him on or laughing as the little calculator-size game beeped under his fingers. The whole scene had changed, everything was cheerful and good-spirited. Erika asked Annie's sister about the baby. Even she brightened and began to relax.

Then it was time to go. Erika smiled bravely at the kids and said, "Ready?"

Mike peeked down at Emma.

"Ready, monkey?"

"I'm not the monkey, silly," she said. "I'm the girl."

"You're the girl? I thought you were the Kong!" and he started making ape noises and all the kids laughed. Nervous laughter, but laughter. It was going to be OK.

Eli went to get their coats and they formed up by the door to put them on. Emma kissed the baby who was holding onto the playpen bars and shaking them and screeching. She didn't want to be left behind. She wanted to come.

Then George looked up at Erika. He was buttoning his coat, and he just stopped dead and looked up. Without hair his face was entirely exposed, his eyes startlingly blue, a sea-green blue unlike either of his parents. He looked at her, she bent down to encourage him to speak. He looked right up into her face.

"Who are you anyway?" he asked.

No one had told them anything.

Erika told him she was a friend of his mommy and daddy and of Bobby and Marlene, his aunt and uncle.

"Oh."

"Is this it?" Mike asked, picking up the three little bags. "No toys?" He had noticed that, too.

"We're leaving our other things here," Emma said. "So we will come back."

Erika told Mike she wanted to drive. Clearly he was better at entertaining kids than she was. He grinned. "It's my life's work."

Erika started up the engine and began backing out of the drive. Eli was next to her in the front, Mike in back with Emma and George. She was concentrating on squeezing the car out between the posts at the end of the short driveway and on nothing else when with a sudden movement George gripped the back of the seat and pulled himself forward. Erika slammed on the brakes.

"Aunt Karen? You're a friend of hers?"

Erika saw the depths of their ignorance and cursed adults, all adults, herself included.

She reminded him of his cousins. She told him his cousins had pretend names just like they did, that Steve's real name was Jesse and Peg's was Winnie, just like theirs had been Brian and Tim and Suzanne, that

192

even the grown-ups had had pretend names. His aunt's had been Karen, but her real name was Marlene.

"Oh," George said, starting to sit back. Then he pulled himself up again. He hung over the seat and looked her right in the eye.

"Is she still alive?" he asked.

Eli sat in front, but he kept one eye on the backseat, monitoring the conversation, asking Emma how she was feeling, did she have to pee, or he would ask George if he had seen that great Corvette or the hawk hanging in the sky. Mostly, though, he listened.

"Where we lived before it was sort of a farm. We had this bull in the field next door. Remember the bull?"

"Are you going to tell them the story about the bull?" Eli asked.

"It's OK, Eli. It's just about the bull. Anyway, Steve....what's his name now? Oh, right, Jesse. Anyway, Jesse didn't know about the bull because they'd just put him in the field a few days before."

"No, no," Emma said. "He knew. He just *forgot*."

"That's right, because after Papa said, Sometimes if you forget what you're supposed to remember.."

"Ssshh," Eli hissed. "Remember!"

"Well, anyway. Papa was home that day. Papa and Uncle...what's his real name?"

"Bobby."

"Uncle Bobby. He saw Jesse in the field and he ran out of the house and jumped over the fence."

"*Papa* jumped over the fence."

"That's what I said. Papa jumped over the fence. Jesse didn't know why Papa was yelling at him. The bull came from the other side of the field. Jesse saw it and he froze, he was so scared. But Papa grabbed him and picked him up and threw him over the fence. Papa was very strong."

193

"My Papa," said Emma, "was stronger than anybody. He did all the hardest things. Mommy said that. He was the one who...."

"Emma, ssshh."

"Well, you said it was OK."

"Ssshh, we're not supposed to talk about it." Eli turned to Erika with an almost apologetic smile. "She's only little. She keeps forgetting the rule," he said. "But *you* know it, right? You're friends of Mom's."

In New Jersey the children fell asleep.

After awhile Erika said, "I'm really surprised they came with us so easily."

"The taboo seems to be what they say, not where they go."

"And Emma sat on your lap right away."

"They're very needy. They'd go with anyone. I've seen the phenomenon before. In Nicaragua. In orphanages."

Erika glanced over at him. He had moved into the front at one of their pit stops, but Emma had stayed glued to his lap. Now she was sleeping with her head on his chest. The boys were stretched out in the back. He met her eyes.

"I'm sorry. It's just what it's like. Listen, I'll go with you to MCC tomorrow if you want."

"They won't let you in. You're not on the visitors list."

"Well, how do I get on? I'll bring the kids up for visits. It's the least I can do."

"How bad will it be, do you think?"

"We'll rent movies for the VCR for when they come home. We'll order pizzas. We'll buy presents. Denora loves toy stores."

"That bad, huh? And Annie's sister, Jesus. It can't make it any better that she's not telling them anything."

194

"Yeah, well what is she supposed to tell them? Congratulations, kids, your mom and dad are heroes of the Revolution. They'll be on stamps someday. Or maybe the other tack. Mom and dad are lousy commie traitors. That's more likely, you know. Maybe we should be thankful she kept her mouth shut. I'd like to make up my own story for them. With a little help from Denora. Though I'm not sure what kind of story we'd come up with. Her idea of a good story is the Big Bang. My idea is the old man with the long white beard saying 'Light!' 'Trees!' 'Elephants!' 'Unicorns!'."

Word has gone out that the enemy is approaching the city. Everyone must leave, evacuate. There is no other choice. But though it is the night before the city must be abandoned, she isn't ready to leave. Nothing is packed, she has no idea even where to go. She and Simon take a walk through the city. It is summer and everyone is out on the street packing their cars, like the whole city is going on vacation. They meet Brenda who tells them she has a place in the country, describes the route to get to it, but Erika knows it's too dangerous to write it down and so she won't be able to remember the way. Morning comes and she still has to pack. She is in the attic with boxes of clothes and dishes. She can't find her jeans, the one thing she absolutely needs. Noah's toys are buried, Becky is searching frantically for something she can't leave behind. British troops playing bagpipes are marching by, but they aren't staying to defend the city, just marching through. Now it is time to leave. But she can't leave without saying goodbye to Marc. She calls him on the phone but all she hears are pieces of other people's conversations. She runs into the street and sees his car driving away from her out of the city. She knows she can't catch up with it and in the chaos of the times she may never see him again. And then the van must be packed (their old one, from fifteen years ago) and suddenly she remembers something she has to find. She runs back into the house, up to the attic. Everyone is yelling at her that it's too late now, it's time to go, but she knows she is forgetting something, the most important thing of all.

They tried to prepare the children a little over breakfast and again over lunch. But since they couldn't explain why Bobby and Marlene were in the correctional center (because they were pleading not guilty, they were admitting nothing), it was difficult to keep the conversation from becoming Kafkaesque. Children, unlike adults, are concrete thinkers.

"OK, they're in prison," Eli said, trying to sum things up. "I got that. But why won't you tell us what they *did*?"

"Maybe it's not so much what they did as what they believe in," Erika suggested.

"No," Eli said. "They can't put you in jail for what you believe in. That's in the Constitution somewhere."

Well, Erika thought, so much for that.

Emma meanwhile was sitting very quietly on Denora's lap.

"What do you think, pumpkin?" Denora asked her.

Emma turned around and put her arms around Denora's neck.

"When those men were asking me questions," she said in a loud whisper, "they wanted to know where my mommy was, but I didn't know. I think my mommy is lost, but someday we'll find her. If I pray to Jesus he'll help us. But until we find our mommy, do *you* want us?"

"*I* want you!" cried Mike, scooping her up and tickling her so that she laughed and laughed and the awkwardness of the moment dissipated into giggles. Only George remained quiet, sitting with his Donkey Kong, seemingly indifferent to everything.

196

The awkwardness of moments.

The children didn't recognize Bobby when the guard brought him in. Emma clung to Erika until Eli shouted, "Uncle Pete!" and then she slipped away and went to him, too. Bobby had grown a beard and lost weight. His hair had been dyed a dark brown, now the lighter color was growing back in. And in an orange jumpsuit...well, it would be hard for children. But even when Marlene was brought in, they hesitated. Could this peaked woman be their Aunt Karen? She hugged and kissed all the children, hugged them so hard it might have hurt. Looked at them hard, too, stroked Eli's nearly shaven head.

"Oh," she said, "your beautiful hair."

"It'll grow again," Eli replied, almost accusingly. "You look different, too."

Then Marlene turned to Erika.

"Thank you," she said. "You're such a good friend."

Erika shrugged, but noticed that Eli had heard and was looking at her with something that might be respect.

She sat over to the side then and watched a phenomenon she would see again and again. She was to become an expert on this, on how adults deal with children in pain, with the most elaborate system of denial and fantasy, like the way they deal with death. Oddly, it is just those terribly important things that adults do, politics and sex, that they are most afraid to hold up to the scrutiny of a child.

"We're going to have pizza after this," Emma said to Marlene. "Want to come with us?"

"I can't, honey. I have to stay here. I'm not allowed to leave."

"Why not?"

"The government won't let me."

"Why? What did you do wrong?"

"I don't agree with their laws."

"Were you speeding?"

"No. The law against speeding is a good law."

"So what did you do?"

"There are other laws that aren't so good. But you know, speeding can hurt people, and that's bad, isn't it? Now tell me what you got for Christmas."

"Why are you wearing those clothes?" George asked Bobby.

"These are the clothes they give the men in here to wear. Pretty sharp, huh?"

"I don't like orange. It's like the clothes hunters wear so other hunters won't shoot them. Why can't you wear blue like Aunt Ka...Marlene?"

"Why can't you wear real clothes?" asked Emma.

"They took them away."

"It's like you're one of those signalmen on the highway."

"Well, I don't know. They're comfortable."

George kept coming back to the orange clothes. Erika knew it was the connection with hunters. Maybe Bobby wore orange so they wouldn't shoot him, or maybe so he would be easier to shoot. But Bobby changed the subject.

Emma, holding Marlene's hand, asked, "What happened to your rings?."

"I lost them."

"I lose everything I love, too," Emma said with a long sigh.

"She means her unicorn," Eli said quickly. "She left it in the grocery store."

He learned fast.

Emma wanted Marlene to take her to the bathroom. Erika was talking to George, Eli was arm wrestling with Bobby, when the guard banged the glass door open and George flinched as though he had been struck.

"Briggs!" the guard yelled. "Briggs, come out here! You know you can't go in there with her. One more trick like that and this visit is over."

Erika took Marlene's place in the bathroom.

Later, when the visit was over, Bobby and Marlene hugged them all tight. "You have to be strong for your papa," Marlene said. "Tell him we love him when you see him. Tell him we love him very, very much."

The breaking away of bodies. You have to be strong. Just holding hands. Then even that clasp breaking.

It really is time to go. Marlene turns to Erika and holds out her arms. She kisses Erika's cheek, her mouth close to Erika's ear, and whispers numbers, a street name, Chicago.

"Goodbye," she says out loud as the guard comes to take her back inside. "Thank you, Erika. And give my love to Ruthie. Be sure to give Ruthie my love."

Mike and Denora are waiting in the car outside. There are three giant teddy bears in the back seat and hot pizza in the front. They all pile in and Mike steers the car onto the West Side Highway and speeds uptown. Eli starts them all singing *The Teddy Bear's Picnic*. When Erika looks in the back she sees Emma is smiling. George is pretending his bear is singing to hers.

They eat pizza in front of the tube and watch *E.T.* Eli is the only one who comments on the visit.

"That place," he says, "that place is like Mars."

But during the night Erika woke up in the darkness and heard somebody sobbing. Before she

199

could move there were whispers and by the time she reached the door to the guest room someone was already comforting the child, another woman who also slept very lightly and listened in the night.

Give my love to Ruthie. Be sure to give Ruthie my love.

CHAPTER 6

The Track of the Fugitive Gods

I

That night Erika has a dream.

She steps off the train onto a platform and notices that she can see the lake from where she stands. She wonders if this is the right stop and if it isn't how she will get onto another train. She takes the stairs down and studies the numbers on the buildings and on the street signs. There are Black men lying asleep in doorways and on the pavement around her, many of the shops are boarded up or have their windows protected by iron grates. She walks and walks until she finds the theatre. There are large posters in the lobby advertizing the production, a series of scenes from *Anna Karenina* entitled *Where Great Waters Meet, Small Creatures Die*. The lobby is crowded, packed with people. How will she ever find Annie here?

Then the chandeliers blink, the lobby empties. She finds herself alone in a huge room. Ushers in blue uniforms with brass buttons are closing the doors to the auditorium, closing door upon door, locking them with their keys. One sees her and says, "Madam, the performance is beginning."

"I'm supposed to be meeting someone here."

"Your friend is evidently late. I won't be able to seat you."

"I don't have a ticket."

He slips his hands into his pockets. "Perhaps they are waiting for you at the box office."

At the box office a man hands her a small envelope. Inside is a ticket with a number scrawled over it in black ink. She goes to the phone and dials. The usher is watching her. The man at the box office window is watching her. People trickle out of the doors, watch her. When the car pulls up she is relieved to be getting inside.

It's a huge car and new. It will take her to Annie. But first the driver wants to see her passport. There are three pictures inside. She has to identify them. One is Simon, one is Marc, the last is Mike. She wonders what Mike is doing on her passport, she hardly knows him. "One of these men," the driver says, "works for the FBI." He knows which one, but he won't tell her. "You'll never see Annie now," he says. "One of these men is a murderer."

She is sitting in the back seat. Now the person sitting in the front on the passenger side turns around to face her. It is Eli. He looks right at her and he says, "One of the men who fucks you murdered my mother."

There is a fourth face on her passport. It is the face of Paul Rousseau.

It had never occurred to her before that she might be that angry at Paul Rousseau. She lies in bed and thinks about this. And what she thinks is that Paul was another one who wanted two lives, who had two lives, an ordinary life and an extraordinary life. He wanted to live like an American and be anti-American at the same time. He wanted to love his wife and kids, play baseball, go to the movies and bars, go camping, paint his house and work in his garden, *and* make the Revolution. He wanted everything and for awhile he had everything. But only the gods can pull off a stunt

202

like that, live two lives, defy the rules. And Paul Rousseau wasn't a god.

Neither was she.

And she remembered something that Simon had said once when he came back from a prison visit. She had asked him how Paul was and he had surprised her by his answer. She wasn't expecting it, not at all. He said, "I think he's relieved that it's finally over."

Of course, it wasn't over. There were the casualties. Erika feels that it's only by chance that the casualties aren't hers.

There are fresh flowers in the vase on the kitchen table. It doesn't assuage her.

"Poets," she says, disgust oozing out of her voice.

Mike looks up from the newspaper. "What about poets?"

"Idiots."

"Fools."

"Morons."

"Imbeciles."

"I don't mean you of course."

"Oh, of course."

"I mean poets who write about love."

"God knows, I never do that."

" 'How do I love thee? Let me count the ways.' "

"You sound a little bitter this morning. Shall I put two spoonsful of sugar in your coffee?"

"People are better off devoting themselves to small animals."

"A roll? A Danish? These bear claws are good for people in rages."

"You don't work for the FBI, do you?"

"Shit! And here I thought I had the perfect cover."

"I had a dream. I just wanted to check."

"You expected a straight answer, of course."

"This is America, right?"

"If it's Monday, it's America. But to set your mind at ease, no. I don't work for the FBI. Sometimes the National Endowment, which might be one huge FBI front, you can never tell. Sometimes the city of New York, which is undoubtedly infiltrated top to bottom with Feds, but one must carry on...."

"I got an address from Marlene."

"Far fucking out. That's great."

"But it's pretty far away. It'll take some time to get there and find her. I don't know what to do with the kids."

"They can stay right here with us. I'm not working this week. We can do New York. Field trips. The Zoo. Erika, I'd love it. Denora would love it. The kids would love it. They're into consumerism, haven't you noticed?"

"The thing is, I don't think they're any more attached to me than to you at this point."

"No, don't worry. You're not deserting them with strangers. We're all equally strangers to them. It'll be OK, Erika. You absolutely have to do this."

"I feel like I do, yes. I couldn't believe she gave it to me."

"Hot shit, is what I say."

He pulled his chair around and straddled it so he was facing her with his head propped up on the chair back. His cheeks were flushed, his hair stood up at odd angles, he probably hadn't shaved in three days, though his beard was hardly noticeable. He hadn't washed his face yet and had that just awakened look about him. Most of all he was so young. Like Marc was young, Erika thought with surprise, looking at him. Though Marc was not raw youth by any means. Raw youth was here, sitting before her with legs almost too long for the kitchen and enormous feet, about to tell her, with great embarrassment, to take care of herself. It was incredible to think that Paul Rousseau had been no older than this when he made the decision that was going to change his entire life and eight other lives besides. It wasn't fair, it wasn't just. If we only had more time, she thought. If only everything we did wasn't so final.

"Take care of yourself, Erika," he says, as she knew he would. "And now listen. We love you and you know we love you and so you aren't going to give me a hard time now when I give you this travelling money which you are going to need and which you will be doing Denora a favor by taking because you know how guilty it makes her feel to live so well off other people's sicknesses. There. Now I've said it, and you'd better take it, too, or I'll never speak to you again except in rhymed couplets."

He unstraddled himself from the chair.

"I'll leave it tacked to the bulletin board in the hallway. Now I'm going to watch morning cartoons with the kids."

He grinned at her and went whistling out the door.

Erika moves from spot to spot in the house following the trail of poems. She does this at some point every day, but because this is the day she is leaving, she takes special pleasure in it. She loves to see the way the poems grow, like watching the growth of plants. He has twenty or so going at once. She has never counted them, she just follows them around the house.

It was an accepted part of life in the apartment that Mike would occasionally stride over to a wall or window or a piece of furniture, a bookcase or cabinet, pull out his pen and write a line or two on the piece of paper taped there. Sometimes he would walk around first or shuffle his feet in front of it, sometimes he would chuckle to himself or say the line out loud a few times, sometimes he would stand scrunched over and scribble for a long time, sometimes he would take the whole poem away with him and retype it, sometimes there would be several versions growing on one spot, like a cluster of grapes or a bunch of rosebuds on a single stem.

Today she notices that sometime during the night or early this morning he added a few lines here and there. One poem in particular sprouted during the night.

President Daniel Ortega Jogging Past the Temple of Dendur
Metropolitan Museum of Art

What are Americans really? you ask.

Rich Egyptians who got buried with all their stuff?
Ancient stuff, transformed, of course—
The laundress a washer/dryer,
The chariot a chevrolet.
State of the Art Slaves made of steel.
Old Horus kept his eyes open, learned a thing or two.
(Wasn't born yesterday, no Sir!)

As for the jewelry, clothes, perfumes, bathtubs,
patios and pools, barges, yachts, pets and palaces,
We've got them all again...

Richer and richer still, Osiris' dead world,
our kas so overjoyed, our little feathered bas
flying piper cubs, Cessnas. Hurrah,
we made it, light-hearted, empty-headed,
reincarnated

206

Dead.

Nicas are born with nothing.
When it was time to weigh their hearts
they had perhaps a sick child, a dying wife,

or maybe a fleeting thought of justice
like why some men spend their lives
working to build a building
other men spend their lives
waiting to lie dead in

And with this stone-sized doubt
their hearts outweighed the feather.

With no more than a book of poems and an M-16,
the kingdom of the dead breathing down their throats,
they travel light-hearted, travel light in the forests,

Now their kas are brothers invisible in the hills

Now their bas fly over them, as parrots and miradors,
the quetzal, the macaw.

They sing to them, the birds sing back.

Now they are barefoot but brilliant, light as air,

with nothing but poems and songs,
babes in their bellies and on their backs,
children in treetops, light as air.

And gringos grow old in houses huge as pyramids,
heavy as tombs,

As Nicaraguans break their bread with death,
offering him poetry and dreams, life, love

that refuse to lie quiet in a tomb

A free man running under falling leaves.

II

City structures will hide the guerrilla as well as the forest. Annie knows this to be true. It was only because of the children that they had abandoned the cities. Cities weren't safe for children and in cities the children made them too conspicuous. They were known in cities, by reputation if not by sight. Once in a city playground Annie had struck up a conversation with another mother. The woman was a graduate student in history or political science, maybe sociology. Annie hadn't paid too much attention, not until she mentioned that she was writing her dissertation on the Weather Underground.

City structures will hide the individual guerrilla of the foco unit as well as the forest. So Annie slips through terminals and train stations, so she makes her way, a fish swimming in the sea, from waystation to waystation, until she finds her place, chooses an identity, a name. She moves into an apartment, gets a job at a public hospital, a place where she is likely to meet people of all kinds, people she needs.

But there is another element at work. Adrift, she was out of contact with everyone, known only in a place inside her husband's mind. Once she links up with the cadre again, she might have a chance to send out a kite, to Paul, to her kids. Just to let them know she loves them.

The duty of a revolutionary is to make the revolution. When she isn't working at the hospital,

208

Annie works on other things. Their unit had been so tight that they had never recruited. Paul had, of course, developed a second unit and a third. She was going to have to do that now. If she wanted a cell, she was going to have to make one herself. To act. She was going to have to act.

The foco is the motor to a general upheaval. She wanted to turn the motor on. Maybe they had been too careful, too controlled. They had hit targets that were important to them, but maybe they were too abstract for people to grasp, maybe they didn't mean the same things to everyone. The names were the names of her enemies: General Dynamics, Honeywell, Union Carbide, the Bank of South Africa, Litton, Coors. The military-industrial complex in all its evil glory. The enemy. Or others: recruiting offices, reserve centers, armories, naval bases. The military itself, masters of war. Even so, they might have been too symbolic. Maybe she needed a new strategy. Maybe what would strike the oppressed poor as just would be not to blow up a bank office, but to blow the bank, blow open the vaults, all the money flying through the air...or to hit one of those three hundred dollar a night luxury hotels, to napalm a golf course, to sink every yacht in every marina along the lake front, to sink a goddam boat that cost more money than a working person might hope to make in his whole lifetime. And Annie thought of Paul and what would make him happy. She tried to imagine him sitting in his cell, in solitary, in lock down, listening to the report on the radio. She tried to imagine his face when he heard the target and the name of the unit responsible. The first action would be for him.

She changed beds and washed floors at the hospital and tried to bring some happiness to the rooms and the people, poor, sick, desperate people, inside them. But at night she would lie in her bed and

209

fill up with such horror and misery, seeing it all around her, hearing its rhythm inside her head, that she found herself praying to the universe, offering anything, everything, only to be back in her kitchen again arguing with Paul over buying too many cucumbers. She couldn't think of the children at all. If she thought about the children she would lose her mind.

January was a month conducive to losing your mind.

The cold. The bitter cold. The long train ride from the north side to the west side to work. The wind crashing down on you from the lake, the wind like an enemy, armed, wanting only to break you, to wear you down until you broke. And everyone dressed in dark colors, in browns and blacks, wrapped up against the cold, immobile, standing beside you like mummies. The other aides at the hospital smoking dope, popping pills, some of them taking care of her because she's special, a white girl, others giving her hell. And she hears everything, too, everything about drugs and busts, about sex, about death, men cutting each other, women getting raped. But what she listens for in particular, what she listens for all the time, she doesn't hear. For pain is internalized first, pain is driven inside to fester, everyone knows that. In the ghetto the enemy, the real enemy, is too big to see, the real enemy is so pervasive, so godlike in its absence, nobody dares raise his eyes and look. They cut each other, they oppress their sisters, they poison themselves, they drive themselves into their graves, without ever once seeing who it is they serve. She listens; sometimes she speaks.

There is an FALN unit operating in this part of the city. Annie knows some of them work at the hospital. She knows they are aware of her, but remain at a distance. But knowing they are there makes Annie

210

feel more powerful, less alone. She cannot recognize them, yet she knows they know exactly who she is, that they are waiting, that she is safe.

It isn't until the middle of January that Raul introduces himself. He approaches her in the cafeteria, also wearing the aqua uniform of an aide. Smiling he explains that there were four of them vying to make first contact, but that he was the only one of the right class. The others are nurses or techs. No sense raising eyebrows. Among the elite, classism runs deep, as does class consciousness among the oppressed. A hospital is just another little world. They smile at each other.

All afternoon the aides on her floor tease her about the good looking young aide who joined her for lunch.

An oppressed class which does not learn to use arms only deserves to be treated like slaves.

Every day they meet for lunch. If there is a free table they sit alone; if they are forced to share, they sit close and whisper together. Everyone enjoys watching the blossoming of this romance, the widowed white woman from the South (her husband dead in a car accident), the young Puerto Rican from the west side.

"You guys goin' at it like this, you gonna tie the knot or what?"

"You ain't even slept with him yet, honey? Don't you believe in squeezin' the tomato?"

"Honey, that old man of yours is dead and gone, now you got to start thinkin' about yourself."

"We got the dynamite, OK? How much experience you have with explosives?"

"Plenty."

"Shit. Let us take this one out, OK?"

"If there's going to be an action, I'm in it."

"You just tell us what you want hit, we hit it."

"No."

"Oh, shit, woman."

"Or I just do it myself, Raul. You give me what I need, I'll take it from there."

"You got a real attitude about this, you know."

"There have to be funerals on both sides."

"There ain't been no funeral yet."

"You can put somebody in the ground without killing him."

"Your husband," Raul says, "ain't never gonna be put in the ground."

Annie strains to hear him. The clatter of dishes, the banging of trays, voices echoing off cement walls, all of it erases some of his words, erases some of hers. They sit as close as lovers, but they still cannot hear. She listens hard, head bent over a plastic plate of white bread, white potatoes, canned vegetables, withered salad greens. *Some day our silence from the grave...* Just lines that come into her head, fly through her mind like lost birds. *There is nothing one man will not do to another.* She wishes she could erase every word she has ever read, every poem, every image. She wishes she could stand up and hurl her plate of food across the room, she wishes she could break something, break walls, prison walls, she wants to open a door in a stone wall, she wants her will to bring him back from the dead.

Erika sits in the waiting area at Gate 6 with a copy of *Vogue* open on her lap. Fifteen minutes to boarding. There is a family across from her, two young children playing with the standing ashtray, a young, flustered mother, a younger-looking father holding an infant. Nearby a few businesswomen in their dark blue suits so like hers, a gay man reading the *New York Native*, an older couple, the rest businessmen with their leather attache cases, their calculators in hand, their *Wall Street Journals* tucked securely under their arms. She gazes around, letting her eyes rest on her fellow travellers, on the ones she can't quite peg, the ones likely to sit beside her in the smoking section, ask her about her family, tell her about theirs, unless she buries herself in her *Vogue*, studies the newest spring make-up techniques. Letting her eyes rest on them. Wondering which of them, how many of them, or if any of them, might be making this trip to Chicago just because of her.

Erika doesn't believe in dreams, but she understands warnings. *One of these men works for the FBI.*

She glances from the page to the material of her skirt, how carefully she dressed that morning, as though a blue suit and a copy of *Vogue* could camouflage her. As though they didn't have her photograph from visiting Marlene at MCC. As though they hadn't staked out the house on the Upper West Side. As though Annie's sister's house wasn't under constant surveillance. A tap on every phone. At least she had sense enough to make the reservations from a pay phone. At least she had taken that precaution. But who knew what they were capable of, laser mics, video cameras....

They are calling for boarding. Erika gets up too quickly, the magazine falls to the floor. Before she can reach for it, one of the businessmen bends down and retrieves it. He straightens up and hands it to her. A young face, cold blue eyes. She takes the magazine but her hand is trembling. *You have no idea what these people are capable of.*

Now she is watchful, alert. She stands innocently in line with her boarding pass in her hand, but every part of her is listening, watching. They can't have tapped every phone in New York City. And even if they had followed her cab to the airport, how would

213

they have managed to get somebody on board the plane?

No, she thinks. This is paranoia. After all, who is she anyway? No one at all. Some lawyer's wife. They will keep tabs on the children, yes. They will follow them to the Statue of Liberty and the Empire State Building. If anything they will expect something to happen in New York. If anything, they will expect Annie to show up by the lion's cage at the Bronx Zoo. If anything, they will see this trip to Chicago as a diversion, a ploy.

And yet.... Erika settles herself in a seat at the back of the plane. Go down with the smokers, in the tail, where the survival rate is highest, since planes tend to go down nose first and in any case you can have a final smoke before checking out. And all she can think is that if Marlene had thought it wasn't safe, if Marlene had any doubts at all, she would never have whispered those numbers to her, numbers that remind her of a historical date—the Great Revolution—and an equally great sea captain, good omens for such a journey, both of them fused into her brain like a destiny she cannot refuse.

O'Hare Airport is set on what was once a prairie, miles away from downtown Chicago. Erika has booked a hotel room and the hotel limo is waiting to take passengers into the city, but she decides to take a cab. She gives the driver an address in Hyde Park near the University of Chicago, miles south of the Loop. It is Denora's old address from her medical school days. Erika visited there once, remembers the bookstores and the cafes and the Illinois Central that passes through the south side along the lake, taking white students and the Black bourgoisie to the Loop without stopping in the Black ghettos of the south side. Erika has convinced herself that she isn't being followed, that she can't be

214

being followed, but just in case she's going the long way around. The hare trying to outwit the fox.

The cabby deposits her in front of a brick three-flat. She walks between two brick gateposts that mark the entry to the courtyard, a lawn, snow-covered, a shovelled path leading to the front door. She waits there, concealed behind brick, and watches the street, watches for another taxi to pull up or for a car to cruise by. But she doesn't know what she's waiting for. Everything she knows comes from old movies, old novels; everything they know, everything they do, comes from a technology she can't begin to understand. They may be tracking her from a car miles away; they may have cameras on her even as she hides behind this brick pedestal with its cement flowerpot on top. Anything is possible.

She waits another few minutes, digs in her overnight bag, changes her tan raincoat for a warmer jacket and then walks down the street toward the avenue. Enough is enough. She leaves her copy of *Vogue* behind her, in the snow.

On busy 53rd Street Erika hails a cab and gives the driver the nearest cross streets to the address she's gotten from Marlene. Better to do it from here than from the hotel. Better to do it now while she still has some daring left, before she loses it entirely, before she becomes paralyzed with fear. Do it and get it over with.

And yet she watches out the back window, watches all the way to the west side, but she doesn't see anything unusual. Not that that means anything. Not that that means anything at all.

She is the only white person on the street. The only white woman with a canvas carry-on bag slung over her shoulder. The only white in sight. Which

215

means that either they've had the foresight to send a Black or Hispanic agent or she's in the clear.

But walking these streets through the west side ghetto makes Erika feel stranger than she's ever felt in her life. For she feels like Switzerland walking, Costa Rica walking, she is a neutral zone and yet she is threatened on all sides, fear coming toward her from everywhere—a woman on a street filled with men, a white on a street filled with Blacks, a member of the affluent middle class in a neighborhood of the abjectly poor, a subversive to the Feds, a collaborator to the underground, to herself, a land-animal out of her element, adrift on the sea with no charts, no life jacket, no survival skills at all. She could die out here, friendless, suspected by everyone, completely alone.

And it was cold. There was no lightness, no music, nothing to mitigate the ugliness of the street, the suffering on the faces of the men gathered in storefronts and around fires burning in trash cans, the dirt, the sense of desolation, stores boarded up and abandoned or chained and barred as though against an onslaught of tanks. And Erika walks through it and doesn't know what to fear. Except that Annie may be here, close by, watching from a window.

But who else may be watching?

And if she's led them to Annie, if she's done that....

She finds the building, a white stone two-flat on a block that looks as though an earthquake had hit it, leaving open lots of rubble and houses boarded up. This building itself seems only half occupied. Graffiti covers the front door, five-pointed stars. This is Vice Lord territory; the Disciples control the south. She remembers this from Denora's days in Hyde Park. And fear swells in her again. She is vulnerable here, and alone.

She goes up the steps, through the front door, into a dark hallway that smells of urine and other things, food she can't identify, or perhaps it's just layers and layers of odors, one on top of another, stuffed into this closed hallway that has neither ventilation nor light. She has to feel her way along the wall to the door to knock and wait. She doesn't realize how scared she is until she tries to swallow and finds her throat blocked, terror crouching there like a scream that can't escape. And her hand is so weak she can barely close it in a fist to knock on the door, can barely raise it to knock on the door, not knowing what lies behind it, not knowing which she fears more: that there is someone there or that there will be no one at all.

"Trouble," Raul announces one lunch time. A woman showed up at his mother's house looking for Ruthie. Left a note with her even though she said she never heard of nobody named Ruthie. Frowning, Raul passes the envelope across the table. "Maybe a kite."

Annie opens the envelope shaking so bad, then smiles so big Raul thinks he's never seen such a shit-eating grin on a woman's face before.

"A sister of mine," Annie says. "A good sister I haven't seen since the days I had nothing better to do than drink wine and listen to Billie Holiday sing the blues."

"How the *fuck* she ever find you?"

"She's my sister. She knew I needed her."

Now because Raul is a sensible man he doesn't understand this. But because he is a passionate man he expects there are things about women he won't understand. And Annie knows this about him. She knows if she had told him, My sister got to you through the MCC grapevine...then he'd get pissed and after he got pissed, he'd get paranoid. Now he won't press her,

217

now he'll just say, Fucking women. Besides, he respects Annie. He admires her. Now, hearing laughter in her voice, he stops himself, doesn't pursue anything else. It's dangerous business, another man's wife.

The message, when it is delivered in a long white box to Erika's hotel room, comes like Annie's own presence: daffodils and irises, smelling like spring, with a note attached that sends love and gives another place and time.

III

Exactly on time, Erika walks through the automatic glass doors and gets on the elevator with half a dozen men and women in white, doctors, nurses, and a few visitors carrying flowers or paper bags. This time she blends in more, feels more at ease. Besides, she knows what she's going to find on the fourth floor, who is waiting there for her. She knows and it feels like destiny, like certainty, something written, like standing beside a man and knowing that very soon he will become your lover.

She is going to Annie now the way she went to Marc: rising up in an elevator, absolutely certain, fearless, thinking of nothing else.

The elevator stops on 3. People peel away from each other, part like the Red Sea for a hospital bed to be wheeled in. A dying man. Erika shifts her gaze.

And then they are on 4. The bed moves out and Erika follows and continues to follow along down the hall. People she passes look on her with the compassion reserved for relatives of the dead and dying; somehow she has become part of his funeral procession, a professional mourner. But then there is

218

the room. Door closed. She opens it without knocking and goes inside.

The small blonde woman standing looking out the window is dressed in prison aqua, like Marlene. For a moment Erika is back in the Correctional Center behind closed doors that will never open again. But then the door clicks closed behind her, the woman turns, and it is Annie, Annie herself, smiling, opening her arms. When they embrace it is as though each of them were hugging a child who had been feared lost and has just been found.

Annie puts on her coat and leads Erika by the arm back to the elevator, leaving a trail of farewells behind her—" 'Bye, darling." "Have a good night now, you hear?"—waving to the ward clerks with one hand, squeezing Erika's arm with the other, walking so close beside her, so close, as though wanting nothing to part them again.

As though nothing could ever part them again.

They walk through a light snowfall toward the el stop, chatting about nothing, each simply listening to the tone of the other's voice, letting past and present wash over them, stick to them like flakes.

"God, Annie, I'm so glad to see you."

"Well, darlin', you're a sight for sore eyes yourself. When did you get so beautiful? And now tell me about my girl Becky."

"She's great, Annie. Disgustingly normal."

"Normal's never disgusting."

"This is. Madonna and hairspray."

"I remember that. Sneaking cigarettes. Oh, yes."

"And there's one you haven't met yet. Noah."

"A girl and a boy. You and Simon always were lucky. And you still are lucky. Still together. It's so beautiful when marriages get deeper and deeper, when people stay faithful to each other. When friends stay faithful, too. It's all we have, you know, that staying power, that's all there really is that counts for anything. You and Simon are such special people to us, always have been. You know, I thought of you two every time I played a Billie Holiday record, which was often, believe me, until we had to leave them behind one time and the Feds grabbed them. I still sing those songs, though. And you, honey, what are you up to these days?"

"God, I can't talk now. I just want to look at you."

"And what do you see?"

"You look, Jesus, so straight."

Annie laughs. "Takes some practice. And my old man, does he still look straight too?"

"No, he's getting pretty shaggy again. Skinny and shaggy, like the old days."

"That's good anyway. I thought those pounds were on for good."

A horn honks on their right and a car pulls up alongside the curb. A third world vehicle, not the Feds. Annie smiles at the driver.

"Come on. We're getting a lift. This is my good friend, Maria."

Annie opens the front door and slides in. Erika follows.

"Missed you in the lot," Maria says. She is a young, dark woman, serious, very thin.

"I thought you were working nights."

"Switched for the day. Goin' home?"

"Yes, ma'am. Maria, meet Erika, an old and dear friend of mine."

Maria glances across Annie to check out Erika. Her expression doesn't change. "Nice to know you," she says.

They drive through the ghetto in silence, salsa music carrying them along, Erika and Annie swaying

220

in tune with the windshield wipers, Maria squinting against the snow.

"Fucking weather," Maria says, lighting a cigarette. "And I got a meeting tonight."

"Say hello to Raul for me," Annie says.

"Sure will."

Annie's apartment is as neat as a pin, as bare as Marc's, though it carries her traces in it, slight ones, but Erika notices them: women's faces on the walls, a young Winnie Mandela with huge liquid eyes, a copy of Tassajara Cooking on the kitchen shelf, Mila Aguilar's *A Comrade is as Precious as a Rice Seedling* on the table, a huge orange, yellow and blue God's eye hanging in the window over a table of lush green plants.

Annie brings out a bottle of wine, Erika digs her Swiss Army knife out of her bag and struggles for awhile with the cork.

"Here," Annie says, "let me try."

"No, no, I can do it," Erika says, holding the bottle between her knees and pulling hard on the corkscrew. "Jesus."

Annie takes the bottle from her and pops the cork out with a single tug. They laugh; they've gone through this ritual a hundred times before, in a time that seems a hundred years ago. Annie pours the wine into water glasses, Erika lights a cigarette. Now alone, face to face for the first time, neither of them knows what to say.

"Salud!"

"Good health!"

"Freedom! We should pour this wine out like at a seder," Annie says, "the whole glass, for all our comrades still held captive."

Erika looks at the floor, imagines a pool of red wine like blood.

"Let's just drink to them instead, Irish style."

They drink and then Annie says, "Tell me about my husband."

And so they come around to reality, to what is real, Paul and the trial, the strategy, hopes and fears. Annie listens carefully, nodding or shaking her head.

"He's a good lawyer, Simon, but he doesn't understand. Good strategy won't help. This is America with a 'k'. There are limits to what he can do."

"He's testing the limits. He's not going to give up."

Annie watches Erika while she speaks about Simon. She notices the lines on Erika's face radiating out from around her eyes. Too much laughter. But there is a sadness there, too, a sadness in her face. Well, it's only to be expected, living in such sad times. But she is here, that's the miracle of it; she has crossed over the line from Annie's past to her present, she has done the impossible, broken through the barrier of time.

"What about my children, Erika. Have you seen them?"

"Yes, I've seen them."

"Oh, God, why do you say it like that? Is anything wrong?"

"Is anything wrong? Annie, everything's wrong. How can you ask me that?"

"Tell me."

"Tell you? OK. They need you. They need you back. They don't know what's happened to you. Emma thinks you're lost. I don't know what the boys think."

"What did you tell them?"

"What did *I* tell them? I told them their father would explain it to them. I told them you were alive, that you loved them. That you had all been living these pretend lives because you and Paul were trying to make

222

the world better. So then Eli asks, Well, why is papa in jail then? Annie, what do you want me to tell them? Why didn't *you* tell them?"

"We couldn't, Erika. It was too much to lay on them. Too dangerous for all of us. But they knew some things."

"More than you think, maybe. They know what not to talk about. Eli still shushes the other kids. It's unnerving."

"Eli knew Paul was doing something secret and important. We told him that we would tell him when he was older, that he'd have to trust us for awhile longer."

Erika puts her lips together and keeps still. Let it pass, she thinks. Let it pass. There isn't enough time to fight. There's no point in fighting.

"It must have been very hard," is all she says. No recriminations. She has no right to judge. But, oh, she wants to say, oh, Annie, wasn't there another way?

"How are they doing with my sister?"

"Ah, yes. We need to talk about this. I don't think they're doing real well with your sister. She doesn't have the resources for one thing, plus she's found Jesus...."

"Shit."

"The position of your family seems to be that you and Paul are as good as dead and the best thing to do is just forget you ever existed. They won't accept Paul's calls. He's written to them, but they never get the letters. They won't let the kids ask questions. They say essentially, Your parents are gone. You have to forget them. Pray for them. So Emma prays for you every night, that God will find you."

Annie stares out the window, biting her lip. "Jesus," she says. "We got to get them away from there."

223

"They're in New York now with some friends of mine. I'm taking them up to see Paul and they'll stay with his mother for awhile until we can figure it out. The main problem with everything now is that nobody's giving them a straight answer. We went in to see Bobby and Marlene and they wanted to know why they're there. That makes sense, right? So Marlene says, We're in jail because we don't agree with the laws. What kind of bullshit is that?"

"Marlene would have a hard time with that. She really sheltered her kids a lot."

Erika can't hold it in any longer. It bursts out of her:

"Annie, what are you talking about? You sheltered yours, too."

They can't look at each other now. They are both staring out the window at the night. Erika, who, if faced with her own children, knows she would have sheltered them too, feels like a hypocrite. And she is thinking how painful this is, how she hates to do this, how after all these years they are still at odds over the same thing, only this time it isn't just an idea—the Red Guards versus the children of America's middle class—no, this time it's real. She thinks that all she has to do is say, I'll take them, Annie, I'll take them and love them and they'll be all right. I'm your friend. And she wants so badly to say these words, she wants so badly to be a woman who could say these words, a strong woman, and yet she knows that she can't, that she can't promise anything, not without talking to Simon, not without thinking hard about Becky and Noah, about the nuclear family (and her heart cringes), not without thinking about money and about time, about her own work, her life. All she can think is, What would I do with five children? How could we support them? And then, I would have no time, no life. I would have to give them everything.

The reality of it. Not impossible, no. But terrifying.

But Annie is only thinking of getting the children away from her family. Two months wasn't so bad, not irrevocable. They are resilient kids, strong kids. Children all over the world are separated from their families. Parents lost in political upheavals, wars, repressions, murdered by death squads, found mutilated on the side of the road, made to disappear. Now that she knows what's happening, she can act. Their support networks stretch across the country. Even right in New York City support households exist and care for the children of political prisoners, engage in collective parenting. Some had won legal custody, others had guardianships. They knew enough lawyers and there was money that could be channelled through them. That way the children would grow up in an activist community, retain ties with Paul in prison, even somehow or other with her, and everything she and Paul believed in would be right there, enacted openly every day. No more clandestinity. The children would be raised by people who openly shared their beliefs and acted on them.

It was the only solution.

"Anyway," Erika said, sighing, breaking the silence, "they'll be seeing Paul soon and I'm sure he'll be able to make it all clearer to them. I wish you'd tell me what I can do, what you want me to tell them...unless you want to tell them yourself."

"Oh, Erika, what an idea that is! I've thought of it so often myself. But, see, you managed to meet me here because the Feds aren't following you around. There was a chance they were, there's always that chance, but they aren't. But my kids, my kids are going to have permanent tails on them probably for the rest of their lives. Just like our families' phones were tapped all these years on the chance we'd call them. They'll have

225

thought of that, believe me, that somebody would try to get the kids to me. The only way it could be done safely would be to set it up outside the country. I've thought about it. I've wished for it, somehow being reunited with them. But where in the world could it be done, Erika? Where could I go and not be extradited? Cuba? Nicaragua?...Maybe sometime. Maybe I could slip out of the country, maybe you could take the kids on a trip, maybe we could meet up in Managua. But there's the war, and you know eventually Reagan's going to send the army in, you know in your heart that's going to happen. Besides, my work is here. This is where I belong."

"There's another way, Annie. If you were to surface. Simon says he thinks he could get you five years on a plea bargain."

"On what charge?"

"Harboring a fugitive."

"Harboring my husband, you mean? I don't admit to that. It's not a crime."

"Paul doesn't think bombing buildings is a crime either."

"It isn't when you're at war."

"War? For Christ sakes, Annie, there's no war. Look around you. Do you see a war going on here? There are two hundred million people in this country. How many of them think there's a war? A dozen? Two dozen? A hundred? Everybody else thinks they're at peace, Annie. And the last fucking thing in the world anybody wants is a war. Why should they? War turns people into animals. Annie, Jesus, just think about it. Three years with good time and you'd be with your kids again. They need you."

"Paul needs me too. Out here. Continuing his work, continuing the struggle."

"Oh, shit, Annie. The Revolution doesn't need you. Your kids need you. Paul would understand that."

"No, you're wrong. He wouldn't understand. And he'd never forgive me either."

"They're his children, too."

"All children are his children."

"Come on, Annie."

"No, see, here's where you're wrong, Erika. Our struggle is for all children, not just our own. Listen: 'A mother is not a woman who gives birth to a child and cares for it. To be a mother is to feel the pain in your own flesh of all children and all peoples as if they had come from your own womb.' That's from a letter a Sandinista combatant wrote to her children before she died in battle. It is very important that you understand this about us. It's what Paul lived for. It's what he expects of me, too."

"But what about your own children?"

"We raised them to be strong."

"You can't ask that kind of strength from a five year old."

"All over the world that's being asked of five year olds."

"This isn't all over the world. This is here..."

"Where it all starts. So it's more vital here." Annie stops. Her face tightens, takes on a sternness, and something enters her voice, suspicion, fear. "It sounds like you're saying you don't accept the validity of what we've been doing."

"I don't understand what you've been doing."

"Understand it? Erika, we have the same enemy. Or we did."

"Yes — General Dynamics. I guess it's hard for me to see how a few bombed out offices are going to cripple General Dynamics."

"We are not so arrogant, Erika. The end result for us is not to cripple the corporate structure, but to inspire a larger struggle. Before a mass movement can be organized, the enemy has to be flushed out and identified. People are too comfortable in this country. They need to be shown how ripped off they really are, what crumbs they're getting — a color TV, a VCR, just plug in and forget what you do every day, the degradation you go through every day. We've been colonized by a handful of corporations. We're slaves to them. White, Black, Hispanic, all of us, here, all around the world. It's the same enemy everywhere."

"I'm not sure it's been made clear to people. I'm not sure the connection has been made."

"Well, you're not going to read an analysis of it in *The New York Times*, but it's reaching people, the people it needs to reach. It's not going to happen overnight, but it will happen. The road to freedom is long and paved with thorns. That's why it's called a struggle. And the biggest struggle is showing people that they have power, they have incredible power if they would only unite and use it. Not sell out and not surrender. It's so simple, Erika. Sometimes don't you just want to shake people and tell them to wake up?"

Erika smiles at her. "Yeah," she says.

"Yeah. Is that hard to understand?"

"No. You need a better P.R. person, that's all."

Annie smiles at that. "Well, there's opportunity...But you *do* see, Erika? You do see?"

"Yes, I see."

"I need you to see this, to understand this. Because if you can't see it, how will our children ever understand it? And they have to, Erika. They have to understand how precious this was to us, that we had to choose it even over them, despite how much we loved them. They have to learn whose children they are. They may suffer, but they'll be better people. I just got to see that they don't go back to my sister. Or to Paul's mom. She's a sweet old lady, you know, but she can't raise three little kids. She's done that already. But there

228

are people in New York, good revolutionary people who are raising children of political prisoners..."

"Oh, no. No, Annie, you can't do that. I've been to that house. I've met them."

"They're good people."

"They're fucking scary people. They're ideologues. You'd hate them. You'd never want your kids raised by people like that. It's like they're Moonies."

"They feel very strongly that they have a responsibility to the parents of those children. Maybe they just came off as too radical for you. But they're dedicated to the struggle and they're...."

"Annie, I...listen, just listen, please. I know I have less than perfect politics and I haven't blown up any buildings lately and I don't even believe in the armed struggle, OK?, because it just seems to bring everybody misery, and I won't bullshit you about that. But I know something about kids, not a lot, but something, and I know how I feel around adults and kids and so believe me when I tell you that there is no love for kids in that house. There's a lot of bullshit about what's politically correct—but, Annie, were you raised by politically correct parents? was Paul?—but there is no love. I can't imagine your kids being happy there. And Annie, it's hard enough for them. They're broken hearted kids, don't make it any harder for them. I'd take them before I'd let you do that. I can't speak for Simon, but I'm sure he'd say yes, you know he's always wanted a million children...."

But now Erika, who has been pacing the room, talking without thinking, letting her frustration fill the room, letting out all her despair, now looks at Annie and sees an expression of such pain on her face that she feels that without thinking she has just slipped a knife into her best friend's heart.

"I never wanted to break their little hearts," Annie says. "We never wanted that. Erika, can't you tell them, please, make them understand. We loved them so much. Paul loved them and I...."

"I know that, Annie. And they're great kids, you made three great kids. They're smart and kind, they love each other...."

What comfort was that? What comfort could Erika find now?

"Annie, this is what I can do. I'll bring them to my house. They can visit Paul, they can visit their grandmother, stay there for awhile, we can switch back and forth. In the meantime I'll talk to Simon and we'll figure it out."

"Just don't separate them Erika. They can't be separated."

"Don't worry. We won't separate them. Will you let me do that, though? Will you give me some time? Will you trust me?"

Annie looked at Erika. Everything came back to her—Simon and Erika, the apartment, the cats, Simon kissing her one night on the porch in the moonlight, Paul Rousseau walking through the door.

"Please, Annie, say you'll trust me."

"I trust you. You love them, too, don't you? You'll do what's best."

"And will you just think about the plea bargain? Will you just think about it? Please?"

Annie hesitated then. She wanted to be upfront with Erika, always upfront. No games.

She knows she can't promise this, can't even think about turning herself in. It goes against everything she's had to hold onto all these years, all her life. No collaboration. No surrender. If you think about collaborating, where do you draw the line? When they capture your man and torture him in front of your eyes? Then? If then, why not when they threaten to rape you or beat your friends with rifle butts or burn your crops? Then? If then, why not when they

230

come to arrest you and torture you by separating you from the people you love? Where do you draw the line? When and where? In Guatemala and in El Salvador, her sisters can say no and keep saying no, when to say no means so much more, everything lost, and if they can say no, if they can keep strong, how can she possibly break ranks here and say yes?

And Annie looks around the room, at the blank walls, the bare floors. She feels so free. It frightens her. What is there to keep her attached to the earth now? Only Paul.

"All right," she says. "I'll think about it. I'll let you know."

"Soon?"

"Soon. Before Paul's trial is over, before then I'll let you know. One way or the other. Listen, I have a letter for you to give to Paul. Simon can get it in to him. I'll just add something. I'll tell him to trust you, to go with whatever you decide."

"If you don't surface."

"If I don't surface. But I won't tell him I'm thinking of that. Oh, Erika, these past few months, since I've been alone, I've thought about him so much. How torn he must have been all those years between his love for us and his work. Now he isn't torn anymore. Now it's out of his hands. And I don't have to worry anymore that he'll leave someday and the next he'll be dead. And now that you're going to work everything out for the children, I don't have anything to worry about, nothing to fear at all."

Erika thinks about Marion, worst Federal pen in the country, but doesn't say anything. Instead she reaches for the bottle.

"Well, what do you say...."

The sound of the phone stops her cold. Annie is already moving, picking up the receiver before the second ring.

231

"Yes."

A few seconds pass, Annie's face showing nothing yet seeming to age before Erika's eyes, becoming stern, hard. Without saying another word she puts the receiver back.

"Get your coat. We have to leave. Now."

Erika can't move, watches Annie slide a leather bag out from behind the couch, pull out a gun, check the cartridge.

"Annie?"

"Come *on*, Erika. The Feds are busting Maria's place right now. It could be a sweep, then we're in it. I'll set you down someplace. You just get back to your hotel, OK? Now let's go."

Annie glances around once more, picks up her coat and Erika's, pulls Erika along with her to the door, Erika who feels as though she is moving in slow motion, thinking in slow motion, never good in an emergency, never able to think under pressure—the cat run over in the street, Noah's broken arm, always terrified someone will begin to choke in front of her, now the Feds.

But Annie pulls her along and they are running now down the back stairs and out into the snowy yard, along a partly trodden path to the alley, down the alley to a lot, across the lot, running, slipping, coats unbuttoned, snow getting into their shoes. Annie pulls a key from her pocket and opens a garage door.

"The closest one I could get that's not stuck in an alley. Still quite a hoofing distance away, huh?"

Annie unlocks the car door, slips over to open Erika's side.

"Hold it. You don't have to come with me at all. Walk down the street there and catch a bus south."

But Annie is already starting the car up, Erika already has her seat belt on. Even in the darkness, they know each other's faces, each other's minds. There's no time to decide. There's no time at all.

"How fast does it go?" Erika asks, knowing she should be walking to the bus stop, knowing in her heart this is a mistake.

"Maybe we'll just have to see."

And Annie pulls the car out and hangs a sharp right into the flow of traffic. Erika wants her to step on it now, wants to go fast, faster than the speed of light. Get away. Just get away.

"Fuck, we're right behind them," Annie says as two cars peel off into the alley they've just run down and Erika, catching a glimpse up Annie's street as they speed through the intersection, sees a convoy of vehicles pulled up in front of the building, lights, men holding shotguns in their hands.

"Holy shit," Annie says, "it's too close."

She switches something on on the dash: male voices, static, numbers, a kind of jibberish to Erika, must be the police channel, but it sounds like babble. Erika is only aware of speed and of craft, of Annie maneuvering the car, of the need to flee, of the men following, maybe following right behind, the snow making tiny circles of liquid on the windshield, the wipers passing by, the circles being erased. She turns half-way around and watches out the back. Only headlights, white headlights, no colors. Still she feels her feet pressing against the floor, her right foot pressing down hard on the floor. Annie glances over.

"Hey, let up on the gas, Rick. No point getting picked up for speeding." And Annie smiles and Erika tries to smile back, but she feels as though she is in one of those dreams, running, running, knowing they're right behind and gaining, and that wherever you hide, there's no escape.

Finally Annie turns the jibberish off. They are farther north now, in the suburbs. Annie makes a

233

series of turns, pulls up in front of another garage, opens it, drives the car into the dark.

"Here we are," she says.

"Where are we?"

"Safe for awhile. Let's go take a look at the manse."

They emerge from the garage into a cold, grey night, into snow, and walk up a few rock steps and along a path, shovelled from the last storm but showing a few inches of new snow, to the side door of a large, single family house. It is very quiet here. Annie unlocks the door.

"The country house," she says softly.

"Who lives here?"

"An old couple who winter in Florida and rent it out in the winter to a visiting professor of English lit. You didn't know about my fondness for Elizabethan sonnets, did you?"

Annie ushers Erika into the kitchen.

"I pay someone to shovel, so the neighbors don't wonder. Neighbors always wonder." Annie goes around switching on the lights. "I haven't been here in ages. But I think there's beer."

But Erika is still, standing completely still, seeing again the lights, the cars at odd angles, the men with shotguns in their hands.

"A safe house," she says, or asks, sounding stupid to herself, trying to understand.

"Let's hope."

It's Annie who goes to the refrigerator and gets out two cans of beer.

"So," she says. "Here we are."

"Yes, here we are."

"There's food. There's TV. There's a ping-pong table in the basement." Like a mother, Erika thinks, a mother trying to divert a child. There's pizza. There's a VCR. There's a big stuffed bear.

And the men with shotguns.

So this is what it was always like.

And then Erika feels it. It sneaks up on her like an orgasm, like laughter, like the punchline of a good joke—the jubilation of it, the exhilaration, like being a kid again and making it to the fort. Her whole body relaxes into the laughter of it, here in this kitchen so like her mother's, here with a cold beer in her hand, both of them together, safe.

Annie is laughing, too.

CHAPTER 7

Everything Human Takes Time

I

Erika is driving again, this time a rented car, forging her way up through league after league of dark, snow-bound forest. Eli, sitting beside her in the front, disconnects himself from his Walkman and finally begins to speak:

"I guess I should tell you this. I'm not really eleven. I'm really nine. When I was Brian I had to be eleven, but that was OK because I was going into fifth grade anyway because I was skipped, so it was like I was a slow eleven instead of a fast nine, see? And I'm tall like my dad so I could pass for being older. Anyway, I didn't tell Aunt Barb. I just let her think I was eleven. We weren't even going to real school there. It was this bible place. It was so weird. Like no science at all. No math. It was really hard on George. He won the math medal in our old school for the lower house. But in this bible place he had to lay low because they didn't even want to know there were such things as Apples, I mean, you couldn't say 'software bank' to them, they'd lose it right on the spot."

"So you're really nine."

"Yeah. Really. My birthday is April 10th. I'll be ten."

"Your mom's birthday is in April, too. April 15th. Income tax day."

"How do you know that?"

"Your mom and I lived together a long time ago. We used to have birthday parties, and April 15th sticks in your mind because it's the day you have to pay your taxes, or not pay them, if you decide not to. Because so much of that money goes to the military. And when we lived together the war in Viet Nam was going on."

"So did you pay them or not?"

"Well, we never made enough money to pay them. They always sent us money back. Then we'd have a party."

"I don't know if my dad paid taxes or not. But he probably didn't. See, I know what my dad did. I know he robbed banks. It's OK. They're asleep back there. They always fall asleep in cars. But I want you to know that I know that so you don't have to make things up or lie to me. George and Emma don't know, but I do. I sort of figured it out, but then I heard Aunt Barb and Grammy Pratt talking about it. But I wasn't really surprised. I mean, why else would we always be running away and changing our names?"

"I hope you'll talk to your dad about this, Eli. There's really more to it than that."

"Yeah, well here's another thing I wanted to talk to you about. It's about going to see him. George is really bummed out about it. He's, well, he's not going in. He says he's not going to go. First he said it was the cross. I said, Hey, dope, just take it off. I'm taking mine off. I thought of that already. We'll all take them off. Grammy Pratt gave them to us for Christmas and it was a real big deal to her that we wore them, it meant a lot to her and she's really nice, so we wore them. But I know Papa would freak out if he saw us wearing crosses. I mean, I've heard enough about religion from him and Mom to know how much he hates it, so I said to George, Easy, we'll just take them off and give them to Erika to take care of for us. You'd do that, right?"

"Of course."

238

"But, see, it's not that. It's his *hair*. He's so scared that Papa is going to say something about his hair. So I said, George, if he's going to freak out about it with you, he'll freak out about it with me, too. We just say, It wasn't *our* idea, you know. I mean, I didn't *ask* to get my head shaved. But George just cries when I say that. He's just turned into such a cry baby."

"How old is George really?"

"Seven. Seven going on three....No, I know. He's just scared of seeing Papa in jail. He just doesn't want to go. Period."

"Maybe Simon can handle this."

"Who's Simon?"

"My husband."

"Oh, right. I talked to him on the phone while you were gone. He's Papa's lawyer, isn't he?"

"Yes. So he sees your dad a lot. And he can talk to him and explain about your buzz cuts—which I hear are very in, by the way. If he knows that you have them, he won't be so freaked out. You probably look different, but then he looks different, too."

"Like Marlene does."

"Well, not exactly. He has a mustache."

She got what she wanted, Eli's smile.

"Will we be staying with you for awhile?"

"With your grandmother first. There's an army of lawyers at my house now because of the trial."

"Oh, right. Sure."

"After that, we'll see what happens. Did you have fun with Mike and Denora while I was gone?"

"Where were you, anyway?"

"I have cousins in New York. I never get to see them, so I went for a little visit."

"Oh. Yeah, we had a good time. Mike took us all over the place. It was pretty cool. I liked the Zoo the best, even though most of the animals were inside. And Mike is really funny. He made up songs for us to sing to the animals so they wouldn't feel so bad having us stare at them. In the monkey house there's this sign that says that monkeys are very sensitive and you shouldn't make fun of them. I liked that. I don't think you should make fun of anything. He took us to the Met, too—you know, that big museum? We saw knights and mummies and pyramids. It was great. George liked that the best. Then we went to this incredible toy store and got to pick whatever we wanted. Though it's funny, you know...when you can have whatever you want, you wind up not really wanting to pick anything."

"What did you pick?"

"Well, Emma knew right away. All she wanted was a Cabbage Patch Kid. George went right to the computer games, of course, but he wound up picking some ultra Donkey Kong. He won't even let me touch it. I got the Walkman. Mike is pretty radical. I really like him a lot. And Denora. And you. I never knew Mom had such neat friends."

And so Eli talked as they drove northward. But Erika remembered what Denora had said to her the night before they left:

"Emma needs somebody to be her mommy. Once she finds that person she'll be needy and demanding for awhile, but eventually she'll be fine. Eli has a lot of anger. Whoever takes on a parenting role with him will bear the brunt of that anger, as soon as he feels safe enough to trust them with it. But he'll be OK, too, I think. It's George I'm most concerned about. Keep an eye on George, Erika. He's been hurt the most and the hurt's right there. Be prepared for it. God, I worry about George...."

Simon met Erika at the door. He was wearing a sweatshirt and jeans; he had been shovelling the

240

driveway and had just come inside to have a beer. He was sweaty, his hair was damp.

"I was just going to get cleaned up for you," he said. "I'm too yukky to hug."

"No you're not," she said, holding him and kissing him out on the front steps. "I love you yukky."

"My God," he said laughing, "you should go away more often. But, boy, did I miss you."

And then the children appeared one by one from the car and he went to welcome them and help them all in from the cold.

Lovingly he took his children onto his lap. Studying them, knowing already.

They were his and not his.

His and not his. Already gone from him. Already he was fading from their lives. As they were from his. He knew. Like the memory of a pleasure. Or the memory that once there had been pleasure, not even the memory of it anymore, just the words about it. Part of all he had to forget to survive—forget the feel of a woman's skin, forget the taste of good food and drink, forget the open sky, the rush of wind, the heat of the sun, running in and out of the shade, the dappled light on the path, the pounding of blood, and how you keep ahead of the ones behind you, how you outpace them, better than they are, stronger, more determined to win, and if they track you, you can escape, outwit them, strike out at them and disappear.

Simon, who had brought the children in for the visit, asked Eli later what he and his dad had talked about.

"Running," Eli said. "Mostly about running."

Paul's mother lived forty miles from the city in a small mill town. She was a thin, nervous woman in her sixties, never sat down for longer than five minutes at a stretch, worked overtime every day, a chain smoker. She spoke in exhales. Sometimes she would get so excited half her sentences would come out in French.

She tells a story of the FBI agent who came to see her a few years after Paul went underground. He arrived at her door one night very late.

"I brought my son up better than this," she told him. Her English was musical, deep throated. "My son would never wake *your* mother up in the middle of the night."

Several years later the same agent returned to her house early in the evening and handed her a manilla envelope.

"I found these in a house your son had been living in," he told her. "My mother would want her son to bring you these pictures of your grandchildren."

She was so touched she invited him in for coffee.

The photos were on the wall around a big framed picture of Paul in his army uniform. They were a good four years old. Emma was a baby; George was missing his front teeth; Eli had his arms wrapped around a big collie.

They were the same pictures Erika had seen on the wanted posters hanging up on the post office wall.

Erika expected that at some point it would be necessary for her and Simon to talk about Marc, but it was difficult to find time alone. There were the three children staying with them at first. Then the visit to the

242

prison. Then taking them back and forth to their grandmother's house, getting them settled there. There was the ongoing preparation for the trial, Dan and Jon in and out of the house, the basketball games on the tube, the long distance phone calls, the pre-trial press conferences. But soon she realized that there was no need to talk, not about that. About other things, yes, about Annie and Annie's children. But one thing at a time. First the trial, and then, only then. But about Marc, nothing. Whatever had to be said had been said.

On her stack of mail and phone messages she found one in Simon's hand saying Marc had called. She wondered what Simon had said over the phone. Then one night when Jon was joking about busting Paul out of jail and asked Simon where he'd stashed the dynamite, Simon had replied, "In some bartender's cellar." Other than that, nothing. Nothing at all. Not even echoes.

Busting Paul out. They hardly even dared to joke about it. Jon was convinced everything was bugged—phones, light fixtures, briefcases. You've been reading too many spy novels, Erika said to him. Wrong, he replied. I've been reading too many trial transcripts.

As the trial date crept closer, they stopped joking entirely.

"I only wish there really was somebody out there," Jon said one night.

They had come home from command headquarters—Simon's office—earlier than usual. Everyone was exhausted, but Jon was wired, too, and went out for a night run. Dan switched on the basketball game. A typical night, Erika thought. A normal night. Except that in less than a week the trial would start, and then in a few weeks more it would be over, and then they would have to figure out what was normal again.

243

Annie's children were staying with their grandmother until the trial was over. Eli wasn't pleased. He wanted to see his father every day (though it was impossible); he wanted to go to court. Erika kept her hand on the pulse of the Rousseau household, talked to Mrs. Rousseau almost every night. There were daily crises. The girl who babysat for the children told Eli she thought his father was a dangerous criminal and Eli had shut himself up in the bedroom and refused to come out, threatened to hitch to the city and move in with Simon and Erika. Erika felt stretched to her limit—part of her in Mrs. Rousseau's house, part in Simon's office, part wandering the streets of Chicago. There was little of her life left for Becky and Noah, for dinner, for laundry, for thinking about art. And then this particular night Jon comes in from his run, stands dripping with moisture—sweat or snow—and says,

"I only wish there was someone out there."

And Dan looks up at him from the TV screen where Larry Bird is careening down the court heading for his third three-pointer of the game, and says,

"I think we should start praying there isn't. Because if there is and they show up, we are all in for some mighty heavy shit."

Simon and Erika drive the children back to their grandmother's house Sunday afternoon after their weekend visit. As usual, Mrs. Rousseau has coffee and cake waiting for them.

"So, how's life at the mill?" Simon asks.

"Eh?" she says, lighting another cigarette and blowing the smoke over the table at him. "That place? I've worked there all my life, you know, but they never fool me, not for a minute. When I read in the papers what my Paul says about the oppressed working class, I know he is talking about that mill. They treat human beings like machines—no, they treat their machines better. But I work. I don't talk to nobody. Work, come home, shut my door, don't think about it no more. I tell you, for years after Paul disappeared and they were all looking for him, you know, I got into the habit of talking to nobody. Because people would ask about him, and what was I supposed to say, eh? Oh, yes, I was famous in this town. More now, with this trial and all. But I say nothing. I keep to myself. Trust nobody. So long as they don't bother the children. I pray they don't. So far there's been no trouble, at school you know. But they are all afraid to say anything. They know my temper. French blood, you know." And she laughs, and they laugh with her. But the laughter is a defense, a covering, and Simon instinctively wants the shields down, wants to know how it really is. And so he prods, gently but relentlessly. Is she getting help from her family, from her friends?

"Friends? Ha. You got trouble, you got no friends. You're too young to know, or maybe you are the lucky ones, like my Paul. He has good friends, you two, others. But for me, no. And for family, most of them are in Canada. My husband is dead so long, Paul was just a baby. So, you know, these children are all the family I got now. But, you know, Simon, this is no life for them, no place for them. Paul calls here and he asks how everything is. I say, Fine, fine. Why upset him? But Erika knows. I lay awake nights and I cry. I can't sleep. I work two shifts, well, why not? Can't sleep anyhow. Listen, I get state aid for them. It's an insult what they give me for three children. How they expect you to support children on that pittance! Oh, I had my eyes closed for a long time, Simon, but now I see things. I read in the papers about Paul, you know, the things he says, and I think, It's true what he's saying. There's a new woman at the mill and the other day she says to me, Are you some relative of that Paul Rousseau they

245

got going to trial there? And I said to her, That Paul Rousseau is my son and I am proud of him.

"You remember, Erika, that day you was here and asked about these potholders, if I made them? And I said, No, they're made by some old lady in town...I think of it, it makes me laugh, you know. What am I, eh? A spring chicken? I'm learning, Simon, I'm no spring chicken anymore."

"Oh, come on now," Simon says, "I bet you can still kick up your heels."

"You get my boy out of this, Simon, you'll see me kick up my heels all right." She pulls a bottle of Canadian Club down off the shelf. "How about a finger of this to toast to our gay youth, eh? You'll take a drink with me, Simon?"

"Any day of the week, Madam," he says, taking the proffered bottle from her and pouring a finger into each of the three plastic glasses she set out on the table. "To our gay youth," he says. "May it last forever."

Soon after Simon and Erika kiss the children goodbye and head toward the door. But Mrs. Rousseau catches Simon by his coat sleeve.

"So, Simon. The truth is hard sometimes."

"Don't worry. Give us a little time. Everything will work out for the best. I promise."

They drive back to the city in silence, both of them occupied with thoughts of their own.

Brenda's dinners were always major culinary events and that Sunday night's was no exception. She had gone ethnic—Greek—and served moussaka and spanikopita, baklava and retsina, a wine that Erika decided tasted like old trees. An acquired taste. The men stuck with beer.

"So," Dan said midway through dinner, "how was Nicaragua?"

"Ah, "Brenda sighed, earrings flashing, "I was wondering when you were going to ask. You didn't even notice my colors." She was wearing her black lace blouse and long red skirt. "But surely you're all sick of politics of any stripe by now. No? I *adore* polite guests. Well, Nicaragua was *wonderful...*"

Brenda talked on and on, recounting her adventures, the coffee harvest, the poetry festival. It had been wonderful, wonderful, better than she had even expected. And sad, too. Of course, with the war, also very, very sad. Bittersweet, in fact, a good Greek word, Erika thinks, sipping her retsina as Brenda describes the women poets she met. Yes, a word coined by Sappho, another woman poet, the first of the line. Bittersweet. Love and hate, that's the insides of me. And armed love, love for the people—to hold a gun in one hand, a child in the other.

Dan sighs, leans back in his chair, lights a cigarette. Erika watches him and waits, but he says nothing. He is looking across the table at Simon. And Simon, crushing out a butt in the ashtray, says with a bitterness Erika has not heard from him in a long time,

"And Paul's going to spend his life in the hole for blowing up a few buildings. I wish to God he'd taken some of those bastards out first."

And Dan, as though waiting for it, as though knowing it was coming, says,

"There's always the temptation to think that. When your man is going down and you think, For *what*? Christ, for *what*? Why the hell didn't he do something worth the price? But, see, Simon, the only thing we got going for us is that our brothers are righteous men, the prisons of America are filling up with righteous men. That's what keeps us going—righteous anger. It's all we've got. Let Jehovah take care of the bastards. Let us just take care of Paul Rousseau."

247

And his children, Erika thought with a bitterness of her own, who's going to take care of them?

Trial date minus five. Erika and Dan sit up late. Erika is wearing a red silk kimono and drinking wine, finishing a bottle she opened at dinner. Dan is smoking a Marlboro and watching her intently. He is thinking that she is simply unaware of her presence, the kimono, hair damp and fragrant from her shower, the glass of wine, now plucking a cigarette from his pack, smiling at him, asking him questions, a woman at ease in her own home, an innocence about it, or perhaps she has no interest in him, thinks he's an old man....And Erika is thinking how she hasn't told Simon about meeting Annie, not about the meeting or the FALN, the bust, their escape, the safe house, nothing. She still has Annie's letter, had tucked it into her pocket when Annie gave it to her (thank God or it would have been left there for the FBI to find), but she can't give it to Simon to bring in to Paul. No, she can't say anything to him at all, can't put him in that position. She has to protect him now. If he were ever subpoenaed and asked about Annie he could answer truthfully that he didn't know anything. And smiling at Dan, she is thinking that he is quite right: nobody should know more than he absolutely needs to know. About anything.

But she is getting high, she wants to speak, she wants to tell Dan, just say her name out loud: Annie.

Instead she asks what happened while she was gone, what did she miss.

"Oh, let's see," he says. "A major upset in the Celtics game against New York. Jonathan almost coming to blows with the assistant D.A. on this issue of keeping Paul in solitary, a press conference on the warden's harassment of counsel. Then we were all set

248

to go to hearing on the suppression motion, and the judge had indicated very strongly that he was going to grant it, when the government decided to withdraw from the evidentiary list anything taken from Paul's house, thus muting the whole question."

"Well, that's great, isn't it? You've won."

"Not exactly. See they have virtually the same stuff that they got out of Bobby's house, all of it as incriminating as hell, but because Bobby isn't charged, we have no standing to move to suppress it."

"Gee, I bet Paul is happy."

Dan smiles somewhat ruefully at her. "And then, let's see, what else? Oh, yes, there was the night Simon beat the shit out of that bartender at the Second Front."

"No he didn't," she says, cool as ice.

"No, he didn't. We did discuss it, though, but ultimately we decided it might prejudice our client's case."

"Three against one, I'd say."

"Jon and I would only have been innocent bystanders."

"And did he tell you why he wanted to beat up the bartender?"

Dan doesn't reply at once. He leans back in his chair and stretches. He is wearing a green t-shirt that says *Free Rice and Poindexter*. The muscles in his arms strain against the sleeves, but his hair hangs to his shoulders. He looks like the Left's answer to Sylvester Stallone.

He finishes his stretch and then lifts his eyebrows back at her. "Some," he says. "Sounds like you're putting your old man through his paces."

"I don't do it often."

"My old lady does it to me now and again too."

"And you survive?"

"Here I am."

"Do you think Simon and I will survive?"

249

"Sure. Just look what you pick for competition."

Erika feels herself bristle. "You don't know him," she says.

"I don't have to know him. I just have to know you."

"Maybe you don't know me either."

He gestures at the room. "*By their works ye shall know them. By their works, Erika.*"

She glances around the room, too. She sees books, newspapers, shelves of records, her drawing table with all her paraphernalia on it and around it—sketch pads, pens, ink. She sees a scattering of children's toys on the rug next to a sleeping cat, Simon's plants by the window, the piano with pictures on it of friends and family and hanging above it on the wall Noah's painting of dinosaurs and flowers entitled *What It's Like In Heaven.*

"It's only stuff," she says. "I didn't make it."

He leans back in his chair, runs his hand through his hair, smiles and shakes his head. She recognizes him now as one of those masked gods, the travelling *kachinas.* She wants him to speak to her from that place of judgement, with all his authority, and to tell her clearly what she already knows.

"Liar," he says.

"Add it to the list."

"I'm not keeping a list. But do I take that as an admission?"

"Sure. I'm lying. I did make it all. Wove the rug. Built the table."

"Made the babies, fed the cats."

"Made the babies, fed the cats. And now you know what it feels like? It feels like a trap."

"It is, if that's what you choose to call it. You could as easily call it a little bit of paradise. Whatever you call it, that's what it will be."

"You believe in the power of words, don't you?"

250

"I have to. Words are the only weapons I carry, and it's a dangerous world. I've known many men who have gone away for many years because of the words they espoused and chose to live by. Paul Rousseau is only one of them. These guys, Poindexter and Rice, two fine men, Black Panthers, framed fifteen years ago because they organized a chapter of the National Committee to Combat Fascism. Elmo Geronimo Pratt, survivor of the FBI raid on the Panthers' L.A. headquarters, four days after the Chicago pigs killed Fred Hampton and Mark Clark. You remember that obscenity, I'm sure. These men are paying dearly, not for anything they did, but because of the words they used, like Paul uses them, the words he uses to describe why. Not what but why. Words. Paul Rousseau's major crime is that he says what he says. He stands up and speaks his mind. The government can't prove their case against him. There are no witnesses. There is no real tangible proof. There's a lot of reasonable doubt, believe me. And yet, just look at the man. He's a defiant son of a bitch. He scares the shit out of them. He looks guilty and he sounds guilty. His very existence threatens something the enemy holds dear: all the lies. The man refuses to join in on the lie. Sure, he'll say he's guilty of no crimes. That's because he doesn't believe bombing a military installation or the Bank of South Africa is a crime. He believes it's a moral act. He believes that if he did anything less, then he'd be guilty, as, by implication, all the rest of us are. Unless we can gag him in the courtroom, he's going to speak his mind and they're going to put him away for it. So now tell me how this beautiful, loving home is a prison, how your old man is the turnkey, how you're trapped in here and can't get out. Use those words for me."

There is a long but not awkward pause. The warmth in the voice takes out the sting of the words. There is a sensuality about Dan's voice. *Use those words for me.* A huskiness, sexual, he would say it the same way making love. Erika plucks another cigarette from his pack, empties the remainder of the wine into her glass. Her judgement about Dan: he is not a man who calculates, who measures. She knows this about him when he tips waitresses at lunch. She wonders if he is like this with women, too, uncalculating, openhearted.

"What's that Blake poem about building a hell in heaven's despite?"

"Yes. I know it. Or I used to."

"I don't want to do that."

"No. You just want to shake Simon off for a little while and see what happens."

"He's different now, you know. He was so grim, before Paul's case. He never laughed."

"My old lady says the same about me."

"So dourness is the price you pay for being politically correct?"

Her sarcasm glances off him. He smiles again, sucks on his cigarette.

"Maybe it's the price of a certain awareness. Look at what we do or what is done by other people in our name. Your name. My name. It's hard to stay lighthearted."

"Well, I'll tell you, if I ever do leave Simon it will be because of that, because he doesn't laugh enough."

"But you never will leave him. Even I can see that. You love each other. 'And stern as death is love, relentless as the nether world is devotion, its flames are a blazing fire. Deep waters cannot quench love nor floods sweep it away.' "

"Makes love sound a little scary."

"Only words. Though Solomon was reputed to be a pretty smart guy."

"Have you memorized the entire Bible?"

252

"Only the good parts." And he laughs a deep laugh like the rumbling of a mountain. A cat perks up its head, listens for a minute, then lies down again. Erika remembers when she thought Dan Weinberg was cold and arrogant. Before he smiled at her.

And while they continued to talk Erika thought again how alike she and Paul Rousseau were, how they both wanted two lives, how they both imprisoned themselves with words. And acts. Words and then acts. Now by another act their lives were going to be forever mingled, as much as if she had slept with him that night twelve years ago and borne his child. If Annie didn't surface, or even if she did, for the time it took her to get out, for those years, if not forever, she would take the children. For Annie.

Trial date minus four. Simon receives a call from New York. Marlene. She tells him she turned down the plea bargain so they went one better. In return for her testimony against Bobby and Paul and information leading to the arrest and conviction of other clandestine resistance groups, they promised her immunity from prosecution, relocation and change of identity for herself and her children under the Witness Protection Act (reunion with her children, that's what they promised her) and a quarter of a million dollars.

There is a pause. Simon thinks of her, thin and quiet, a farm girl from Vermont, avid reader of Gothic romances, faced with smooth talking lawyers from the United States District Attorney's Office. In the pause he thinks how he cannot offer her advice, his own client's interests are at stake, this is altogether different from copping a plea, this is selling out everything. And yet he, Simon Donnis, knowing everything he knows, knowing how difficult everything is, knowing something about suffering and temptation, a little

253

about loyalty and very much about being torn, finds that despite what it might mean, he is ready to forgive, to comfort and forgive. In the pause. And then she says,

"I just wanted you to know, Simon. If they're trying to buy me it must mean they don't have a rat. But what an insult, huh? I couldn't believe it. I said, 'I'd tell you boys to go fuck yourselves, but you'd probably enjoy it too much.' Oh, Simon, the world really sucks."

Trial date minus three. The living room has been transformed into a war room. Folding tables with stacks of paper. Boxes of discovery lined up on the couch, sharing space with sleeping cats. Children are asked not to play in this room; children are bribed.

The indictment against Paul is for two counts of malicious damage to United States property by means of explosives and one count of conspiracy to commit malicious damage to government property by means of explosives. The alleged overt acts include bombings at a naval shipyard and a marine recruitment center; the conspiracy charge involves planning the bombing of the National Guard Armory with two confederates. One of these so-called confederates was killed in a car crash after a police chase. The other turned weasel and is the government's chief and only witness in the case. The indictments are now ten years old. The government's evidence consists of the testimony of the fink and corroborating evidence from Bobby and Marlene's house, attenuated at best. But the government is in a bind. Under the provisions of the Speedy Trial Act, they either have to go to trial or dismiss the charges and until the New York grand jury returns indictments, these old ones are all the government has on Paul Rousseau, terrorist, insurgent and incendiary, all that's keeping him from walking.

254

The judge, despite government objections, has ordered that Paul will enter his courtroom without physical restraints and without an overt security presence to influence the jury. The judge insists that the case be presented to the jury as an ordinary criminal case and reminds the prosecution that any violation of his orders may result in a defense motion for a mistrial.

A mistrial, however, is not what the defense wants. The defense is in a race against time. If they can keep their client quiet, if he will let them use the law to his advantage, if the grand jury in New York drags its feet, they may yet see Paul Rousseau walk out of the courtroom a free man.

Time is of utmost importance. They have divied up the cross examinations and figured out the time each will take. Foundation witnesses—the fire chiefs, the local police, the officers in charge of the various bombing sites, the investigating FBI agents—are Jonathan's. Two days. The corroborating witnesses—Rousseau's old landlord from ten years ago and the FBI agents who searched Bobby and Marlene's house—are Simon's. Two days. But the plum, the virtuoso cross, is reserved for Dan who has taken government spies apart on the stand before and is looking forward to making a meal out of this one, the government's star, Frankie DeRose. Three days. No, better make it four.

Simon will do the opening, Dan the close. The defense will call no witnesses. The government will not be able to prove its case. If by some miracle they get an acquittal before the grand jury returns indictments in New York, Paul Rousseau will be free.

Trial date minus two. Night. The lawyers sit around the living room in various positions reading through the discovery for the fifth or sixth time. The

255

most important document is the statement made by DeRose when he was picked up by the State Police ten years ago. Running away from a burning car that his best friend was dying inside of. A nice guy from the word go. It was some statement, too. Two hundred odd pages. Called spilling your guts. They had to know it by heart, every word of it. They had to trip him up in his own words.

There were medical records on Frankie, too. While Erika talked to Denora about George's insomnia, Dan would get on the phone and ask her what she knew about manipulative personalities and pathological liars.

Then there were the somewhat damaging contents of Bobby's house which included a manual written by Paul with detailed instructions on how to form a revolutionary cell and a draft of an essay in Paul's own writing on the necessity of armed resistance.

The only other evidence the government had was the testimony of Paul's landlord who identified Paul as his tenant right after he went underground and let the Feds search his apartment. They found blasting caps, but in the basement, and the basement was kept unlocked and was easily accessible to anyone including six different sets of tenants. In the apartment itself they found too many pocket watches for one normal man to need and political writings that the government would say bore a striking similarity to the political statement found at the bombing sites and in Frankie DeRose's burnt Chevrolet.

Trial date minus one. They work at the office through dinner, come home, open a few beers, watch the game. They are too tense to do anything more. Jury selection starts the next day.

Paul is talking again about politics in command. He isn't happy with the thrust of the defense. And word from New York isn't good either. The grand jury is working overtime, but what exactly it is they are working on no one seems to know.

The subtext of the household is mournful, too. Arnold the goldfish died during the night. Becky spent the evening sobbing in her room. Noah tried to make it make sense by asking, "If we called it something else would Arnold still be dead? Like instead of *dead*, if we called it *balloon*?"

Erika doesn't know what to do about death, what to say. She cannot find the right words of comfort. She says, Some people say...Some people think...They look at her and say, But what really happens, Mommy? What do *you* say?

And she thinks of Socrates' saying, *Swans sing before they die...No evil can happen to a good man.* She says, "I think if you love something enough nothing really bad can happen. If you love something enough, it matters. Anything is possible."

And Becky, sobbing deeply but recovering, says, "God didn't die, you know. He did die first, then he came back to life. That happens if you're good."

"Where did you hear that?" Erika asks.

"At recess."

And Noah says, "What about cats? They're good. What about Arnold? He was good."

Erika goes to the bathroom, locks the door, sits on the edge of the tub and cries.

II

A rainy Valentine's Day. Every year the mysterious Valentine Bandit strikes the city in dead of night leaving behind him a trail of red hearts taped up all over the city, on windows and doors, on walls and posts, under windshield wipers, even manages under cover of darkness to scale the side of the museum and drape a red heart banner from the roof, hangs another from the wall of the abandoned civil war fort in the harbor. The loveliness of it, every year, rain or shine, to wake up in a city decked out in hearts. But there are no soggy red hearts gracing the peninsula this year. Instead there are barricades sealing off a six block area around the Federal Courthouse, and the streets are patrolled by city cops and state troopers, by U.S. Marshalls and undercover Feds, and vans of helmeted riot police squat all around the old section of the city, waiting. Sharp- shooters are up on the roofs. The city feels like an armed camp. There are some exploits even the Valentine Bandit will not attempt.

Like a regicide or the leader of a peasant revolt, Paul Rousseau is brought to the Federal Courthouse in chains.

On the other side of the barricades, sad-faced people gather. Middle-aged Viet Nam vets, old time Diggers, mountain men after twenty years gathered together again, remembering other days, their whole life stories reenacted here. There are no Valentine Day hearts hanging on the doors of the courthouse. The drizzle becomes heavier by noon.

Among the suits, speculation is that the Dead are in town. The suits, as usual, are wrong.

On the second day there is a slight scuffle at one of the barricades, some shouting, the threat of an arrest.

Reporters congregate like vultures around the courthouse. They surround Simon as he comes out. He refuses to talk to them. But Erika, watching the news that night, gets a glimpse of him and the swarm of reporters and the phalanx of armed marshalls. On the

258

other side of the barricades, as the camera pans, she sees veterans in combat fatigues and war paint, fists raised, and supporters with their banners (*Paul Rousseau is a Prisoner of War*), new recruits radicalized by Reagan and nuclear power and Nicaragua. Then someone off screen yells out, *Right on, brother!*, and Simon turns toward the voice and smiles and raises his hand, not in a clenched fist but in a V and Erika feels her heart go out to him complete and entire, their past rushing back to meet their present, all of it of a piece again.

At each entrance to the courthouse a portable metal detector has been set up and every person coming into the building for any business must pass through. Another is set up directly outside the courtroom door where security officers also hand-search packs, bags, briefcases, and women's purses. The courtroom itself is on the second floor, a high-ceilinged, wood-panelled room decorated with the portraits of former judges in heavy, gilded frames. The courtroom is tense. Glancing around, Erika realizes that a good number of the men in blue suits are probably plainclothesmen or Feds armed to the teeth. She goes up to the low railing which separates the spectators from the inner sanctum of the court and says hello to Simon and Company who look positively cheerful. On the other side of the aisle the government attorneys are scowling into their papers.

"What's new? The other side looks like it has gas."

"We just had a little session in chambers. The judge doesn't like the security arrangements. The marshalls are too overt and the jury's picking up on it. If Paul sneezes too loud some asshole in the back makes a lunge for him."

The side door opened then and a gang of marshalls came in with an unshackled, unhandcuffed Paul Rousseau. He entered like a monarch, a king in exile, dignified, proud, his eye taking in the room, the spectators, seeing immediately, so Erika imagines, those who were his enemies and those who were his vassals. A few minutes later the bailiff sang out the litany of the court: Oyez, oyez, the District Court of the United States....and everyone stood for the gaunt, white-haired judge who himself remained standing as the jury entered and took their seats. Only then did the bailiff give the call that permitted the rest of the room to sit down. It was the jury, not the judge, that was the honorable body here, the ones whose duty it was to try to see with the eyes of god.

"Good morning, ladies and gentlemen," says the judge to the jury.

"Good morning, judge," the jury replies.

"Good morning, counsel. Mr. Donnis, are you ready for your opening?"

"Yes, Your Honor."

"Proceed."

And Simon proceeds. His task is to lay out the elements of the defense: Paul's background, familiar to at least two members of the jury, the two with French surnames who came from mill towns similar to Paul's; his years in Viet Nam, familiar to the veteran on the jury, who watches Simon intently; his organizing for the VVAW around military installations in the South and his bust for three marijuana cigarettes that led to a conviction and a five year sentence in one of the toughest penitentiaries in the South. His return to New England after his release, his organizing efforts around prison reform, his work with the state legislature, his membership on the boards of various community organizations, his public positions opposed to militarism and police brutality.

"So public," Simon said, "that some of the so-called clandestine meetings upon which the government's conspiracy charge rests were actually written up and published in a monthly newsletter distributed across the state."

Up until this point, Paul Rousseau was no different from any number of other men whose experience in the late '60s and early 70s made them realize that something somewhere had to change.

And then what happened?

Then there were three bombings in the state. After one of them a certain Frankie DeRose was busted speeding through a police barricade. Arrested and interrogated, he confessed everything, incriminating a pal of his, a comrade, a friend, Paul Rousseau.

"That was ten years ago, ladies and gentlemen. The basis of the government's case against this defendant was then and still is now the testimony of one man and that man is a convicted felon."

Simon talks, Erika watches. She wants to try to see him as the jury sees him. She wants to feel his weight as the jury might feel it. To weigh him. Is he the sort of man a stranger would believe? Is he the sort of man a stranger would trust? How, after all, does a jury make up its mind? Erika tries to separate herself from him to see him, to hear what his voice says without the words. She thinks: this man is my husband. She hasn't thought of Simon as her husband in a long time. She hasn't used that word. The word itself offended her, suggested duty and obligation. The word lover appealed to her more. A lover wasn't obligated, a lover's love was freely given, was deserved not simply expected, or was undeserved, simply given not bartered. When, she wonders, when did she ever become such a purveyor of words?

Now finally she allows herself to think of Marc. She thinks of him and to her surprise she finds herself

261

diminishing. She sits on the hard bench and feels herself begin to shrink. Instead of expanding to include him, her world reduces itself for him, she steps out of it entirely to meet him on neutral ground. But on neutral ground she is empty-handed, lost, alone. She has nothing to give him. The lilacs from her garden seemed poisonous when she put them on his table, the birthday cake she baked him made her gag. Her own creatures, her creations, betray her. She becomes someone she can't recognize, someone she can't expect him to love. The one thing she had always refused to see, but that he saw so clearly, is now revealed to her: the relationship itself, its very existence, is a lie.

Simon finishes and sits down. The government calls its first witness. The trial of anti-U.S. terrorist/revolutionary Paul Rousseau has finally begun.

It is two days later, the day that Frankie DeRose takes the stand, that the first bomb threat is received. The judge calls for a recess, the jury leaves, the courtroom is cleared. No bomb is found.

The next day there is another call. Scuttlebutt has it that even the judge has been threatened. Then on the seventh day of the trial a new set of demonstrators appears on the street, the neo-fascists with their own banners proclaiming Rousseau a communist, demanding the death penalty, a public execution, for his treason against his country. There are clashes between left and right, the police move in to separate the two groups, a veteran in his army uniform decks one of the fascists, a skinhead kid young enough to be his son. The city cops have been holding back but this time there are a few arrests. It is a situation with the potential of turning very nasty at any moment.

262

So many armed marshalls surround the defendant when he is moved back and forth from the courthouse that he can barely be picked up by the television cameras. Erika notices that two plainclothesmen are staying close to Simon, too.

During the day he is frantically busy, during the evening, too. By the time he finally comes to bed, he cannot begin to make love to her. She doesn't expect him to. One night he asks her if she's called Marc yet. She tells him, truthfully, that she hasn't thought about it.

"Who *are* these people?" Jon asks at breakfast, looking over the newspaper's front page photograph of the latest of the daily noon-time street demonstrations and counter-demonstrations outside the courthouse.

"I don't know about all of them, but I'd guess that from one half to two-thirds of them are employees of the United States government," Dan says.

"On both sides, too, I'll bet."

"Absolutely. Who's phoning in bomb threats? It's not our side, I'll tell you that much. If they intend to strike, they're not going to call in first and announce it."

"So what's the scenario here? I just don't get it."

"Paul Rousseau is a dangerous man. See how powerful he is? He can drive other men to kill each other on the streets." And Dan lifts his eyebrow, gives Jon a nod. *Get it, Jon?* Jon scrunches up his long, scholar's face. He gets it but he doesn't like it one bit.

"So what do we do then? I mean, something's bound to happen out there, you know, and it's going to fuck up the whole case. I'm pretty optimistic at this point, but, like, if some asshole starts shooting.... Can't we just tell our people to go home?"

"If you can find our people out there, you can go ahead and tell them."

"What do you know that we don't?" Erika asks.

"The size of the FBI's payroll."

"But you said yourself, they can't *all*...."

"No, not all. But the ones who are know exactly what to say to people to make them do exactly the worst things, the most destructive things to their own cause, to twist words so that the worst possible scenario seems the best. Our people aren't out on the street. Mine aren't, anyway. I don't know what to tell them. I think we just ignore them. The jury are the only important people right now. Those twelve people, those are the only ones who count."

The eighth day of the trial. Still the courthouse is surrounded, still spectators are scanned, still at noon groups of people gather in the chill February sleet and hurl words at each other. Paul Rousseau sits quietly at the defense table, writes copious notes to his lawyers, seethes. The jury watches him more than they watch the witness on the stand. There is something magnetic about him. He has refused to speak to the press. He will not take the stand in his own defense. No one can figure out what makes him tick. But his eyes fascinate them, deep set, dark, burning eyes under bushy brows, the scar on his cheek, the face of someone who could as easily be a madman or a saint.

The eighth day, the day Daniel Weinberg of the silver tongue takes on Frankie DeRose, murderer, perjurer, snitch. Frankie is being guarded as heavily as Paul Rousseau. There are more reasons to guard him. Only the Feds are after Rousseau's blood, but the whole city is crawling with men who would love to get their hands on Frankie DeRose. Left unprotected on a city street, he wouldn't last a minute and he knows it.

264

He is a sallow, skinny man, thirty-three years old, most of them spent in one institution or another. But he's clever, has an intelligent face, a faultless delivery, directing his answers not to the questioning attorney but to the jury itself. He has been well-schooled in the tricks of the trade and has developed a charming manner. Yes, sir. No, sir. Humble yet assertive. Wears a blue suit to bring out the color of his eyes. His shoes shine. The prosecutor's last question would have made even a professional actor gag, but DeRose answers it without skipping a beat:

"Now will you tell the court, Mr. DeRose, why it was you agreed to cooperate with the government in the investigation of this defendant?"

"I agreed to it, sir, because I love my country."

Dan rises from the defense table to begin his cross.

I'd like to pick up just where my respected colleague left off, Mr. DeRose. You stated that you love your country, is that right?

Yes, sir.

Did you serve your country in the armed forces, Mr. DeRose?

No, sir.

Not in the army?

No, sir.

The Navy, the Marines?

No, sir.

Why not, Mr. DeRose?

I wasn't able to serve.

And why was that? Isn't it because you were in prison at the time other young men of your age were serving their country in the military? Men like Mr. Rousseau, for example. Isn't that the case, Mr. DeRose?

Yes, sir.

You do have a felony record, Mr. DeRose?

265

Yes, sir.

Can you tell me how long ago that record started?

In 1970.

How old were you then?

Seventeen.

And that first conviction, Mr. DeRose, what was the charge?

Breaking and entering.

Breaking and entering. And you served eighteen months on that charge, isn't that correct?

Yes, sir.

You served eighteen months, you were on the street approximately three months and then you were arrested on another felony charge, weren't you, Mr. DeRose?

Yes, sir.

And do you recall what that charge was?

It was an assault charge.

Assault on a police officer, wasn't it?

Yes, I believe it was.

And you were convicted on that charge and you did some more time, didn't you?

Yes, sir.

You were released in 1973, weren't you?

Yes, sir.

All right. Now I want to skip over the period between 1973 and 1975—but don't worry, we'll get back to it—and continue with this examination of your felony record. In 1981 you were charged and convicted on another felony charge, were you not?

Yes, sir.

Armed robbery, wasn't it?

I believe so, yes.

Armed robbery and assault with intent to kill, wasn't it, Mr. DeRose?

I believe that was the charge, yes.

266

And you are currently serving time on that conviction, Mr. DeRose?

Yes, sir.

Have you ever killed anyone, Mr. DeRose.

Yes, sir. But it was....

Just answer the question, Mr. DeRose. You have killed...someone?

Yes.

So, let's see what we have here, Mr. DeRose. We have breaking and entering, armed robbery, assault, assault with intent to kill, and manslaughter. Now, Mr. DeRose, when you talk about loving your country, as you did earlier today, I have to wonder what exactly you mean by that. Do you think committing crimes against your fellow citizens is a reasonable way of showing love for your country? Or was lying to the state police about Paul Rousseau a way of showing your love for your country?

Rousseau was a terrorist.

Given your record, Mr. DeRose, I can only say that you have a strange way of defining terms. Can you define terrorist for me, Mr. DeRose? Could it be someone who terrorizes people by assaulting them and robbing them and...

Objection. Mr. Weinberg is testifying, Your Honor.

Mr. Weinberg, you will refrain from answering your own questions. Sustained.

Now, you testified earlier that on October 12, 1974 you placed a bomb at the National Guard Armory, is that correct?

Yes.

And you constructed that bomb?

Yes.

Will you tell the jury exactly how that bomb was constructed?

You tape the sticks of dynamite together with a nine volt battery, a blasting cap in the middle of the sticks. Then you tape a Westclock pocket watch to the dynamite, attach the wire leading from the battery to the metal part at the back of the watch. Then at the site, you take the two wires from the blasting cap—you put alligator clips on them—place one on the front of the watch on the screw in the face and the second on the second lead of the battery. Then you wind the clock. When the minute hand winds down and touches the screw, the current comes from the battery, circulates around from the battery to the watch to the blasting cap back to the second lead of the blasting cap and completes the circuit. You set it for a twenty minute lead time, so you place it and then you have twenty minutes to make your calls.

After you placed the bomb at the armory, you called the local police station?

Yes, sir.

Then you drove the car back?

Yes, sir.

But you didn't get back, did you?

No, sir.

You picked up a state trooper on the highway, didn't you?

Yes, sir.

You ran a police barricade?

Yes, sir.

And the car you were driving crashed and your passenger, your buddy, died.

Yes, sir.

Now, after they brought you back from the hospital, where did they put you?

I was in a cell.

And where was the cell located?

At the state police barracks.

And two detectives arrived?

268

Yes, sir.

And what did they do?

They asked me what I wanted and I said I wanted to talk to them and see if we could make an arrangement. I said I wanted to confess.

What do you mean, 'make an arrangement'?"

I asked about leniency.

And what did they say to that?

They said they'd have to talk it over with the DA.

What did you have in mind when you were talking about leniency?

I had in mind confessing and getting some leniency in return for testimony.

Testimony against people you claim had been with you on these events?

Yes, sir.

But the man who had been with you was dead, wasn't he?

Yes, sir.

So it wouldn't do any good to testify against him, would it?

No, sir.

So you had to think of somebody else to testify against, didn't you? Some other friend of yours you could testify against, Mr. DeRose, isn't that right?

Objection, Your Honor.

You are badgering, Mr. Weinberg. Strike that last remark.

You had in mind confessing in return for leniency and giving testimony against friends of yours you claim participated in these events with you. Is that correct?

Yes, sir.

Is that correct: your friends?

Yes.

People you had known for a long time.

Yes, sir.

People you had eaten with?

Yes.

And shared roofs with?

Yes.

Shared experiences with?

Yes.

People who had taken care of you when you were sick?

Yes.

People who took care of you when you were down and hurting.

Yes.

And you were going to turn these people in for some silver coins?

I object, Your Honor.

Sustained.

Have you received any money, Mr. DeRose, for your testimony?

No, sir.

I notice you are wearing a very nice suit. Did you own that suit two months ago?

No, sir.

And the grey one you were wearing yesterday? Is that a fairly new suit as well?

Yes, sir.

Are you being housed in the county jail during your stay in the city?

No, sir.

At the state prison?

No, sir.

In fact, you're staying at a hotel, aren't you, Mr. DeRose?

Objection.

Sustained.

Have you been offered a change of identity for your testimony?

Yes, sir.

270

Have you been offered protection?

Yes, sir.

Mr. DeRose, did you stab a fellow inmate to death in the state prison?

Yes, sir.

Were you prosecuted?

No, sir.

The police knew of the incident, didn't they?

Yes, sir. It was self-defense.

You claimed it was self-defense, is that correct?

Yes, sir.

I see. Now were you aware back in 1974 that the FBI was interested in making an arrest of Mr. Rousseau?

Not until I was arrested.

You never heard it on the street?

I don't recall.

Anyone ever come up to you and offer you money if you would turn him in or set him up?

Prior to my arrest?

Prior.

No, sir.

Only afterwards?

I haven't been offered money.

Only leniency.

Yes, sir.

Did you ever turn anyone in before?

No.

Never set up a drug deal?

I was questioned once.

Did you give information to the police that led to an arrest?

Yes, sir.

Did you testify in that case?

Yes, sir.

Now to get back to your conversation in the state police barracks. This transcript, Mr. DeRose, reads like a slice of Swiss cheese, every five minutes or so the transcript indicates you went off the record. Do you recall what transpired in those times?

I think I went to the bathroom.

Do you recall the detectives telling you to rephrase something you said or to say it in a different way?

I don't recall that.

What can these expressions mean, Mr. DeRose: references to 'earlier talks', references to 'no more slipups'?

I have no idea.

How was it explained to you that the FBI was involved in picking you up for highway speeding?

I don't remember.

It didn't strike you as odd that within twenty minutes of planting an exploding device at a National Guard Armory, before the bomb had even gone off, in fact, you're picked up for speeding and the FBI is right there, waiting for you at the state police barracks. That didn't strike you as odd, Mr. DeRose?

I don't remember that it did.

It's hard to remember back over all these years, isn't it?

Yes, sir.

It's hard to remember all the facts, isn't it?

Yes, sir.

And to separate the truth from the version of the story you have been asked to tell.

I object, Your Honor.

Mr. Weinberg, you will refrain from commenting. That will be stricken.

The judge took that opportunity, since it was quite late in the afternoon, to recess until the following day.

You testified that Mr. Rousseau recruited you in 1974 and trained you to be a revolutionary, is that correct?

Yes, sir.

That you considered yourself a member of his group, his cell, as you put it?

Yes, sir.

That you took your orders from him?

Yes, sir.

Now could you explain to the jury how Mr. Rousseau trained you to be a revolutionary?

Yes. While I was in the state prison, the defendant would come in to visit and he started teaching me his revolutionary philosophy and I identified with what he was saying and upon my release I began working with him in his political action.

All right. Now you said Mr. Rousseau started teaching you his revolutionary philosophy. Could you tell us what this was, explain it to us a little bit?

Rousseau told us it wasn't our fault that we were in prison, we were there because we were poor and we committed crimes because we were trying to survive. That the only way to stop this from happening was to overthrow the government. A lot of this was based on the ideas of Che Guevara and George Jackson.

Did Mr. Rousseau ever invite you to go with him to lobby at the state legislature?

Yes.

Did you go with him?

Once or twice.

What did you do there?

We spoke to people. To the legislature up there.

Did he mention getting various laws passed to help people in prison?

Yes.

273

Did he suggest to you that you should testify before the legislature on these laws that would make prisons better for prisoners?

Yes, he did.

Did he himself testify at these hearings?

I believe he did, yes.

Now, when you discussed overthrowing the government, how were you intending to do this?

By attacking various important targets.

Who determined which targets were the important ones?

We decided the military and big business.

How did you determine this?

Rousseau did that.

First you said 'we', now it's Rousseau alone. Who chose the targets?

We made up a list.

You and he together?

Yes.

Was anyone else present?

Yes.

How many would you say?

Ten, fifteen.

This was a fairly large group of people making up this list, wasn't it?

Yes, sir.

Do you recall the names of the companies on the list?

Polaroid, General Electric...

Now, just a moment. Do you know why, for example, Polaroid was on the list?

No, sir. I have no idea.

Do you know that Polaroid is a large employer in South Africa?

No, sir.

Do you know anything about General Electric and its foreign investments?

No, sir.

Now this original list that you say was compiled by ten or fifteen people, was this list made available to people?

To us, yes.

Was it given to each of you?

Yes.

Was it made public in any other way?

I don't know.

May I approach the witness? Mr. DeRose, this is a copy of a newspaper called *The Prison Advocate* dated July 1974. Will you look at the article on page two entitled Notes from a Revolutionary Cell written under Paul Rousseau's byline and look at the names of companies on that list under the heading *Targets: Enemies of the People*? Would you mind reading those out loud, please.

Polaroid, General Electric, General Dynamics, Litton Industries....

Thank you. Now, did Mr. Rousseau explain to you why these companies—the list is quite long—were enemies of the people?

He told us that we were victims of the justice system. The justice system is supported by big business. The laws are made to protect the rich and imprison the poor.

Do you still believe that?

Not as much as I did.

What's changed your mind?

I think things have changed for the better.

Better for you?

For the country.

And this is what you were thinking when you agreed to talk to the FBI?

I wasn't thinking so much about that at the time.

You were thinking about yourself, is that correct?

Yes.

About how life might be better for you?

Yes.

Now in respect to the revolutionary cell that you claim to have been a part of, what was your function in that cell?

I mostly constructed explosives.

At that time you were the only member of the group who knew how to construct these devices, were you not?

Yes.

You taught Paul Rousseau how to make that type of bomb you described to the jury?

Yes.

Now when it came time to choose targets for these bombs, you stated that you had the list of companies compiled at a meeting in July 1974, the same list that was subsequently published in *The Prison Advocate,* is that correct?

Yes, sir.

Now, Mr. DeRose, you stated in your previous testimony that after you and Mr. Rousseau and ten to fifteen other people made up this list, and after you taught them all to construct bombs, that you then did nothing until October when word reached you, as you said during your direct examination, word reached you that 'Rousseau says it's time to act'. Is this an accurate summary of your testimony in this court, Mr. DeRose?

Yes, sir.

Would you explain to the jury how word reached you?

Through Ouellette.

Through Robert Ouellette.

Yes, sir.

He told you 'Rousseau says it's time to act'?

Yes, sir.

Can you recollect his exact words?

Yes, sir. He said, Rousseau hit the shipyard last week. He says it's time to act.

I see. And on the word of Mr. Ouellette you and he set off the next morning with your bomb to blow up the National Guard Armory. Did you attempt to contact Mr. Rousseau?

No, sir.

Why not?

I didn't know exactly where he was.

Ouellette knew, didn't he?

Yes, sir. Well, he had spoken to him a few days before, but he didn't know his exact location either.

So solely on the word of Robert Ouellette, without checking it out with Mr. Rousseau, you and he placed a bomb at the National Guard Armory?

Yes, sir.

And in the process of the police chase afterwards, Mr. Ouellette was killed?

Yes, sir.

At no time prior to October 12th did you yourself speak to Mr. Rousseau about the bombing of the shipyard?

No, sir. It was Ouellette who spoke....

Excuse me. You did not speak to Mr. Rousseau about the bombing of the shipyard, did you, Mr. DeRose?

No, sir.

And have you spoken with Mr. Rousseau since October 12, 1974?

No, sir.

Now, Mr. DeRose, you are serving a prison sentence at this time, are you not?

Yes, sir.

For armed robbery, is that correct?

Yes, sir.

A crime that was committed subsequent to the events of October, 1974?

Yes, sir.

In other words, you served time, some time, for this bombing, you were released, and then you committed the robbery for which you are currently serving time, is that correct?

Yes, sir.

The time you're serving, the sentence is considerably lighter than the maximum penalty under law, isn't that true?

I object, Your Honor. Counsel is testifying.

Rephrase the question, Mr. Weinberg.

What was the sentence you received, Mr. DeRose, for that last armed robbery committed in 1981, six months after your release from prison on several other felony counts?

Seven years.

Are you aware that the maximum sentence in this state for armed robbery is twenty years?

Yes, sir.

Thank you. Now, Mr. DeRose, you have been in and out of jail since you were seventeen years old. And during those periods when you're not in jail, you're pretty much out on the street, aren't you?

More or less, yes.

It's hard to live on the street, isn't it?

I don't know what you mean.

I mean, when you don't have an education, your family has no money, your family, in fact, is broken, you don't have a home that's safe and secure, you have to depend on yourself from the time you're very young, you don't have any job experience or training, in such a case, you have to learn to use everything for your own advantage, don't you?

Yes.

Otherwise you don't survive, isn't that true?

Yes.

And in jail, it's the same way, isn't it?

Yes.

You have to use everything to protect yourself?

Yes.

Do you recall when you were in the state hospital any one of your doctors or therapists telling you you were a manipulative person?

No.

A pathological liar?

No.

Now these agreements you made with the state and the U.S. Attorney's office, do you recall these agreements?

Yes, sir.

You were offered a change of identity, weren't you?

Yes.

You were offered concurrent time?

Yes.

Protection in prison?

Yes.

Relocation after release?

Yes.

They were going to set you up someplace, is that correct?

They were going to bring me to a new town.

They weren't going to just drop you out of a speeding car, were they?

No, sir.

No, they're going to set you up, find you a place to live, find you a job.

I believe so, yes.

You were going to have a new life for yourself, is that right?

Yes, sir.

And you hope to be successful in your new life?

Yes, sir.

And the people who used to be your friends, people who took care of you, have you thought what kind of life they're going to have?

Yes, sir.

Your new life is going to be laid on the bones of these people, is that correct?

I feel they always had the opportunity to work something out.

They can turn around and tell lies about you?

They can tell lies, but if they tell lies, they'll know they're lies.

Yes, that's true. When people tell lies they know they're lies, don't they?

Yes, sir.

Judge, I have no further questions.

The defense team is cheerful. Simon smiles to reporters outside and Dan even says, "I am optimistic that this jury will find that the government is quite literally trying to hang an innocent man."

They go to check in at Simon's office; Erika picks Noah up and goes home. She is there only a few minutes when the phone rings. Simon.

"The New York grand jury came back with indictments this afternoon," Simon says. His voice is emotionless. "They've indicted Paul on ten counts of bombing and seditious conspiracy to overthrow the government by force. That's it, Erika. It's over."

III

The eleventh day. The government's corroborating witnesses. Paul's landlord from ten years ago who claims there were bomb-makings in his cellar. His memory is bad, the police report is lost, and no one has kept copies of the political tracts the police found in the apartment. Then the Feds who searched Bobby and Marlene's house. The claim is made that political writings found in their house and authored by Paul Rousseau himself are identical in style and content to the communique found at the armory site and in Frankie DeRose's car. The government is permitted to enter the writings themselves into evidence over the objections of the defense. It's powerful stuff. The writings in conjunction with other items found in Bobby's house—a small arsenal, the government calls it, a small munitions factory—lend credence to the government's contention that Paul Rousseau is not an innocent victim of the lies and perjuries of Frankie DeRose.

Simon takes the agent out on the issue of political writing styles, proving that DeRose's statement could as easily have issued forth from the pens of the Black Liberation Army, the Red Brigade, the FALN, the ghost of Che or Fidel himself. As to the relevance of any of the things in Bobby's house to an explosion that occurred ten years earlier and twelve hundred miles away, he can leave that to the intelligence of the jury.

Contained. Not annihilated but contained. The government rests its case. The defense has no case to present. The prosecution will spend the following day on its closing arguments. The jury is excused for the night, instructed as always not to read the newspaper or watch TV news, not to discuss the case with anyone, to sleep well.

That night, in the wake of the New York indictments, Paul Rousseau announces to the defense team during their usual nightly conference that he has decided to fire them and take up his own defense. He wants the opportunity to address the jury in a closing statement. There are some things he has to say.

"Why can't he win this one?" Erika asks Simon. "He's got lots more trials he can lose. Why can't he wait until he's in New York to say the United States government sucks?"

"It's one of the tenets of the movement," Dan answers, "that it is not possible for a revolutionary to get a fair trial. So if for a moment it seems like he might, then it is politically expedient to make sure it doesn't happen."

"Expedient for whom?"

"Expedient for him. I'm afraid Paul can't allow himself to be found not guilty."

The trial is almost over and still no word from Annie.

Of the events of the following morning, the twelfth day of the trial, Erika remembers everything.

It is such a normal morning: the alarms sound, people get up, breakfast gets made, *He Man* is on TV. The weather is ominous as it has been all month, grey, gloomy, bitter. One more day of this trial. No, this trial is over. Today and tomorrow will be different. Politics in command.

Erika watched them tie their ties, shut their briefcases, put on their coats. Noah, who has just learned the word, asks why Jon looks so glum.

"Because the bad guys are going to win, Noah."

"The bad guys never win."

"They do if the good guys give up."

"But the good guys never give up."

282

Dan picks Noah up and holds him, squirming like a little eel, at eye level.

"Young man," he says, "you've been watching too much TV."

"No I haven't," Noah replies stoutly, "I've been watching too many lawyers."

She tries to work, but everything she draws she hates.

She takes her pad into the bedroom, curls up on the bed and starts to sketch. She hasn't played like this in a long time. From memory she makes sketches of people she knows. They appear almost miraculously on the white paper—Simon, Dan, Brenda, Paul, Annie. Annie as she's seen her last. She stares at the page and then tears it up. Destroy the evidence. Create. Erase. Create. Erase.

Around noon the phone rings. Simon.

"Turn on the news," he says.

"What?"

"Turn on the TV news and then call me back. I'm at the office. Quick."

She turns on the news and sees a picture of a half-demolished building. Shell Oil's corporate headquarters in Houston, Texas. Hit by terrorists in one of the most daring attacks on an American corporation within the United States. At the same time smaller explosions damaged Shell offices in New York and Oak Brook, Illinois. Responsibility for the bombings was taken by the August 7th Brigade in a taped message. While the camera pans the rubble, a voice is heard:

We will resist American corporate imperialism which grows fat off the broken lives of Black South Africans. Shell Oil defies global boycotts. Shell Oil breaks Black unions. Shell Oil supports the White racist government of South Africa in its ongoing campaign of militarism and genocide. Shell Oil murders Black children in Soweto...

The newscaster reiterates that the August 7th Brigade has taken credit for the blasts that severely damaged three offices of Shell Oil, including the corporate headquarters in Houston. There were no injuries.

Erika switches stations and catches the taped message again. She sits and listens. The message is not for everyone. The message has a particular meaning, a subtext. It is a sort of cryptogram. What it really says is:

This is my answer. No compromise. No surrender.

The voice on the tape is a soft voice, a woman's voice. Annie's.

Later that afternoon Eli calls. He is desperate. He begs Erika to bring him to see his father in court the next day. He wants to hear the closing argument. He has talked to Paul on the phone every night, but he wants to see him, has to see him. He pleads, Erika can't say no. She drives the forty miles or so to Paul's mother's house with the radio on, brings Eli back to the city with the radio switched off.

"It's Annie you know. On the tape. It's Annie."
"Yes.
"What does Paul say?"
"He says it's Annie, too."
"No, I mean about the thing itself."
"He's pleased. Good choice of target. Successful operation. He's feeling pretty good tonight. Smug, I'd say. Happy."
"And what about you? What do you think?" She props herself up on her elbow and looks down on his face, even though she can't see him very well in the dark.
"I'm just thinking about tomorrow."

284

"The jury you mean?"

"Yeah, the jury. Paul. They'll know of course, and even if by some chance they don't, he's sure to tell them."

"What do you think it will do to the case?"

He sighs. He has spent the last few hours trying to calculate what the bombings of Shell Oil will do to the case. All the care, all the preparation, the grand scheme of seeing Paul walk out of the courtroom a free man, that was a fantasy from the first. He sees that now. They would never let that happen, never. So the grand jury was pressured into returning indictments and they did and that blew that dream out of the water. But it doesn't mean that the verdict doesn't matter here. It matters a great deal. For a conspiracy charge to stick, the government needs to prove predicate acts and here were three charges of predicate acts that could come in handy for them. Simon can't see making it any easier for them. That was point one. Then there was point two: the idea of going to trial in New York with a prior acquittal instead of a conviction, with a defendant who had just been found innocent by a jury. It gave the defense a psychological advantage and a strategic one. And then there was three: he just wanted to win.

His whole life was on the line, everything he had ever done, every choice he had made, the whole ballgame.

"If the August 7th Brigade is still active and Paul Rousseau is not, well that means somebody else is blowing things up, right?"

"Unless he has bilocation."

"And they haven't argued that he has. So in that sense it may help us. On the merits we should win. He should be acquitted. There's no reason why he shouldn't. Unless it's all bullshit."

"Unless Paul's right, you mean."

"Yes. He's right. I'm wrong."

285

"You're not wrong."

"Yeah? Who says?"

"Me. I say. I'm your wife and I say you're not wrong." She bends down and kisses him. It is hard to find his mouth in the dark. Once she does, to find the rest of him is not hard at all.

The next morning every major news service, every TV station and radio station, and every free lancer in the state wanted to talk to Simon about Paul Rousseau and the August 7th Brigade. Erika took the phone off the hook after the second 6 A.M. call. Simon had no comment anyway. Everything spoke for itself.

They descended on the courthouse and vied for position outside with the pro- and contra-forces; inside they vied with each other for seats, all these newspeople from away. The city had never seen the likes of it before. TV crews waited in the dreary chill outside, standing with the demonstators who were also out that morning in full strength, all of them waiting for Paul Rousseau to arrive in his armored car with his small army of guards, in his shackles and chains.

On the way to the courthouse Erika notices the Night Writer's latest work.

DEFINE TERRORISM
FREE PAUL ROUSSEAU

Security cannot be any more intense. Erika, holding Eli tightly by the hand, passes through the security checks. The marshalls and the court security men all know her by now. ("Good morning, Mrs. Donnis. And who is this young man? Not your son, is it?...Better grab a seat while you can. Going to be a full house this morning.")

286

Inside the courtroom there is a sense of excitement, a new energy. The bailiff calls for order. The room rises for the judge, remains standing for the jury, sits down again. But the ambiance is different. Newspeople may even outnumber Federal agents this morning. Everyone is squeezed together on the hard benches—friends and supporters cheek by jowl with U.S. marshalls, reporters, the FBI. And sitting close beside Erika, Paul Rousseau's eldest child, Eli Fidel.

"Mr. Rousseau," says the judge, "are you ready to proceed?"

Paul stands. "Yes," he says. He walks over from the defense table to be closer to the jury. She watches them, how they respond, whether they move their bodies away from him or lean closer. The foreman, code name Santa Claus for his florid cheeks and white beard, sits back in his chair, but keeps his eyes on Paul's face. They all make eye contact with him, the veteran, the two Francos, the young woman, the housewife. They are open to him. They haven't dismissed him yet.

Good morning, members of the jury. After all these days being in the same room together, I am pleased to finally have a chance to introduce myself to you. My name is Paul Rousseau. I am not a criminal.

I am not a criminal and this has not been a criminal trial. The evidence that has been presented against me is evidence that supports one thing: my long struggle against the imperialist policies of the United States government. This struggle is political and this has been a political trial. There has been no evidence presented during this trial that I did anything but speak and write and defend myself. Speaking and writing and defending oneself are not crimes in this country—not yet.

The prosecution has presented certain information about me, that I served in Viet Nam, for example, that I

287

have been a so-called fugitive from justice, and I would like to say a few things about these facts before discussing the charges themselves.

Yes, I served in Viet Nam. I did not learn demolition techniques there as the prosecution suggested. What I learned was what an invading army does to a small, poor country. I learned what the United States military could inflict on people, the pain, the suffering, the slaughter the United States military has the power to inflict. My best friend, a Black man, was killed in front of my eyes in Viet Nam. He was nineteen years old. I named my first child after him because if it hadn't been for him I wouldn't have lived to have a first child. There is no racism on the battlefield and the United States Army didn't care if Black men died side by side with whites, if we saved each other's lives or died for each other—that was OK with the United States Army. But just come home again, just come back to this country and see if there is no racism on the campuses, on the streets, in the job market, in politics, in where people can live and where they can go to school and how they feel walking down the street.

I didn't learn how to make bombs in Viet Nam. What I learned was the horror of war and the horror of greed which inspires war. I learned to hate that greed. Then I came home and I saw that it didn't just exist in other places, that greed and that war. It was right here, right in this state, right in my home town, right in the mill, where the owners oppress and abuse and have no respect for their own workers. You take that attitude and transport it across the ocean and you have Viet Nam.

This was not a very pleasant realization. I didn't want to come home from one war and jump into another. I wanted peace like everybody else. But I came

288

back and what I saw made it impossible for me to close my eyes.

I moved to the South after I was discharged, to organize against the war in Viet Nam. I was set up by an informant for the FBI, I was charged with selling three dollars worth of marijuana, and sentenced to five years. I had never been in prison before. It was a shocking experience. But I learned something there, too. I looked around and what I saw was a prison filled with poor men and working men serving time for economic crimes, taking because you're hungry, your family is hungry, and you can't provide for them in any other way.

Viet Nam and prison and my own home town taught me that the idea of justice and human dignity and freedom of expression—all those ideas we all believe in and were brought up believing in—have no real existence in this country except for a very small group of people. But for poor people, for working people, for Black and Hispanic people, in this state, for Franco-American people, for them there is no justice and no dignity and no freedom.

I realized there was no choice for me except to work however I could against those who make themselves rich off the labor and pain of others. My dream was to create a world in which no child would ever have to suffer from oppression and exploitation, from racism, from the domination of the few. This is the movement of which I am a part. I am a revolutionary. I resist the United States government in its imperialism abroad and its exploitation through corporate greed of its own people at home. But I am not a criminal.

Yesterday the attorney for the government pointed toward me and suggested to you that because I was a fugitive from justice I was a guilty man, because innocent men, says the attorney for the government, do not flee from justice.

This is true. Innocent men do not flee from justice. If there were justice, I would not have had to spend ten years of my life, my wife's life and my children's lives underground. But I also spent five years of my life in one of the worst prisons in this country for the crime of buying three joints, and there were men in that prison doing more time than I was for the crime of being Black and being on the wrong street at the wrong time. I knew what sort of justice I could expect. I can reel off names for you of men and women, political people, who have been captured by the government and haven't seen an ounce of justice. It may be hard for you to understand, hard for you to believe—it was hard for me to believe at first, too—but for some people it is not safe in this country, it is not safe to speak, it is not safe to be seen with certain people or to go to certain meetings. In Arizona, ladies and gentlemen, it is not even safe for people to speak their minds inside their own churches because of government spies...

Objection.

Sustained. This is not in evidence, Mr. Rousseau. The jury will disregard that statement.

What kind of justice can we expect from the FBI whose thirty or more agents armed to the teeth are in this very room today?

Objection.

Sustained.

These same men who in order to capture me and my family conducted a sweep operation in which they questioned hundreds of ordinary citizens, intimidated them, threatened them...

Objection.

Sustained. Mr. Rousseau, you cannot refer to information or alleged facts that have not been properly introduced into evidence during this trial.

When these agents arrested me, I was in the home of a friend with my three children. You heard testimony from the agent in charge of that arrest. You heard him say that there were forty agents on the scene. You heard him say they were armed with 12-gauge shotguns, and M-16's. You heard him testify that he knew that there were five young children in that house, my own and two others who lived there. You heard him testify that he knew the safest way to make the arrest would have been to call in, to telephone in to that house and inform us that the house was surrounded and the children were to be sent out. But this agent did not think we would have sent the children out. This agent thought we would have tried to shoot our way out or used our own children as hostages, and so he chose, in his own words, the most dangerous way. He assaulted the house, crashed through doors and windows, into a house with five children inside, all under ten years old. Now I will ask you, ladies and gentlemen, who are the terrorists?

Members of the jury, I have been charged with conspiracy. You have heard the evidence, or lack of evidence, in respect to this charge. But I would like to say a few things about conspiracy, and I would like you to think about them.

When whites stole Native American lands and the Indian people started fighting back, the government called that conspiracy.

When whites stole Black people from Africa and brought them here to be slaves and the Black people started fighting back, rebelled, escaped, and other people helped them and developed the Underground Railroad to get these fugitives out of the slave states and sometimes out of the country, the government called that conspiracy.

When a cross-section of people in this country organized to stop the war in Viet Nam, the government called that conspiracy.

291

When a cross-section of people today organize to stop the United States aggression in Central America, the government calls that conspiracy.

And every time, every time Black people try to organize their communities, the government calls that conspiracy.

The government's concept of conspiracy, members of the jury, is anything which is an organized resistance to its exploitation and injustice. The government's response to resistance of any kind is to criminalize it, destroy it or buy it off.

Please consider this when you come to decide whether I am innocent or guilty of conspiracy.

The defense in this case has taken the position that the government has no case against me. We do not bring into this courtroom witnesses who lie, who are bribed to lie. We do not report hearsay testimony of dead men. We do not offer you pieces of paper and tell you the similarities of phrasing mean that one piece of paper is the same as the other, or that it means a crime has been committed. We respect your intelligence too much to do that.

At the same time I am not going to stand here and distance myself from the people who wrote those words. Some of those words are mine and I believe in them. I am part of the resistance in this country. I support the armed struggle of the Black Liberation Army and the Fuerzas Armadas de Liberacion Nacional and the August 7th Brigade. I support them for the sake of my own children and all children, all over the world.

A world in which no child will ever have to suffer. Eli, fixed like a star beside her, does not move an inch.

292

It is over. An almost universal sigh goes up from the room. Erika is thinking of the squads. Eli begins to squirm, but she is thinking of something else, the armed resistance spread out across the country. The house in the west side ghetto of Chicago. The old woman who met her at the door. Ruth? Ain't no Ruth here. And how many sticks of dynamite in her cellar? And how many others like her? And Annie, at this very moment, where is she?

They stand for the jury to leave for recess, and in the shuffle of bodies, Eli slips away. She reaches out to grab him—"Eli, stay here!"—but he shakes her off—"He's *my* father!"—and begins to move forward. And Paul, hearing something behind him (Eli's voice perhaps) turns around, sees his son, reaches out for him.

As though the very air around them had convulsed and begun to move, four shapes erupt from the sides of the room and rush toward the center. Quick on his feet, Dan puts his body in front of Paul's and cries, "Your Honor!" Simon puts his hands out to the others as though to stop an avalanche with his bare hands. One of the men wields a stun gun, the others Simon cannot even see.

But the judge is hammering with his gavel and calling out for order and the convulsion eases, the head marshall gives the signal to back off.

Paul remains standing with Eli in his arms, the boy's body wrapped around his father's as though he were a tree while all around them the air still quakes. Foolishly, by moving forward like a tidal wave, scores of agents have made their presences known. Some spectators, expecting the worst, crouching down to the floor, sheepishly rise again. Eli holds on tight. Order is restored.

The judge orders counsel into chambers.

For Simon this is what it has been about all the time and now he was witnessing something he had only hoped to see: a Federal Court judge lambast a United States Attorney in chambers. He had never seen this judge so irate before, had never heard any judge castigate an attorney so severely. There had very nearly been a melee in his courtroom, there had very nearly been violence, unprovoked by the defendant, and due entirely to the government's insistence on placing so many armed marshalls in the courtroom

The essence of the scene, everything it represented, everything it said, spoke directly to Simon's heart. "The rights of the defendant to a fair trial have been severely jeopardized." He glances around. The white-haired patrician judge. The red-faced U.S. Attorney, shaken, speechless. Dan, leaning against a wall, relaxed, smoking a cigarette (something no other attorney would dare do in chambers), taking it all in. Paul, there by virtue of acting as his own counsel, in his chinos and red and black plaid flannel shirt (he wouldn't allow them to put him into a suit), managing to look like a Sandinista and a native son at the same time. And Simon himself, standing on the brink, watching all his loyalties being put to the test.

And Simon remembers the day in the prison so long ago, before he had found Erika and himself again, before she had exposed him, before he had been exposed to himself, before he realized he loved her and how much and why, so that all that was real was letting the past go and loving her again, so long ago it was that Paul Rousseau had looked at him and smiled, and yet that for him was a turning point, a moment of sight. He remembers what he realized then, that no matter how—or if—history would judge them, they were locked into a historical moment, their personal struggle was one that repeated itself over and over again throughout time, both archetypal and unique, both

294

universal and specific. Paul had taken one path, Simon had taken another. Now the paths were being judged, both paths, his as well as Paul's. Just as Paul needed to lose, Simon needed to win. Every man, Simon knew, lives in a historical moment, but not every man has the chance to have his choice within that moment judged. Soon he would hear his own verdict. Had he mistaken the moment? Had he chosen the right way? Was the time to be seized or assuaged? Was there justice here among these men in this frail ceremony of evidence and reasonable doubt, or was there only force, violence, the risk of starting again?

Risk. It was all risk. He was going to let the jury decide for them both.

But now he remembers the look on the face of the marshall, his ferocity. He feels his body react again as it had in that moment, his own ferocity rising to meet the enemy's. Like being ten years old again and being jumped on the way home from school, how from out of nowhere a dark inner place opens up and ferocity pours out. To feel that in a courtroom where reason must prevail was like having someone introduce his erect penis into a conversation. Now all sides had to reassert the presence of the civilized veneer, as though that cock had never shown up, that stun gun didn't exist, there was no brutality lurking beneath the order in the court. Simon, having recently examined photographs from El Salvador of what happens when the veneer is completely peeled away (ditches filled with mutilated corpses), could not say that he was displeased. When it came to brutality, the other side had a leg up on him and Simon had always been one of those kids smart enough to arrange things so he was always fighting it out on his own turf.

Paul had a different turf. His appeal was to that dark place wherever he found it, wherever he was, and he was a master at arousing it. He only had to touch the place and it moistened and came to life.

"No," he heard Paul say to the judge. "No mistrial. We don't have to confer on it. The jury has it all. It's up to them to decide."

Simon looks over at Dan. Dan nods. Yes, it's what they would have decided, too. But, Simon thinks, not for the same reasons.

Politics in command.

Erika and Eli leave the courthouse by a labyrinthine way to escape the reporters at the door. They are led through the maze by one of the courthouse security men who, at the door, pauses to wish them a good day. They are not planning to return for the government's rebuttal or the jury instructions. They are going to the country again to pick up Emma and George so all the children can hear the verdict. Erika is no longer ambivalent about this. They have a right to be there.

They stop at the house first for lunch. Erika puts the phone back on the hook and it rings in her hand.

"Hello, stranger, where have you been?"

It takes her a good ten seconds to recognize Marc's voice.

"Right here for the past three weeks."

"Not when I've called you haven't."

"Well, I'm here now for a few minutes."

"When can we see each other?"

"I don't know. Not right away. The trial's almost over."

"OK. Well, will you call me when you have time? Please, Erika."

Please.

"Sure. Or you call me. It's just not a good time now."

She hung up not knowing what exactly she had heard in his voice, hoping it wasn't what she thought, what she had always wanted to hear before, the last thing she wanted to hear now.

Over lunch Erika talks to Eli about what happened in the courtroom, about Paul, about how he feels.

"He said a lot of things," Eli says, carefully, slowly. "I've never heard him talk like that before. Is that why he's in jail, really?"

"There are a lot of reasons, Eli. But yes, I think so."

"I didn't know I was named after a friend of his. Is that why he likes Black people so much? It sounds like he does. We lived in a place with lots of Black people when I was little. I had fun there...I guess he sort of kept a lot of stuff pretty secret, huh?"

"He felt he had to."

"He still does."

"Does he?"

"Yeah. Like where Mom is."

"Maybe he doesn't know, Eli."

"Oh, he knows. He knows." And Eli's face becomes hard, for a few seconds, closed, hard, and Erika can see why from that look Paul himself had once recoiled.

The jury deliberated through dinner and at eight o'clock were sent home. The lawyers came home, too. They looked worried, all of them. None of the omens, as they read them anyway, were good.

After a quick dinner, Erika and Simon took the children back to the prison to see Paul. It was the first time Paul and Eli talked about politics. But Emma wanted to sit on his lap and George wanted to talk about going to the movies. So Eli contented himself with sitting near Paul as though he could absorb his thoughts by being close. He had discovered his father,

297

his real father, finally discovered him now that it was almost too late.

"But the jury could find him not guilty, right?" Eli asked Dan when they got home an hour later. "I mean, he isn't guilty, right, so why can't they just let him go?"

"You're right, Eli. The jury may find him not guilty. But there are other trials ahead. There's an indictment in New York, there may be a trial later in Massachusetts. There are grand juries meeting in Ohio and Illinois. So, see, even if we get an acquittal, they won't let your dad out of custody. They'll just move him to New York."

It was so depressing that even Eli looked like he might begin to cry.

They lie in bed together in the dark but neither of them can sleep.

"Have we ever talked about raising sheep?" Simon asks.

"No, I don't think so."

"No, I suppose not."

"Do you want to raise sheep?"

Simon reaches down to his pack of cigarettes, fishes one out, finds the match, strikes one, lights up.

"I want to stop smoking," he says. "When the trial's over. My lungs hurt."

"Simon, when the trial's over we have something to talk about."

"Let me guess."

There is a long silence while Simon smokes and Erika listens to the throbbing of her heart.

"Can this house get any bigger?" she asks finally.

"Any house can get bigger."

"After I'm going to ask you a question and if you say yes, we're going to need a bigger house."

"Ask me now."

"No, later."

"No, now. Come on, Erika. What are you thinking about?"

"Children."

Simon let the word hover in the air, settle in the dark somewhere in front of him at about eye level, where he could study it blindly while he smoked. So this is what had been on Erika's mind while he had been reading transcripts until he couldn't see, shaping cross-examination questions until he couldn't think, plotting strategy in his sleep. The important thing, the really important thing, and he had left it to her.

And then rushing in...the questions he hadn't asked, the argument he had neglected to make, all he had neglected, the threads slipping out of his hands, the threads he couldn't even see. But what did it matter anyway, what did any of it matter? Paul was doomed. His life wasted, his life gone, years and years, all his years, whatever else he might have done, whatever dreams he might have dreamt. In Marion, nothing to do, nothing to dream, terminal solitude, solitude at best, at worst, death. Death anyway. However you look at it, death.

...and the walls, the closed, lit spaces, never a moment of darkness, of soothing darkness, the pleasure of darkness, of slipping into it, like slipping into her body, the warmth and the dark, holding on and then letting go, letting it all go...

Erika took the cigarette out of his hand and eased him down, covered him, kissed him, let him sleep.

When by noon the next day the jury still hadn't come in, Erika put the kids in the car and took them to the movies. It was a school day, so they were virtually the only people in the theatre.

"We should've brought Noah," George said. "He'd love this movie."

Erika smiled. It was a good sign that George liked Noah so much.

Then, because she didn't want the pleasure of the afternoon to end quite yet, she brought them all to Brenda's house. Brenda was delighted. She hugged and kissed them, made them hot chocolate and served them cookies. Emma fixed herself like glue to Brenda's lap until Brenda suggested she look through the trunk of long skirts and old dresses and the boxes of jewelry, much of which Brenda wrapped up for her to take home. George sat in a corner and played with the Tarot cards. Eli looked through the binoculars at the birds and through the books at pictures of animals and knights.

"So are they living with their grandmother now permanently?" Brenda asked over tea, making sure the kids were out of earshot.

"No, they're on loan from Annie's sister. But I think that Simon and I might...."

"Oh, Erika!"

"What do you think?"

"You'll never come back as a rock."

"I might long to come back as a rock."

"You'll never have to do another good thing in your life if you do this."

"I won't have time to do another good thing in my life."

"They're wonderful kids."

"You might have to move in with us, though. As spiritual consultant."

"Buy a dishwasher right off. And some lottery tickets."

"Give me some numbers."

"Erika, seriously, I'll do whatever I can. If you really want me to move in with you...."

"I'm serious. We'll build you a room."

"God knows your kids are the only ones I'll ever have."

"I'll share. Gladly."

"You're a peach," Brenda said, pouring more tea into their cups. "You finally dumped him I take it."

"I guess I did."

"Wise woman. If you're going to put all that energy into kids, they might as well be under twelve."

Erika laughed and drank her tea. Outside the sea was high and grey, strong, ominous, like an act of will.

The phone rang three times that night. The first call, around six, was Brenda.

"I have a good feeling about Paul. Any news?"

"No. Did you do a reading?"

"Well, actually I tried. But I couldn't do it. Or rather, I could at last, you see. It had been arranged so that I could."

"You lost me."

"George, the lamb, tore up every bad card in the deck. Every single one of them. Ripped them right up."

"Oh, Brenda. I'm sorry!"

"No, don't be sorry. It's amazing, Erika. He knew which ones were the bad cards, not just the obvious ones like Death and the Devil, but the real esoteric ones, like the Hermit. He's a natural. You know, I myself have wanted to do that for years."

The second call, at seven—

"Hi, hon. How's it going?" Marc.

The third, a few minutes later, Simon.

"Jury's coming in. Get down here fast."

Erika arrives at the courthouse with her brood of five children and immediately asks to speak with the head marshall. She wants him to search the children himself, to see them, to know who they are. She doesn't mean to confront him, just to avoid any misunderstandings. She explains she may not be able to hold onto them all when they're inside and she wants his assurances that...."Don't worry, Mrs. Donnis," he says, though his tone is not conducive to tranquility and calm, "nothing like that's going to happen again."

The room is only half-filled tonight for the last act in the drama, reporters and FBI. She sits on a bench right behind the defense table. Marshalls move over for her, have gotten the high sign to be polite.

The bailiff gives his muezzin call, the judge enters, they all stand and remain standing as the jury files in. The jury sits. Everyone sits. Erika feels the tension in the room, in her stomach, in the small bodies beside her. She studies the backs in front of her: Jon's, slightly round-shouldered; Dan's, four-square; Simon's stiff; Paul's, completely relaxed. Then the clerk stands up and asks, "Mr. Foreman, have you reached a verdict?" and the foreman, nicknamed by them Santa Claus but considered non-sympathetic despite his benevolent looks, stands also.

Erika's heart is pounding now, unexpectedly, and her throat is tight. Even sitting she can feel her knees weaken. She finds she is holding three hands. How has she done this? Why did she bring them here? Emma is too young, doesn't understand it, still asks every night where her papa is, why he can't be home with them, why her mother is lost.

Meanwhile the foreman, at the judge's direction, or perhaps on his own initiative, turns to the defense table. He locks eyes with Paul Rousseau and Erika sees Daniel's hand grasp Simon's arm because the foreman is looking right at Paul and that means something but she can't remember what and the foreman clears his throat and says, "We have."

302

"As to count one," says the clerk (that he did knowingly and wilfully combine, confederate and agree with others to commit offenses against the United States by conspiring to maliciously damage by means of explosives...), "what is your verdict?"

"As to count one," says the foreman, looking now toward the clerk, while Erika steels herself, trying not to squeeze their hands, concentrating on relaxing her grip on the children's hands, "our verdict is not guilty."

Eli and George spring forward, but she holds them. "Not yet. Wait," she says.

"As to count two," asks the clerk (that he did wilfully and maliciously do damage by means of explosives...) "what is your verdict?"

"Not guilty."

"As to count three?"

"Not guilty."

And the cheery foreman smiles right at Erika who lets the children slip off the bench and go to their father like, Annie would say, sweet syrup goes to pancakes.

And Erika watches as Paul turns to Simon, to Simon first, and holds out his hand. She freezes that picture in her mind, forever, along with the faces of the men she loves, Paul and Simon shaking hands.

Then the gavel again. The judge thanks the jury and excuses them. Counsel is asked to remain. The jury departs. The judge sits.

"Mr. Rousseau," he says, (Mr. Rousseau now has a child in his arms, but he is not guilty; for a moment, for this one moment, he is free), "I discharge you from these charges. On these charges you are free to go. However I have been informed by the bailiff that there is an outstanding warrant for your arrest issued by the United States District Court for the Eastern District of New York and that there are agents of the Federal Government in this courtroom—I suspect you do not need me to tell you this, sir—and these men are authorized to take you into custody on that warrant.

"I wish to take a moment to congratulate you, Mr. Rousseau, and defense counsel, Mr. Donnis, Mr. Golden and Mr. Weinberg, for a very fine job, a very well-run trial. Mr. Rousseau, you probably are aware that this Court was under tremendous pressure to treat you as a particular threat to the judicial system in general and the order of this courtroom in particular and that I refused to bend to that pressure on the grounds that my courtroom would never be one in which a defendant could claim that he was deprived of his right to a fair and impartial hearing. I now know, after the incident here the other day, that you were under similar pressures and were oftentimes goaded into making theirs a self-fulfilling prophecy. I want to compliment you for resisting this pressure and maintaining your equanimity throughout this trial. I hope that the outcome tonight has revived some faith you may still have in our judicial system and I wish you good luck in New York. Gentlemen, again, my compliments and thank you all."

And Simon turns to Erika, who is both smiling and crying, and calls her name and she gets up and goes to him through the low swinging door.

It is with a certain amount of reluctance that she goes to his apartment.

She drives and she remembers what she would think as she left her house on those nights she spent with him. This is my home, she would think going down the front steps. My husband who loves me. My children who love me. It is warm and bright and cheerful here. Why am I leaving?

And then in the car she would think, Why am I going to him? It will be so strange there.

304

But she would keep driving. Like tonight she would keep driving, up the hill, cresting it, starting the slow descent, sometimes in snow, sometimes in rain, or like tonight in another thick mist, the peninsula shrouded in cloud, the late February thaw, rivers of melting snow running along the curbs following her own way down toward the sea. Midway she would see his building and the window with the light shining out and she would cut off that part of herself that longed for home, she would slice it off and open her heart to the light from the window and the man who lived inside. And once she opened the door and walked in, the barrenness of the rooms, the emptiness, the silence, all of it would be transformed.

She crests the hill and sees his building, but she does not feel that drunken, crazy joy.

And she remembers the first time she came this way. She didn't know what she wanted from him or what she was willing to give. She simply went and by that act of going allowed fate to play out her hand, abrogated responsibility, thinking it was either in the cards or it wasn't, abandoning herself to the moment the way a drowning man abandons himself to the sea, blindingly, achingly, in hope and faith or maybe in despair, faithlessly, breaking every rule, every law of survival, willing himself out of existence for this one moment. For her, the moment was like a door opening, that simple, that uncomplicated. The door opened, she walked in.

Now she parks the car in a familiar spot, turns off the engine, pulls the key from the ignition. But she cannot move, cannot will herself to move. Does she want to go up again only to say goodbye?

And the night is enveloping, the night is a dark fragrance, mildness, thaw. Soon the rains will begin. And after the rains they will build onto the house, home improvement loans, two bedrooms in the attic, another in the new wing, extend the kitchen. And a bigger car, maybe a van.

The night is magical, like a screen upon which she can project images, Eli close beside her on the hard bench, George tearing Tarot cards in half, Emma curled up into a tight ball on her lap.

He will understand what it means that she doesn't come.

She drives back the long way through the old district, passing block upon block of brick walls.

WHO ARE THE TERRORISTS?

IS THERE A PRISON BEHIND THIS WALL?

GOD IS DEAD

ROUSSEAU LIVES

The Night Writer has been at work.

Related Fiction Titles from Curbstone Press

UNITED STATES:

BEASTS, stories by Harold Jaffe. "*Beasts* is a blessing, a dazzling construction of fiction that resurrects the genre."—John A. Williams. $9.00pa.

THE BOX & OTHER STORIES, by Victor Kaplan. A trio of witty and fascinating stories. $6.00pa.

CENTRALIA DEAD MARCH, by Thomas Churchill. A historical novel about the Wobblies & the struggle to form labor unions in the U.S. $9.95pa.

LATIN AMERICA:

ASHES OF IZALCO, a novel by Claribel Alegría and Darwin J. Flakoll. A love story which unfolds during the bloody events of 1932, when 30,000 Indians and peasants were massacred inEl Salvador. $17.95cl./$9.95pa.

LUISA IN REALITYLAND, a prose/verse novel by Claribel Alegría. A retrospect of the real, surreal and magical memories of childhood in El Salvador. $9.95 pa./$17.95 cl.

THE SHADOW BY THE DOOR, a novel by Gerardo di Masso. A superb piece of writing about torture and disappearance during Argentina's "dirty war". $6.95pa.

DENMARK:

ANNA (I) ANNA, a novel by Klaus Rifbjerg. A story filled with adventure, suspense, and a poetic evocation of places and times, by a leader among contemporary Danish writers. $9.95pa.

COMPLETE FREEDOM, stories by Tove Ditlevsen. "Quietly impressive, from the work of a shrewd, ironic writer."—*Kirkus Review.* $7.00pa.

IF IT REALLY WERE A FILM, stories by Dorrit Willumsen. A selection of stories by one of Denmark's prize-winning authors. $7.00pa.

THE PILLOWS, stories by Benny Andersen, "The results are sometimes bizarre, often comic, but always affecting."—*Booklist.* $7.50pa.

SELECTED STORIES by Benny Andersen. His sense of humor, insight into the human personality and acute observation are well represented in this collection. $6.00pa.

FOR A COMPLETE CATALOG, SEND A REQUEST TO:
Curbstone Press, 321 Jackson St., Willimantic, CT 06226